MW01533179

blurred LINES

ANDI JAXON

Cover Designer: Y'all That Graphic

Models:

Photographer: Wander Aguiar

Editing: Candace Royer and Rumi Khan

Formatting: Andi Jaxon

For all the readers who begged for Brendon and Paul's story.

PROLOGUE
june – seven years ago

Paul

T he radio is blasting as we head down the highway. Mom's singing at the top of her lungs as we head out of town for hockey camp. She loves her early 2000s songs, so I know them all. Green Day, Beyoncé, Radiohead, Britney Spears. My gear bag and duffle are in the back of our Ford that's older than Mom, and we drive with the windows down since there's no air conditioning.

These are the moments I love the most with her. It's just us, laughing and having a good time. A lot of my friends are embarrassed by their parents, but I'm not. Mom is the best, and Dad loves her more than life. They are relationship goals.

Someday, I'll find a love like theirs, and life will be perfect.

"Okay, big man," Mom says as she turns down the music. "What are you most looking forward to during camp?"

"Playing hockey. Duh." I roll my eyes but laugh.

"Well obviously, smartass." She huffs at me. "What

specifically? Is there a skill you're looking forward to perfecting or a coach you want to work with?"

I shrug. "I dunno. I'm just happy I get to go. I'm gonna be a hockey star one day, you'll see."

She smiles at me, taking her eyes off the road for just a second, but that's all it takes for the world to turn upside down. In the blink of an eye we crash into something big and lose control.

"Mom!" The scream rips from my throat as fear like I've never experienced before chokes me. The unimaginable force of the crash jerks me forward on my seat belt. The screeching of tires overwhelms my head; burning rubber and hot radiator fluid fill my nose before my brain can process that we've stopped moving.

My head is buzzing, and my body trembles as I look around. My eyes are wide with adrenaline and fear. We're off the road, facing a ditch next to a field.

"Mom." My voice is small and cracks as I turn to check on her. She's slumped over, leaning against the steering wheel. "Mom!"

I fumble with my seat belt, but I can't get it to unlock.

"Mom!" I lean as far over as I can, forcing the seat belt over my head to give me more room while a white-hot pain high on my chest steals my breath for a second. Clutching my right arm against my chest, I shuffle my way across the bench seat until I can reach Mom. Her face is turned away from me, and I'm afraid to move her. Reaching a shaking hand to her neck, I feel for a pulse, but I can't find one.

Am I in the right spot? Tears are making it hard to see, and the knot in my throat is making it hard to breathe.

"Momma," I sob. "Please wake up."

I shake her shoulder a little, but she doesn't respond. Pressing my ear to her back, I listen for any kind of noise, but there's nothing.

Picking up her hand, I hold it against my cheek and sob until my throat is raw and my eyes hurt, rocking back and forth.

I know I should call 911, but I can't see anything through the tears. Nothing is where it was, so I don't see her phone. How can I call for help if I don't have a phone?

"Hey!" There's a male voice outside the truck. "You guys okay?"

A man in a John Deere ball cap appears at my window, takes one look at me, and wrenches the door open. "Hey, man, come on. Let's get you out of here and I'll help her. Okay?" He reaches for me, but I scream.

He holds up both hands like he means no harm, then backs up.

"Bethany!" he yells up toward the road. "Call 911. There's a kid in here and a woman, I think. The driver doesn't look good."

He moves around the truck to Mom's side and reaches in through the window to touch her neck. His shoulders drop, and I know before he says anything what he knows. She's dead.

Part of me knows it, but my brain can't accept it as truth.

"Come on, Mom. Wake up. Please." The adrenaline is fading, zapping my energy, and dropping me into shock, I guess. Numb is better, right? Easier.

The next few hours are a blur. From the side of the road, to an ambulance, to the hospital. The seat belt broke my collarbone, so my arm is in a sling. I'm sitting on a hospital bed with Grandma, picking dirt and grass from my clothes when Dad comes in.

"Heather?!" His panicked voice echoes in the space, and I look up to see him frantically looking for Mom while staff follow behind him telling him he can't be back here.

3

"Dad!" I get up off the bed and run for him. I wrap my arm around him for a hug. He wraps an arm around me, patting me on the back, then steps back and holds my good shoulder.

"Where is your mother?"

Tears fill my eyes, and my lip trembles as I shake my head. I can't say the words. A couple of nurses in green-blue scrubs pull him off me.

"Sir, you can't just burst back here! Who are you looking for?" the lady with black glasses and long brown hair in a ponytail asks him.

"Heather Johnson. She was in an accident with my son." He points to me, almost angry as he demands answers.

The nurses look at each other for a second before the same one speaks again. "Sir, if you'll come with us, we'll fill you in on the situation."

"No! Where is my wife?" He's yelling now, and I flinch back. I've never heard him like this, and honestly, it scares me. Grandma wraps an arm around my shoulders and pulls me into her while I cry on her shirt.

"Ryan." Grandma uses that soft tone she uses with me when she knows something is about to hurt my feelings. "Please go with them."

He stares at her, red-faced and breathing too hard with his hands on his hips before his face falls.

"No. She's not." He drops to his knees, and a heart-shattering yell echoes in the room. Grandma approaches him and wraps her arms around his shoulders with tears running down her face.

"I'm so sorry," she repeats like this is her fault.

It was my fault, though, wasn't it? Because she turned to look at me. I'm the reason we crashed.

Guilt eats at me. *I'm the reason Mom died.*

4

"They hit a bear on the highway doing sixty-five." Grandma's words are quiet but teary while I'm frozen to the floor. I've never seen my father break down like this. It's terrifying and has me sinking to the floor with tears once again streaming down my face but no sound coming from my mouth.

Grandma reaches for me, but I can't move. All I can do is stare at my father while he grieves the loss of Mom. Maybe I don't want to find a love like theirs after all. If this is what it feels like when I lose them, I don't want anything like it.

Dad starts banging his fists on the floor as he yells, then stands abruptly and storms out. Grandma gasps and covers her mouth with her hand as she watches him leave. The door slams against the wall on his way out, and all I can do is stare.

He left me here.

Happy birthday to me.

five years ago
Brendon

The game is over, and we're trudging back to the locker room, sweaty and exhausted, but everyone is happy. We won, even though we were a mess out there. I was anyway. Every fuckup plays on repeat in my head, and I know Chad and his goons will take it out on me. They always do. My gut tightens, and my mouth goes dry at the thought. I don't want to deal with them today. They've been getting worse lately, leaving marks that I've lied to my parents about, just brushing the bruises off as hockey injuries.

At my cubby, I strip as fast as I can, shower and get dressed with anxiety nipping at my heels to make me move faster. I keep count of how many teammates are still around and where the coaches are. Who's still around and how long I have before I'm alone with my terrors.

Get out while you still can.

After pulling my jacket on, I'm straightening my tie when the laughter that haunts me echoes in the locker room.

My stomach rolls, and bile threatens to choke me as my hands pause on the silk. Fear has me freezing, gluing me in place despite knowing that makes me an easy target. My ears pick up every footfall from the four of them, their breathing, the smacking of bubble gum in John's mouth. I'm hyperaware of everything but can't do anything to stop whatever is about to happen.

The blank mask I've perfected since starting on this team falls over my face on instinct. Can't let anyone know about the pain, the bullying, the terror. *Be a man. Don't show any weakness. Weakness makes you a pussy.*

Chad steps in front of me with a smile that promises pain on his face. His friends create a shield around us, like I have any chance of getting away, and crowd my space. I never had claustrophobia issues, but the last few months, I do. I hate feeling trapped.

"M-my mom is waiting." I stumble through the lie and hope like hell it works. Almost everyone knows my parents work full-time to put food on the table and rarely make it on time for pickup.

Chad is always the last one here since he's Coach Williams's stepson. That man shouldn't be in charge of kids. He doesn't give a fuck about the bullying his stepson doles out. I've tried talking to him about it, and he tells me to stop being a pussy.

"You know, birdy, you're a shitty liar."

"You know what my mom used to do to me when she caught me lying?" Garret, the black-haired boy with evil in his eyes, says. "Washed my mouth out with soap."

My body feels like I'm vibrating, but my hands are surprisingly steady. I do everything I can not to react to them. They want a reaction, and by denying them, maybe they'll get bored. So far, this theory isn't panning out.

Delight brightens the muddy brown of Chad's eyes, and the urge to cry or beg is so strong I almost give in to it. But it won't make a difference. If anything, it'll just make it worse.

"John, grab the bar of soap from my bag." Chad doesn't look away from me when he says it, watching for my reaction. The boys laugh, and John turns away to do as he was told. They are probably all victims of Chad as well if they don't do what he wants.

"Are you gonna chirp for us? Squawk?" Chad moves in closer to me as John shows up with a blue plastic soap box. Chad holds his hand out, and John gives it to him without a word.

Without thinking about it, I step back, right into Andrew. The curly-haired blond guy is the biggest guy on our team and is known for being a bruiser. His arms band around me, forcing what little air I was able to manage from my lungs.

I'm going to throw up. I can't do this.

I yell as loud as I can, hoping someone will hear me, but they never fucking do. It's not fair! Why am I always the damn target? I hate this place and everyone in it.

Chad shoves the bar of soap into my mouth so deep I choke on it, but he won't let me spit it out. He holds it in as I gag, tears running down my cheeks as I try to breathe and not throw up. My body tries to save itself, turning and squirming, trying to get away, but Andrew is fucking strong and has the upper hand. They all laugh at my pain, at my fear, at my humiliation. The bitter taste of soap fills my mouth, bubbles forming on my tongue and around my lips from the movement. Chunks of the bar wear onto my teeth too, and I will never be able to get it all out of my mouth.

"No one will ever believe you." Chad finally moves his hand and the bar falls, leaving me panting and coughing with drool dripping down my chin.

I used to love coming to practice, lacing up my skates, and taking to the ice like a bat out of hell, but now I dread it, and I can't even tell anyone why. I'm lying to everyone because I'm so fucking ashamed of what I've let them do to me.

Someone punches me in the stomach, but I don't see who it is, and it doesn't matter. Andrew lets go of me, and I drop onto my knees hard enough for the sound to echo.

"I hate you," I manage to get out. Chad grips my hair in a tight fist and jerks my head up.

"Look at you, birdy. Crying, on your knees like a bitch." He backhands me. Hot, sharp pain explodes across my cheek. "If you want to act like a little bitch, I'll treat you like one."

Dread settles like an iceberg in my stomach. What does that mean?

"Hold him still," Chad says, and it feels like Andrew

grabbing a hold of my elbows and pulling them behind me.

Fuck. Fuck. Fuck.

I start to tremble and try to pull away from Chad, but all it does is put me closer to Andrew.

Chad unzips his pants and pulls his dick out, stroking it until it starts to thicken.

"You aren't exactly my normal type, but a mouth is a mouth, right?"

The pull of my hair and saliva on my chin don't matter, but I choke and cough when he finishes. My stomach rolling at the bitter taste on my tongue. The bang of the locker door closing makes me jump, and for a second, hope blossoms in my chest. Is someone going to find us and help me?

No one can know about this.

I hold my breath, both wanting to be saved and hoping no one finds me like this.

Coach Williams comes around the corner, lifts an eyebrow, but doesn't say anything about me on the floor, probably looking distraught and a complete mess.

"Boys, time to go. Come on." Coach Williams meets my eyes for a second, then turns and leaves. My heart breaks, shatters in my chest. How is this my life?

"You'll make someone a good pussy if you practice." Chad puts himself away, ruffles my hair, then turns and strides down the aisle with his lackeys following along behind him.

Scrambling on my hands and knees, I grab my gear bag from the now empty locker room and run outside to

9

wait for my mom. It's cold, but I don't care. It's better than being in there.

I sit on the dirt next to the building where the wind is blocked, and my stomach rolls. Saliva pools in my mouth, and I race for the garbage can, throwing up everything in my stomach. Water, my protein bar, soap, and *him*. It burns my nose and throat and leaves me gasping for breath. My abs ache, but it's better this way. I don't want any part of today left in my body.

A shiver races up my spine at the thought, and I settle back against the wall, using my shirt to wipe my face.

I don't want to do this anymore, but I don't know how to make it stop either. The coach doesn't care, clearly. He's supposed to support us, shape us into the best players we can be, but he's allowing his kid to torment me.

I've been playing hockey since I was five. I love the game. But I need to get off this team. For two years, I've dealt with this, and it's steadily gotten worse. I can't do it anymore. If I can't switch teams, I'll have to quit playing. The thought makes me sob. I don't want to give up hockey. Pulling my knees to my chest, I wrap my arms around my legs and cry. In the shadow of the ice rink where they encourage us to play injured and to suck it up, I'm weak.

A while later, Mom pulls up to the curb, and I make my way to the car. After dropping my bag in the back, I sink in the front seat and force an air of excitement I don't feel. I don't know if she can smell *him* on me or not, but the need to shower again and brush my teeth is so heavy on my shoulders. I'm exhausted, and I'm sure my eyes are red from crying, but she's too distracted by driving to notice.

"How was the game?" she asks as she gets us turned toward home.

"We won." I smile and start talking about the game. I

tell her about the shots our goalie blocked and the times we managed to hit the net.

"Sounds like you guys played a great game. I'm sorry I had to miss it." She pats my knee as she pulls into the driveway, and I jump out of the car, galloping toward the house like I'm riding a horse or something. She laughs behind me, and I dance on the porch as I wait for her. I'm exhausted and want to crawl into bed, but if I'm making her laugh, maybe she won't look too closely and see how broken I am. I can't let her down. She's a good mom, and I don't want her to be ashamed of me.

"What do you want to eat?" She unlocks the door, and I bow.

"Ladies first." I extend my hand, and she heads inside. I'm not at all hungry. The idea of eating turns my stomach again.

"I'm good, Momma. I'm gonna change and take a nap." I kiss her cheek quickly and bound up the stairs to the bathroom. Once the door is closed behind me, I lean against it and let the mask fall. Since I showered at practice, my mom will probably inquire if I take another one, so I grab a washcloth and scrub my face, neck, and hands, then brush my teeth until my gums bleed and I can't taste him lingering anymore.

My shoulders sag once I'm cleanish, and my eyes close as I suck in a deep breath. Slowly, I make my way to my room and pull off my suit. I hate that thing. Nothing good ever comes from wearing it.

Lying down on my messy bed, I pull the blanket over my head, curl into a ball, and cry until I pass out.

CHAPTER 1

january – present

Paul

B eing in love with one of your best friends fucking
sucks. I tried to avoid it. Most of the time I can
ignore the fact that I'm a sap for him. At this
point, I'm faking it through every day of my life. Even I
don't know who I am anymore.

It was hard knowing that he was fooling around with
our other best friend. They didn't rub it in my face or
anything, but I knew. They would disappear for twenty
minutes, then come back flushed and relaxed. Jealousy
definitely reared its ugly head more than once.

I've known they've been fooling around since it started
when we were still in Michigan, playing for the
Lumberjacks, not long after Jeremy Albrooke joined our
team.

I'm a year older than them, so I moved out here to
Darby University last year to play hockey while they stayed
in Muskegon, but I'm really glad they're here. I hoped the
time away would give me a chance to get the hell over the
redhead I pined over, but the second he showed up as my

roommate, I knew I was fucked. All those feelings came rushing back, and I hate myself for it.

I spent a damn year trying to fuck around when time allowed, but every time I tried, it felt off. Like something was missing. I couldn't get Brendon Oiler out of my head, so I never went past kissing. That definitely didn't help me get over him. I've always been weird about hookups. Sure, getting off is great and all, but without a connection to your partner, what's the point?

I love having Jeremy and Brendon here, though. Last year was boring without them, and I never gelled as well with the other guys as I do with them on the ice. We're perfect together.

Sitting cross-legged on the bed, I'm up to my armpits in biology homework when I'm startled by Brendon yelling instead of the lyrics from Tarzan he was just singing.

"Why am I so fucking stupid?" He throws his pencil across the room and drops his head into his hands.

"What have I told you about that?" I give him a stern look to match my tone. I've worked hard to make him stop with the negative self-talk.

"It's true. Fuck off!" he snaps and shoves his chair back from the desk, heading toward the door.

I fling the book aside and stalk after him. When he reaches the door, I grab his shoulder and flip him around. He startles a little, and the anger fades from his face before he waggles his eyebrows at me.

"Oh Daddy." Brendon bites his lip and winks at me. "You gonna spank me?"

I try not to react to him. It only encourages him to act like a brat. When I cross my arms and give him an unamused look, he drops the smart-ass act, and a softer side of him comes out.

Fuck, I love the way he melts for me. He's such a big

personality normally, loud and joking around, while I'm in the background, but here, like this, he's quiet and reserved. Does he like it as much as I do? The big personality is a front, at least part of the time.

"You are not dumb. The next time I hear you say something like that, I'll make sure you're up at four to work out with Preston."

His expression morphs to scandalized, complete with the hand to his chest.

"For a week," I tell him.

He crosses his arms and glares at me. "That's just cruel."

"If that's what it takes, that's what I'll do." My hands ache to touch him, to cup his jaw or run through his floppy red hair. I've made peace with the fact that I'm not straight. I'm still figuring out where I fall on the spectrum of LGBTQIA+, but I also don't really care to label myself.

"You wouldn't do that to me." He's not confident about his words.

I lift an eyebrow and stare at him. "You sure about that?"

He deflates and looks like a spoiled brat about ready to stomp his foot. It's harder than it should be not to smile at him.

"Pizza will be here soon, then sleep. We have a game tomorrow."

He rolls his eyes. "I know."

Brendon slithers past me, his body brushing mine, then there's a knock on the door. I open it and take the pizza boxes from the delivery guy.

Brendon grabs them from me and rushes toward my bed, cackling like a lunatic when he opens them. The delivery guy watches him warily for a second, then hands me the receipt to sign.

"Have a good night," I say and close the door.

Brendon is sitting cross-legged on my bed, a garlic twist in one hand and a slice of pizza shoved into his mouth with the other. I sigh and shake my head.

He looks up at me and tries to say "what" around the mouthful of food, but it's just a garbled sound.

"Why do you always make a mess on *my* bed?" I reach for a garlic twist and take a big bite.

"Why would I make a mess of my own bed?" he scoffs. "That doesn't make any sense."

I shove him over, and he laughs but moves enough for me to be able to sit down. Once one of his hands is empty, he turns on my Xbox and TV, then flips through shit even though I know he's going to pick something from the *Star Wars* universe because he always does.

After ten minutes, he settles on Disney+ and turns on *The Mandalorian*. Brendon scarfs down half the pizza and three twists before laying back on my pillows and rubbing his stomach. I move the pizza boxes, and he stretches out, pulling my blanket over him.

"I ate too much," he whines. "My stomach hurts."

He pulls his shirt up to show me how round his stomach is as I lay down next to him.

"You shouldn't have eaten the last two garlic twists."

Brendon scoffs, "But they're so tasty."

He reaches for my hand and places it on his stomach. I lift an eyebrow and look up at him.

"Am I waiting to feel the baby kick?"

"Rub it; it hurts."

I sigh but readjust on the bed so I can rub his stomach, the big baby. Secretly, I love it. I like taking care of him. I like that I can touch him sometimes, and I like that he only lets *me* do this for him.

We make it halfway through an episode before he falls

asleep and rolls over, dragging me in behind him to spoon. He mumbles something in his sleep, and I smile into his shoulder when he settles and snores softly.

For a little while, I can almost pretend like he's mine and fall asleep with him in my bed.

CHAPTER 2

Brendon

I n the locker room two days later, we're all stripping out of our suits and changing into workout gear to prepare for the second game against Maine. There's an excited buzz to the locker room like always. Every athlete thinks they're going to win the game. There's a pressure we put on ourselves to perform perfectly, or we've let everyone down. Logically, we know it's a team sport and not one person wins or loses a game, but in our heads, we know the truth. If we lose, it's our own fault.

"God*damn*, Albrooke!" Willis, one of our defenders, calls a few cubbies down from me. "Wild night, buddy?"

Everyone turns to look at Jeremy, and when I step back to get a look at him, I can see why. He's absolutely covered in hickies, bite marks, and scratches. Now that everyone knows Jeremy and Preston Carmichael are together, the ribbing over the sex marks is worse. Preston says nothing, only smirks if someone comes up with something clever, but Jeremy blushes like a virgin. I have to admit, it's pretty fucking hilarious.

"Definitely looks like it." I laugh, leaning my forearm

19

against Paul's back. Paul lifts an eyebrow at me, then gets back to changing.

Our captain, Joey Carpenter laughs at the mess that is Jeremy's skin and claps him on the shoulder, then turns to Preston. "Perhaps you should take it easy the night before a game, huh?"

Preston just lifts his uninjured shoulder but says nothing. Since Preston dislocated his shoulder last weekend, he's not playing for a while, but he's still here to fuck with everyone.

"Make sure the reporters still stalking around outside don't see them, or you'll have to explain how you got them." Carp shakes his head and heads back to his cubby to finish getting ready.

Preston's dad being a world-known surgeon with skeletons—and sexual assault charges—in his closet has created a tizzy in the media. Luckily, the school isn't interested in them harassing students, so most get kicked off campus pretty quick.

I finish getting dressed and grab a roll of tape and my hockey sticks. Everyone has three sticks for the game, since breaking them is common. Everyone is particular about how the tape is applied, so we all do it ourselves, not trusting anyone else to do it right. Since we've all been playing since we were kids, it's pretty quick, and we have multiple rolls of tape circulating the room.

Someone stands over me as I finish wrapping my last one. I don't have to look up to know it's Paul Johnson. I'm the dumbass, Jeremy is the good boy, and Paul is the one that keeps me out of trouble. Usually. He has some type-A personality quirks that keep my ass on time unless I can manage to distract him with what I lovingly call a side quest. Aka food.

He runs his hand over my hair and walks away. After

all the years of playing, there's still anxiety before a game. You never know how it's going to go, who will get hurt, which team will be hungrier for the win. Paul knows physical touch helps calm me, so he always makes sure to do something before we start warmups.

We've gotten comments over the years from players about us fucking. Sports are notorious for being homophobic and full of toxic masculinity, so most of us that are part of the alphabet mafia tend to keep it pretty quiet. I'm bi, and only a handful of people know. Not because I'm embarrassed or ashamed; I just don't want to deal with the bullshit in the locker room.

Once all the sticks are ready for the game and stored, we drop off our skates to be sharpened, and we head to the gym for off-the-ice warmups. Some guys have music playing in their ears, others are joking around or trash talking. I tell jokes and make an ass out of myself. We all have what works for us.

"Ten minutes, boys!" Coach yells, and we finish what we're doing, then head out to the hallway that leads to the rink.

My skates hit the ice for warmups, and the rush of cold air on my cheeks has me smiling. This feeling right here is my addiction. It's the calm before the storm. That adrenaline rush and butterflies in your stomach. It's almost time. It's the last few moments before we have to battle another twenty men for the win. When my skates hit the ice, my heart soars. There's nothing out here but teamwork, blood, and victory.

The ice will be resurfaced after warmups, and the stands will be full when the game starts. We're on our home turf, so the cheers will be deafening, the lights bright on the ice, and the fight for victory will begin.

"Everyone take a piss, let's go," Coach announces from

the doorway. "And if you need to shit, better do it now or shit your pants on the ice."

In shifts, we all go to the bathroom since there is nothing worse than playing while prairie dogging.

The last guys finish up, and we're told to get our sticks and head to the hallway. The commentators are announcing the schools, and the crowd roars to life. Paul and Jeremy turn, and we slap our sticks together before hustling down the shoot and onto the ice.

My blades hit the ice, and I let out a loud, "Ca-caw!" which makes Jeremy and Paul chuckle.

I love the rush of the game. The way a well-gelled team moves, anticipating their teammates thoughts, and being ready—it's beautiful. Hockey is such a physical game, we leave the arena bruised and sometimes bloody, with aches and pains from being thrown into the boards or a fight. I love it. You have to be hungry for that win, or you're not going to get it. It's a brutal fight to the death out here, and it hums in my blood.

Out here, the game moves fast. You can't take your mind off it for a second. The puck moves across the ice, players fight for control, and lines switch out quickly. Your entire mind must be focused on what's in front you, the next move, looking for an opening, or you'll miss everything.

This game is fun. Maine is a good team, and we have to work for our win. Albrooke, Johnson, and I are back on the ice together, anticipating each other's next move like we never spent any time apart. It's perfect. I get lost in the hum of the crowd and sounds of skates and sticks on the ice. Adrenaline courses through me, and my love for the sport lights me up inside.

By the end of the game, we're exhausted but happy. We won, and that's what matters. And tomorrow we'll get up and do it all over again. The locker room is rowdy with the boys celebrating. A smile is plastered on my face as we strip down and talk about the highlights of the game.

Until Jeremy strips out of his gear and I see Preston pause at his damage to my friend's skin. It's such a clear sign that Jeremy and I were not right for each other, and that's fine. It was fun and convenient while it lasted. When they first got started, I thought Preston was abusing Jeremy. Not in a fun, sexy way. Our arrangement was never permanent, and yeah, I struggled to share him with someone else. He's one of my best friends, and I'm used to having complete access to him, but I want my dude to be happy.

Jeremy's naked ass walks past me toward the shower, and with my eyes locked with Preston's, I slap Jeremy's ass. Preston tenses and steps toward me. Jeremy spins and punches me in the arm, and I run toward the showers still with some of my clothes on just to get away from Preston. But I'm laughing.

"You know he's going to snap one day and take your head off, right?" Jeremy says before he steps under the shower.

"Yeah, but it'll probably be worth it."

Paul gives me a *you're so dumb* look and leaves the showers to get dressed. Jeremy and I do a quick scrub down, and when I turn toward the doorway, Preston is leaning against the wall watching. Probably making sure I don't touch Jeremy. A smile turns up the corner of my lips, but Jeremy sees it and says, "Don't even think about it."

Paul is dressed and waiting for me when I get back to my cubby. I guess I took longer than I thought. He looks sexy as fuck in his suit and tie. There's an air to him that makes it hard for me not to stare. For some reason, I can picture him watching me with hunger in his eyes, not ashamed for anyone to see. What I wouldn't give for someone to claim me publicly. I'm tired of being a dirty secret. Like who I stick my dick in is shameful. It's bullshit.

He commands the room in that damn outfit, and it's a mind fuck. He's my friend, and at this point, I'm scared he's going to drop me too. He knows me better than most and lets me drop the mask to be my true self.

I pull on my own suit and fall back into the character everyone expects from me. With a quick movement, I smack Paul's stomach with the back of my hand and wag my eyebrows at him.

"I'm hungry. Feed me."

He smirks and shakes his head. "Are you ever *not* hungry?"

"That's a big negative, good buddy."

I follow him from the locker room and out to the walkway that will lead us to the dorms.

"Pizza?" he asks with his face buried in his phone.

"Have I ever said no to pizza? I think the fuck not." I smack his ass, and he flushes a little.

"You're a pain in my ass," he grumbles.

I laugh and squeeze his ass this time. "I'm not, but I could be."

Paul stops walking, turns to face me, and straightens up. He's only two inches taller than me, but he's slimmer. All lean muscle and power, but wrapped in that suit, I can't look at anything else. There is nothing else but him and the air in my lungs that's trapped there.

His eyes drop to my mouth, and for a second, I think he's going to kiss me. I want him to. Take control of me so I get out of my own head. Make the inner monologue stop for just a minute.

Please.

I've always thought he was straight, but since I moved

here a few months ago, I've caught him looking at me. Watching me. I know how men look at other men when there's interest, but he's never said anything or done anything else, so I just wait.

"Get your ass back to the dorm." Paul's voice is low and dangerous. That tone has never been directed at me, but fuck, it's so sexy I want to hear it again. It sends a shiver up my spine and goose bumps across my skin. What would it feel like to have his hands on my skin? To have him controlling my body?

My phone buzzes in my pocket, and I'm ripped away from the spell he's put on me. Reaching for it, I answer the phone call from my mom.

"Hey, Mo—"

"Brendon!" Mom's excited voice is so loud I jerk the phone from my ear. "Do you remember that coach you had in high school? Craig Williams?"

I hated that team. Dude was a drill sergeant, and it was not effective. Not to mention the menace his stepson was.

"Uh, yeah."

"He got hired to coach at UM!"

My body moves on instinct, getting me away from the crowd of people and into a corner where I won't have anyone surprise me from behind. The memories of my worst days flood my brain, the taste of Irish Spring a ghost on my tongue. Hit, tripped, humiliated. That team was the worst two years of my life.

Squawk for me, birdy.

I shiver at the words and the history attached to them.

"Brendon? Did you hear me?" she says when I don't respond, but I can barely hear her over the voices in my head. We play UM later in the season.

My stomach is tight with tension. I hate that I'm afraid of him. That after all this time, just hearing his fucking

25

name turns me back to that person. Terrorized and jumping at shadows. I don't know if I'll have to see Chad again, if he plays NCAA hockey. It's likely I will at some point, and I dread the day it happens. But seeing Coach Williams is enough to fuck me up.

He knew Chad was targeting me, making me a victim, and did nothing.

A warm hand grips the back of my neck, and I flinch. Paul pulls me against him, grounding me in the present.

"Breathe," he whispers, and my body trembles. I close my eyes and rest my forehead against his chest, the phone basically forgotten against my ear. He squeezes my nape, giving my mind something to focus on instead of the memories.

I have exactly one secret from Paul, and it's this. I don't want him to know how weak I really am.

"Hey, you okay?" Jeremy's voice is close and concerned. I reach for him, too, and he wraps an arm around me, but when Preston growls, I snort. I don't know why it's so funny when he gets territorial over Jeremy, but it is.

"Yeah, Mom, that's great for him." I lift my head off Paul's chest and see Preston watching me, but with concern this time. "I've gotta go, I'll talk to you later. Love you."

"Love you!" The call ends, and I roll my shoulders, then shove my phone back in my pocket. I don't want to talk about what this was or what it means. I don't want them picking at me all fucking night, so I do the only thing I can think of. Act normal.

"All right, pizza. Feed me."

Paul steps back and shakes his head. I head out after him with Preston and Jeremy following along after us.

"Come to Rocky's with us," Jeremy says. They're walking close together but not holding hands, just in case a blood-sucking reporter catches pictures or whatever. Preston doesn't want any of us getting caught in his drama, but especially not Jeremy.

"Isn't there a rule about feeding the Gremlins after midnight?" Preston says.

"It's not midnight!" I pull out my phone to check the time just in case because time has zero meaning to me.

"It's midnight somewhere . . ."

I flip him off over my shoulder.

"No thanks. I think I'll pass," he deadpans.

"It was *definitely not* an offer. I'm not into pain."

"Children!" Paul says, and Jeremy snickers. "I swear you're as bad as siblings."

I wrap my arm around Paul's and give him a big-eyed innocent look. "Sorry, Daddy."

Jeremy cackles, and Preston shudders while Paul looks like he's going to murder me.

He sighs but keeps walking. He never tells me to stop or tells me that I'm being too much. Sometimes I wonder when it'll start, though. I know I'm a lot. I'm over the top, change topics quickly, have big emotions and a smart mouth. But after a lifetime of being told to lower my voice, sit still, relax because it's not that big of a deal, I struggle to know where to draw the line.

My family loves me; I've never doubted that, but I know they get annoyed with me. The impulsive, loud, random noises get overwhelming. My parents are quiet people. They're content to sit on the couch and watch TV or read or whatever. Sometimes that quiet is great, but then I walk through the room and squawk for no reason at all, leave half the cabinet doors open, and leave the juice container on the counter because I forgot to put it away. I know it's frustrating for them. They've nagged me my entire life to be quiet, sit still, close the doors, and I still can't get it right.

We make it to the dorms, and when the elevator doors close behind us, my head has to ask the same questions it always does on elevators.

If you stuck your hand through the door, where the doors were closed on your palm, would you break your fingers when we moved? How close to the walls are we really? If we got stuck in here in between floors, could the four of us pry the doors open and climb out? Does that theory about jumping right before the car hits the springy thing at the bottom of the shaft actually work? How would you know—

"Brendon." Paul snaps his fingers in my face, interrupting the tirade of intrusive thoughts.

I blink, not realizing I was disassociating, and head down the hallway with Paul.

"You okay?" he asks when we get inside.

"Me? Yeah." I slide my jacket off my shoulders and toss it on my bed to take off the tie and unbutton my shirt. "Why?"

"You seem off." Paul shrugs and strips off his shirt. I find myself eyeing him semi covertly, then force myself to turn away from him. I shouldn't be looking at my friend like that. Doesn't matter that he's hot as fuck.

Paul pulls on old jeans that do amazing things for his ass and a thermal shirt that hugs his frame. With a backward black hockey ball cap, he looks at me and laughs at my yellow ducky underwear.

"I'll go grab us seats at Rocky's." And he's gone.

CHAPTER 3

Paul

Rocky's is busy tonight as we celebrate our second win of the weekend. We've just gotten food delivered to the table when the door opens and a frazzled Brendon walks in. Preston and Jeremy are nowhere in sight, which isn't exactly abnormal.

"You all right, man?" I ask him as he drops into the seat next to me and grabs my beer out of my hand to take a swig. I sigh but don't fight him. It's just how he is. Secretly, I love it. That possessive side of me likes that he reaches for me when he needs or wants something. There's an easy intimacy that I don't have with anyone else, and after being alone last year, I crave him being near me.

"Fine," he snaps. That's not normal for him.

"You wanna tell your face that?" I snatch my beer back, but he's drained it. Fucker. "The lovebirds coming?" I signal the waitress for another beer and turn back to him.

"I don't know." Brendon gets up and orders himself a beer.

He drops back into his chair a few minutes later and grabs some fries from the basket sitting in front of him as

Jeremy and Preston come in and sit across from us. Preston is sporting an arm sling since he dislocated his shoulder about two weeks ago.

"Started without me, huh?" Jeremy ribs me, grabbing fries from the basket, and signals for a beer. Preston sighs but doesn't say what we all know he wants to.

There's a tension between Brendon and Jeremy, but Preston looks like the cat who caught the canary. My gaze flits between them, and I can't quite figure out what is going on.

"All right, out with it," I demand. Preston's lips lift in a slow, knowing smile while Brendon's face turns red, and Jeremy chokes on his water.

"What?" Jeremy coughs. I turn and stare at Brendon, waiting for him to break. It won't take long. About sixty seconds later, Brendon slams his hands down on the table and exclaims. "I walked in on them fucking, and I'm going to have nightmares."

Preston laughs and wraps a hand around Jeremy's thigh, pulling him closer. Jeremy's face pales, then turns pink while Brendon stares at nothing.

"I'm a little afraid to ask what you actually saw . . ." I look between the three of them, and Preston's smug expression makes me a little nervous.

Brendon finally turns and looks at me. "We've all seen the marks, but watching how he gets them is a little scary. Preston is not nice."

The waitress puts my beer down in front of me and brushes her hand against my arm. When I look up at her, she gives me a shy smile, and I tell her thanks. I'm not interested, but maybe I should give it a shot. No one but me has touched my dick in way too long.

The noise around us rises as Carpenter comes in, and

the team cheers him on with drinks in the air. He smiles and bows dramatically before taking a seat.

One of the guys from the team last year slaps him on the shoulder and puts a drink in front of him. "First one's on me."

Our team captain takes it and lifts it to the team. "Thanks. I'm damn proud of you guys."

Brendon and Jeremy are trying too hard to be normal but won't actually look at each other, which I now find hilarious. Brendon's red hair is rumpled like he's been running his hands through it, and it makes my palm itch to do the same. I love Jeremy like a brother, but I'm kind of afraid of his sex life.

Brendon tries to grab my plate, but I slap his hand and move it out of his reach.

"Touch my food and lose a hand." I glare at him, but he laughs, some of the rough edges smoothing out.

"I'm hungry. Feed me, Daddy." He opens his mouth like a baby bird, and I pick up a fry to shove in his mouth. It goes too far, and he chokes but laughs along with the guys around us who heard him. "Dick."

"Get your own damn food," I say around a mouthful of my burger.

He huffs but flags down a waitress to put in a burger order, and Jeremy does as well. Preston gets a chicken salad and water because, of course he does. Brendon continues to eye my food, but I'm not sharing. I'm starving.

We all chat and eat while we sit around the bar. Brendon puts his arm around the back of my chair like he usually does. He's a toucher, and over the last few months of living together, I've gotten so used to it that I miss it when I don't have it. It's also why I can't fucking get over him. He's in my space all the time, so fucking close, touching me, but I can't have him. Not really. Not the way I crave.

Since Jeremy got with Preston and is no longer hooking up with Brendon, he's been making out with a lot of sorority girls from what I've seen, but I'm not sure if he's actually having sex with them or not.

A few hours later, Brendon is sulking into his beer, tossing back shots here and there, while some girl is attempting to flirt with him. He's not stumbling drunk, but he's on his way. If he doesn't slow down, he'll be there in an hour or so.

I order him a basket of fries to help soak up the liquor and tell the waitress to put it in front of him.

He's not great at taking care of himself. So sometimes I have to do it for him. I like doing it.

As I lift my beer to my lips, I see the woman slide a hand on his thigh, and I want to rip it off. I have no claim to him, but tomorrow when he feels like shit with a hangover, he'll climb into my bed and lay his head on my shoulder. He'll let me take care of him, get his food, water, and meds, then demand I lie in bed all day with him. But he won't kiss me. The man who has come to mean more to me than anyone else wants intimacy, but not sex. I can care for him, about him, but I can't be in love with him.

She shakes her head and giggles, which grates on my nerves. She's beautiful, though. Curly blonde hair that hangs past her shoulders, a sweet face with plush lips, and obviously isn't afraid to make moves. That confidence will get you everywhere.

The waitress drops the fries in front of him and walks off without a word.

"Did you order me food?" He leans closer to the woman with that sexy smile on his face that I want directed at me.

"I did," I snap before she has a chance to say anything.

Brendon's eyes meet mine, and the smile changes to his normal dopey one.

"Aw, thanks, buddy." He kisses my cheek and wraps an arm around my neck. "I knew you loved me."

More than you know.

I lift my beer at him and take another drink so I don't say something I'll regret.

Willis climbs on a table and lifts his beer. He's a bit wobbly, and I really hope he doesn't fall and bust his head. I really don't want to hear Coach yell at us because he's a dumbass.

"Hey, shut up!" Everyone quiets down, and I turn to face him completely. "I'm proud to play with you fuck nuggets." Everyone chuckles, and he continues. "Let's have a toast to Captain Carp for being the coolest, level-headedest, ass-kickingest dude."

"Hear, hear," the team cheers, lifting their glasses.

"Yay! Carppy!" Brendon yells, standing abruptly and spilling his beer on Carpenter. "My bad, dawg."

Brendon leans down with his tongue out like he's going to lick the beer from our captain's neck. Leaping forward, I grab Brendon's shirt and jerk him backward into me. He stumbles and leans on my chest for a second, cackling.

"We don't lick people," I say in his ear.

"Maybe you don't, but I definitely do." He licks my cheek, and I force myself to move back away from him. His mouth is so fucking close to mine. It would be easy to press our lips together.

"Act right before someone punches you in the face."

Brendon salutes me and pulls the blonde woman against him. They sway to the music, and she reaches back to hook her arm around his neck. He drags his lips against her neck, and she smiles, pushing back into him.

"I'm surprised he's gone after so many chicks." Jeremy's voice makes me jump, and I lift my beer to my lips just for something to do.

"I'm not." I give him the side-eye. "You hurt him, so he's finding a distraction that won't come back to bite him in the ass." *And I hate it.* It's a dig at Jeremy because I'm jealous, but oh well. The alcohol is not helping me keep control of my pissy mood, and if I don't watch it, I'll end up outing myself to the team before I'm ready.

I get dragged into a game of darts with some of the guys, and by the time I get back to the bar, Brendon has disappeared. Great.

I scan the room but don't see any sign of his bright red hair or the blonde he was wrapped around. Did he leave with her? Did he take her back to our dorm? Is he getting a blowie in the bathroom or behind the bar?

I shove a hand through my hair and pull on the strands in frustration. Fuck. If he disappeared with that girl, I don't know how I'll be able to keep my jealousy under wraps.

A warm body presses against me, making me jump, but a quick look over my shoulder and getting an eyeful of red hair has me relaxing. Brendon's arms come around my waist, and his face presses to the back of my shoulder. He's my comfort, and he doesn't even know it.

"Take me home," he mumbles.

I smile a little and pat his hand. "Okay, let me make sure Jeremy and Preston are good, then we can go."

Brendon presses a soft, quick kiss to my neck, and goose bumps break out along my skin. That was much more arousing than it should be. I force my body to not react to it or to think too much into it. He doesn't mean it to be sexual or a come-on. He's just an affectionate guy.

As much as I don't want him to let me go, I know he

has to. I pat his hands again, and he slides them back, dragging them along my sides. I glance back at him for a second before moving through the crowd to find Jeremy.

He's at a table with Willis and Carpenter sitting on Preston's lap, laughing and having a good time. I lean close to his ear so he can hear me over the noise.

"Brendon is ready to go, so I'm taking him back to the dorms. You guys good?"

"I'll head back with Preston." Jeremy pats my arm, Preston growls, and I nod, then find Brendon again.

We say goodbye to the guys we pass on the way to the door, and I breathe a sigh of relief when we get into the quiet of the night. Brendon follows behind me a few steps, then grabs my hand and holds it.

Butterflies tickle my stomach, and I give his hand a light squeeze. I don't think he's ever held my hand before. Is it the booze?

"I'm sorry, Pauly boy," he sighs, lifting the back of my hand to rub his prickly cheek against.

"Sorry for what?" My voice is a little shaky, but I doubt he notices.

"That I can't love you the way you deserve." He pulls me along with him across campus to our building.

Uh. Excuse me? Fucking *what?!*

My feet stop moving as I stare at the beautiful man rubbing his face along my skin.

"What does that mean?"

He continues to nuzzle my hand until the skin gets sensitive, but I don't pull it from his grip. There's something bouncing around his busy brain, and I want to know what it is. I need answers.

"I don't know what I'm going to do after college." Brendon sighs dramatically.

"I don't think any of us really know. I certainly don't."

Brendon gasps and spins around, grabbing my shoulders. "You bought me food!" His expression gets soft and swoony. "Aww, you love me."

"Yeah, I bought you food." I chuckle at his rapid change of subject. I wonder if I could get him to answer the question later when he's sobered up some. Will I have the guts to ask him when he's sober?

"I'm so fucking horny," he groans and turns back around, walking toward the dorms again.

He's going to give me whiplash.

"Why didn't you hook up with that chick at the bar? She was clearly interested." That sounded jealous. Maybe he won't remember it tomorrow.

Brendon shakes his head and wraps an arm around my shoulders. "Nah, I wasn't feeling girls tonight."

My dick twitches, and I turn my head just enough to catch a look at his face in the corner of my eye. He's such a beautiful man. His pale skin, some light freckles along his cheeks, and the soft swoop of his lips. He's strong and solid. While I'm long and lean, he's powerful and sturdy. Not only can he take a lot of damage on the ice, but he can cause it too. I'm fast and agile but easier to break.

Brendon starts singing "Welcome to My Life" by Simple Plan, which I haven't heard in years. He mumbles the words while we're in the elevator, and I follow him down the hallway to our room where he promptly takes off his pants because, of course he does. I swear he spends more time without pants on than the reverse. His dark blue briefs with yellow ducks cup his ass in the most maddening way, and forcing myself to not react is exhausting. At least he has a shirt on this time. Half the time he doesn't even have that on, and it's hell on my self-control.

There's a vibe surrounding him that I can't quite figure

out, sadness or hopelessness, maybe. It makes a sharp pain appear in my chest.

Before he can drop down onto my bed, I reach for his arm and pull him into me. I wrap my arms around his shoulders, our bodies pressed together, and his face is in my neck. There's nothing sexual about the contact, it's just comfort and friendship.

Brendon hesitates but slides his arms around me and squeezes me back, releasing a sigh, and relaxing into my hold. I close my eyes and just exist in the moment with him. I know he's struggling with something, but I'm not sure what it is. His brain is so busy usually that it's hard to tell when he's just exhausted from it or if there's something really bothering him.

I'm not sure how long we stand there, just breathing, but he pulls his face from the crook of my neck and looks at me. My eyes drop to his lips. I'm desperate to know what he tastes like, how he kisses, how he feels.

In the next breath, our lips meet in a soft brush, and I don't know who moved first. It doesn't matter. I have limited experience kissing guys, and this is so much different than any of the others that I want to remember it for the rest of my life. It's Brendon. My Brendon.

With nerves fluttering in my stomach, I kiss my best friend and hope he doesn't hate me for it in the morning.

I love the way he feels against me. Sturdy but vulnerable. I know he can handle whatever life throws at him. I've seen him take command on the ice, watched him take hits and bounce back, then turn around and need comfort for an internal wound he wasn't ready to talk about at that moment.

It's not a deep kiss, a barely-there contact, but it steals my breath. I hold his head in my hands and slant my mouth over his, needing more from him.

Nothing has ever felt as right as this moment, with this man, in this room. He's my everything.

And that terrifies me.

I'm so gone for this boy.

The kiss ends the same way it began, and he steps back with a sigh, running his hand through his hair, like my world isn't crashing down around me.

The anguish of losing my mom and my dad spirals inside of me. After Mom died, Dad pulled back, left me with my grandparents most of the time while he went out fishing or hunting or whatever he was doing. Even now he rarely calls or texts to check in. He's been a shell of a man since she died, and I swore when I watched him walk away that I wouldn't allow myself to fall that hard for anyone.

But I did.

Brendon drops onto my bed, and I kick off my shoes despite my hands shaking. I crawl over him and lay next to the wall, one arm behind my head while he grabs the Xbox controller and flips through the apps to find something. As he watches the TV, I can't help but watch him. I can only see a sliver of his face and the broad expanse of his back, but I watch the muscles move under his T-shirt. I both want to pull him against me so I can breathe him in and push him as far away from me as possible.

He puts on *The Mandalorian* for the hundredth time and lays back against my shoulder. Part of his body is on mine, and I hate how much I like it. Somewhere along the way, I fell hard for him, but I can't keep him.

Having the pressure of him against me is calming, reassuring. Brendon is a toucher, it's just how he is. He needs it, but it's killing me.

CHAPTER 4

Brendon

I *kissed Paul.*

What the fuck?

My lips tingle, and as badly as I want to brush my thumb over them, I force myself to hold still. I don't know what I was thinking when I leaned into him, but it just felt right. I meant it to just be a quick, soft kiss, but the way he cupped my face and deepened it was hot as fuck.

And now I'm confused.

Before tonight, I never thought he was interested in me, but now I'm not so sure.

I hook my leg over his, wanting more of my body touching his but not comfortable enough to wrap myself around him the way I crave. I hate how fucking needy I am sometimes. That shit with Jeremy fucked up my head and left me spiraling. Even months later, I'm still struggling a bit.

These twin-sized beds are bullshit. There's barely enough room for one jock, much less two. Though I guess they don't really expect two of us to be laying in one. Still. I'm a cuddler. I need human touch, the more the better, and because society is homophobic as shit, I usually have to fuck to get that need met.

After all the shit that went down with Chad and his goons, I was afraid for anyone to touch me. For months, I shut that part of me off, told myself I didn't need it. It was a lie. I started to get angry and depressed from the lack of human contact. It didn't take me long to figure out sex worked, but being with men terrified me, so I stuck to women for a while.

Until Jeremy joined the Lumberjacks and I found myself with him and Paul all the time. They respected the fact that I didn't want to be touched more than high fives or knuckle bumps. Neither of them was weird about touch and freely gave it to the other guys on the team. Hugs, pats, just lying next to each other on the bed so everyone would fit, and they always let me have the edge so I didn't feel trapped. After a while, I learned to trust them, and I've never looked back.

But moving in with Paul made me so much worse. I *crave* his touch.

Being this close to him after that kiss is killing me. God, I want to touch myself right now. The mental image of Paul sliding his hand into my underwear to fondle me flashes in my mind and has blood rushing to my dick.

I shift against Paul, turning onto my hip a little and leaning more of my back and ass against him, hopefully hiding some of the bulge now in the front of my boxer briefs. Fuck, I like laying with him like this more than I probably should. He's my safe space. He never wants anything from me, just lets me touch him when I need it— which is always—and doesn't complain or make it weird. It's not sexual, just comforting.

My family are big huggers. My cousins or friends and I were always in dog piles on top of one another. It's just how we are, so moving out here was difficult. Luckily, Paul and Jeremy know this about me and are used to it, but I know I touch Paul more than I probably should. Is me being so touchy making him question his sexuality?

A cold shiver of guilt runs down my spine, and my breathing hitches for a minute. Paul's arm wraps around me until his palm is on my chest.

"You okay?"

I clear my throat and force a smile. "Yeah, all good. Just got the chills."

He sits up a little and looks at my face. Fuck, I hope I'm masking my emotions hard enough. I want to bury my face in his neck and have him wrap his arms around me again, tell me I'm enough.

A knot forms in my throat, but I keep my face passive.

"Are you cold?" He lifts the orange-and-red crocheted blanket from the end of his bed with his foot and covers us with it. His grandma made it for him a few years ago, and he loves it, so it stays on the bed. Grandmas are the best.

"Thanks," I murmur, accepting it. There aren't many people he allows to use it. Just Jeremy and me, now that I think about it. "You talk to your grandma lately?"

"Yeah." He lays back and pulls me more solidly against him. I'm not sure he notices that he does it, but it makes my soul a little brighter when he does. "She's good. The chickens stopped laying, so she's threatening to use them for bear bait."

I laugh. That old lady is the coolest person ever.

Paul starts talking about his grandparents and the shit they're getting into. It's clear in the way he talks about them that he loves them. I know his relationship with his dad is hard, so I'm really glad he has them. His mom's parents stepped up and helped out a lot after the car accident that he and his mom were in. His dad mentally checked out and couldn't handle the loss of his wife. Paul was fourteen when it happened, on his birthday, so it's a hard day for him. His grandparents always call, but his dad never does, and I really think it causes him to question what's wrong with him.

His voice soothes the edges of my consciousness, lulling me toward sleep. I lift his hand off my chest and put it on my head for him to run his fingers through my hair. I love having someone play with my hair.

Without direction, Paul does it, dragging his nails lightly over my scalp until goose bumps make me shudder and finally, I fall asleep.

Paul is on top of me, naked, riding my dick like a fucking pro. His body rolls, grinding hard against me. My body is hot, sweaty with lust, and I'm desperate to come. The erotic flutter low in my pelvis starts, the tingling along my skin that centers in my groin . . .

My eyes shoot open as I groan, my dick pulsing in my underwear.

I'm breathing too hard, and my skin is sticky with sweat.

Shit.

When was the last time I had a damn wet dream?

Paul adjusts against my back, draping an arm around my waist. My heart is pounding, and my hands are shaky as I lift his arm and slide out of the bed, barely avoiding crashing to the floor.

In the bathroom, I strip off my clothes and take a quick shower.

Paul is one of the few people who sees me. Really sees me and accepts me. I'm a mess. He already puts up with so much shit from me that's not normal, I can't start lusting after him too.

I really hope he didn't wake up when I got up. He doesn't need to know I had a fucking wet dream or that it starred him.

When I get out of the shower and dry off, I pull on a pair of underwear and pajama pants and climb into my bed. It's not as comforting as Paul's warm bed, but I need some space, I think. I have to get my feelings under control before I ruin this.

CHAPTER 5

Paul

W hen I climb out of bed in the morning, I scrub a hand over my face and ignore the dread sitting heavy in my stomach. It looks like Brendon moved back to his bed at some point and is still sleeping, so I grab my phone, slip on some shoes, and head down to the dining hall to grab us some breakfast.

I tossed and turned for a while but finally fell asleep around one. Questioning what happened and how we got here. Nothing has felt as right as when Brendon's lips touched mine. I've come to peace with being attracted to him. Most people don't really do it for me. I can appreciate an attractive human, but I don't want to fuck them. I crave the connection more than anything else. I've never had that before. Not like this. Brendon and I have been friends for years and are comfortable with each other. That connection makes me ache for him, heats my blood.

I've always felt weird about it. Growing up, my friends were always obsessed with girls, and while I appreciated them, I didn't get the appeal of random hookups. I still don't. What's the point?

I rub at the throb in my chest. Since we're athletes, they let us eat pretty much anything we want down there and don't argue too much when we take more than we should. We're supposed to stick to a strict diet that's put together by the dietitians, but the dining hall doesn't rat us out if we grab pastries sometimes.

Since Sundays are rest days and we can sleep in, I don't see many people from the jock dorm and make it back to the room quickly. But in the hallway outside our room is a curly-haired blonde chick, staring at the door.

"Uh, can I help you?" I try not to sound like a dick, but she's in my damn way, and I'm pretty sure it's the same girl that was all over Brendon last night at the bar.

"Oh, hi." Her smile is huge, but something about it makes me uneasy. I don't trust it. "I'm Nikki." She offers her hand, but since mine are full, I just raise an eyebrow at her. She laughs, and it grates on every one of my nerves. "Oh, silly me. I can get the door for you."

The last thing I want is for her to touch my door.

"That's all right, I got it." I move between her and my room. "My roommate is still sleeping."

"Oh, okay. I was wondering why Brendon wasn't responding to my texts." She shrugs like it isn't the creepiest sentence I've ever heard. "I guess I'll just wait a while longer."

With another smile and a wave, she walks away, and I find myself watching her go. What the fuck was that? Once she's out of sight, I shake my head. Puck bunnies are crazy.

When I open the door and find Brendon's bed empty, I stop short and look around. The bathroom door swings open, and he steps out wearing jeans and a hoodie.

Disappointment and unease tense my stomach, and I busy myself with closing the door, then shove his food into his chest.

"Oh," Brendon grunts at the impact and takes the bag. "Thanks."

"No problem," I mutter and sit on my bed to eat my eggs. Brendon sits on his bed and opens the oatmeal with berries on top, stirring it around with his spoon but not actually eating it.

"I thought you went down without me," he says quietly, looking at his bowl.

I glance over at him, and the uncertainty of our situation turns my stomach.

"I'm sorry, I . . ." I don't know what to say to make this better. Do I admit that I've wanted to touch him for too damn long? Is it better to pretend it didn't happen? I don't know what to do, and it's eating at me. Will he pull away now and find someone else to comfort him when he needs it? It was a kiss. I can't lose him as my best friend over a fucking kiss.

That would crush me. If he wants to pretend it didn't happen, I would deal with it, but if he stops touching me altogether, I would die.

"What are you apologizing for?" Brendon's forehead scrunches up like he's confused but keeps his eyes on his bowl. He scoops up a bite of oatmeal and shoves it into his mouth, but he still won't look at me.

My heart thunders in my chest, and fear tickles my stomach. Does he not remember? He wasn't that drunk, was he?

Do I tell him and make it worse if he did forget? Is he pretending like he doesn't know? What the fuck do I do? I want him. Full stop. But I will take any part of him he's willing to give me. If that means I'm relegated to just cuddles, so be it. I'm not sure how a future love interest will like that, but that is a bridge we will have to cross when we get to it. Will he stop cuddling with me when he finds a partner? I don't think I'll survive.

Brendon finally looks at me, and in the blink of an eye, he's set his food down and is wrapping his arms around me.

"Hey." He takes my food and moves it aside to straddle my lap and wrap himself around me. I shove my face in his neck and wrap my arms around his back. "What did I miss?"

The weight on my chest eases, and I suck in a deep breath. My lungs fill with the scent of Brendon: Tide laundry soap, team shower body wash, and the smoky pine of his deodorant.

"We kissed last night. Do you remember?" I say into his shirt.

Brendon relaxes a bit, and he chuckles. "Oh. That. It's fine, dude. No big deal, really." Leaning back, I look up at him, and God I want to kiss him right now to show him just how big of a deal it really is.

Brendon's smile falls, and he looks at me much more seriously now. "Wait, have you kissed a dude before?"

I force myself to swallow and focus. "Uh yeah, I did last year."

Brendon smirks, lifting an eyebrow. "Look at you, getting a little slutty. I'm so proud of you."

I roll my eyes but can't stop the blush from heating my cheeks. "Shut up."

"Did you get laid? Handies? Blowies? Come on, gimmie the deets, my dude!" Brendon shakes me, and I laugh at him.

"What? No." I push on his hips, but he wraps around me tighter. "I'm not telling you shit."

"Just whisper it in my ear. It'll be our little secret." He turns his head so I can do just that, and something about the movement has me wanting to nip at his neck, suck on his skin, and whisper dirty words for him. I wonder if he likes dirty talking . . .

"You're a menace," I whisper in his ear, and he shivers on my lap.

"Okay, fine. We can reenact what happened. You twisted my arm, but I accept." He wags his eyebrows with a stupid smile on his lips.

"Real funny." I dig my fingers into his ribs, and he screams, jerking away from me and falling onto the floor with a loud thud.

He lays on the floor for a minute, looking up at me, and flips me off.

"I hate being tickled."

I smirk at him and pick up my now cold eggs. "I know."

Brendon grabs his oatmeal and sits next to me on my bed.

"There's a Bears game on soon. Wanna watch it?" He doesn't wait for me to respond, just turns on the Xbox and TV and flips to Hulu, then settles on the channel it'll be on in a few minutes.

We finish our breakfast, and he watches the game while I get caught up on homework. At one point, Brendon stands on the bed and cheers, arms raised in the air and yelling like his ass is on fire.

"Did you see that pass? It was fucking beautiful!" he shouts at me, pointing at the TV while standing above me. I smile at him and shake my head, turning back to my book. A pillow smacks me, making my pen draw a line across my paper.

"Hey!" I toss my stuff aside, grab the pillow and stand up, swinging it at him like a bat.

It hits him in the stomach, and he launches himself at me, knocking me back into his bed, then to the floor.

"You think you can take on the pillow fight champion?" I holler at him, cackling with laughter when I get my fingers in his armpit, and he shrieks.

"Who the fuck gave you that title? Your grandma? She was probably being nice!" he yells back, red faced and smiling. He comes for me again, grabbing my T-shirt in his hands and rolling us, but he must have forgotten how small our space is, and we end up with me straddling him, trapping him against the leg of my bed with my hands on the carpet next to his head.

We're both breathing hard, smiling and sweating from roughhousing, when the air around us shifts. I am very aware of him below me, my ass pressed against his hips, and his hands still holding my shirt so I can't move away. My skin heats, and it has nothing to do with the physical exertion, but the arousal humming through me. I rock my hips back, just a little, more on instinct than anything else.

Brendon's breathing hitches, and his hands grip my hips. Leaning on his chest, I rock against him again, and he thrusts up against me. Anticipation and rightness blossom in my chest. This is what I've been missing. The connection and intimacy and acceptance that I've never had with anyone before, that I've craved my entire life.

"Paul." Brendon's voice is guttural and heavy. It sends shivers up my spine. I roll my hips harder against him and smile when his eyes heat. I feel victorious, like I won a battle. Fuck, this is magical. I had girlfriends in high school that I fooled around and had sex with, but it wasn't like this. The connection I have with Brendon is different. It was there before anything sexual happened. It makes this more important. Stronger.

But is it the same for him? Is this once again a causal thing that he'll walk away from? The thought stings.

Grabbing his wrists, I hold them above his head. The move lowers my head, and I drag my nose against his. His breath comes in pants with little whimpers, the warm air fanning over my cheeks, and I can feel him harden under me.

I love him like this, at my mercy and waiting for what I'll do next. I've imagined touching him so many times over the last few years, but I never thought it would actually happen. Now that it's here, I'm almost afraid of it. What if I do something he doesn't like? What if he decides we aren't compatible? Can I go back to just being his friend now that I know what his lips taste like?

I don't think I can.

For months, since he moved in here at the beginning of summer, I feel like I've been edged. Pining after him, getting closer and closer to him seeing me as something more than just his friend, but I'm fucking scared. What if it's just me? What if I'm reading into shit that's not really there?

"Are you gonna kiss me or just stare at me?" Brendon plants his feet on the floor and uses the position to grind up against me.

"I'll kiss you when I'm good and goddamn ready." I nip at his bottom lip, and he hisses. Dragging the tip of my tongue along the edge, I soothe the sting.

I stare at his mouth, moving so close there's barely a whisper between us, and Brendon balls his hands into fists. I can't help but smirk at the frustration radiating from him. *Now you know how I've felt for months.* Knowing I'm getting to him is a special kind of high I wasn't expecting.

The shrill of an old telephone rings out, and we both freeze. Fuck.

I hurriedly climb off Brendon and dig through the blankets on his bed for my phone.

"Hey, Grandma," I say, a little breathless.

"Pauly, how are you?" Her voice usually wraps around me like a warm hug, but since I'm still hard, it's just awkward.

"I'm good, how are you? Are the chickens laying eggs?"

Brendon forces himself off the floor and gets back onto my bed to watch the game again. He not-so-subtly adjusts himself while giving me the side-eye, and I smile at him. I'm not sorry he's hard because of me, but I also don't really know what to do about it. I have no experience here.

"The damn hens started laying but one is broody." She sighs. "Damn birds."

There's a crash in the background followed by my grandpa's laughter.

"Richard!" Grandma hollers. "Stop playing with the dog in the house!"

I chuckle at her exasperated tone. She's been telling him the same thing my entire life. Grandpa has always been a big kid; it's one of the things I love about him. He would take me out fishing, and we'd screw around all afternoon, coming back filthy, sunburnt, and starving but laughing. He tried so hard to make up for the fact that my dad wasn't around much after Mom died.

"Fucking hell," Grandma says under her breath. "I gotta go. They broke a glass."

"All right, I love you."

"Love you, Pauly boy."

We hang up, and I settle back on the disaster that is Brendon's bed. He never makes the damn thing, which drives me crazy, but whatever. I grab my school stuff and get back to work, ignoring Brendon's hooting and hollering at the TV.

Images of Brendon keep filtering through my head, though. Naked, tied to his bed, at my mercy while I ride his dick and not letting him come. Does his entire body flush red? Would he let me tie him up? Would he let me fuck him?

Picking up my phone, I find a sex toy store and browse for butt plugs and prostate massagers. I wonder what that feels like . . . Not giving myself time to think about it, I add two toys and some lube to my cart and check out.

My face is on fire, and I really fucking hope he doesn't look over here.

There's a knock on the door, and we look at each other. Neither of us is expecting anyone. I shrug, and Brendon gets up to answer it.

"Oh good, you are awake." That sickly sweet, fake voice from earlier hits my ears, and I lift my lip in irritation. "Did you get my messages?"

Brendon stands there in the doorway awkwardly. "Uh . . ."

I drop my head to hide my smile but peer at them and watch her face fall a little.

"I'm Nikki, from Rocky's last night? We exchanged Snapchat handles."

"Oh right, right." His tone says he has no memory of this, and it takes all my self-control not to snort.

"So did you not get my messages? Maybe you have to accept the friendship first," she explains as she reaches for her phone. It's a bright pink catastrophe with shit hanging off it and fake diamonds and shit glued to it. Pretty sure my fourteen-year-old niece has a phone case like that.

She shows him her screen, and Brendon nods.

"Oh yeah, maybe." Brendon scratches the back of his

neck as she types out something on her phone. A second later, his phone pings. Busted.

"Oh good, my messages are going through." She stares at him with an intensity that's uncomfortable.

"I haven't really looked at my phone today," he tries.

"Well, why don't you look now?"

The silence between them is awkward before he mutters, "Okay," and turns around to grab his phone off the bed. He gives me a *WTF* look and checks his phone.

"There they are," he says, kind of waving his phone awkwardly in the air. "I'm in the middle of watching a game, so I'll talk—"

"The Bears game? Cool, I'll watch with you." She strides into the room and sits on the edge of my bed like she can't read the damn room. This chick is weird.

"Uh, okay." Brendon closes the door and climbs back on my bed, carefully not touching her, but she shifts closer to him. My body tenses at her movement, wanting to yell at her to get off my bed and to get away from him. I want to wrap myself around him to keep her away, but I don't. I sit and stare at my books, sulking.

For a while, the room is quiet. Nikki tries to start a conversation a few times and even lays on her side to rest her head on Brendon's leg. Something happens on the TV, and Brendon jumps up, jostling her, and I snort at the affronted expression on her face. Brendon is standing on the bed, arms raised, cheering.

Nikki reaches for my crocheted blanket, pulling it toward her, and Brendon doesn't hesitate, just rips it from her grasp.

"No. No one touches that." He cradles it against his chest in a ball and turns his body away from her like she'll reach around his arm to take it back. Fuck, I love him.

"Oh, I'm so sorry." She puts her hand on her chest. "I didn't know."

I sigh and put my stuff away. Watching this is painful, and since I can't focus, I'll go somewhere else.

I swing my backpack over my shoulder and slip my shoes on. Brendon looks at me like I'm leaving him to face a monster on his own. "I'm going to the library."

Snagging my ball cap on the way out, I put it on and close the door behind me. He's not interested in anything serious. I know that. He never has been. But watching him with someone else hurts.

CHAPTER 6

Brendon

I stare at the back of my best friend as he leaves me alone with this girl in our room. Does he think I want to be alone with her? I barely remember her despite her showing me pictures that she took on her phone at the bar last night. While I had been drunk, I wasn't blackout. She just didn't make it past short-term memory.

Unlike the kiss I had with Paul when we got back.

This girl, Nikki, seems nice enough, kind of intense, but I don't want to be in here with her.

"Is your roommate always like that?" she asks once the door is closed behind him.

"What do you mean? Like what?"

"Quiet? Standoffish? Anti-social?" There's a judgey tone in her voice I don't like.

"He's not any of those things." I shake my head and struggle not to get defensive. "He's just trying to work."

I settle back on the bed and face the TV, but I'm not paying attention. My head is spinning with what Paul is doing, where he really went, what is he thinking? I pop my knuckles and circle my wrists, pop my elbows and my neck.

All nervous habits when I can't get up and pace or tap my foot.

"Are you okay?" Nikki asks, putting her hand on my knee. I stop fidgeting and stare at it for a minute. I am a big fan of human touch, but this feels off.

"Uh yeah, I'm okay." *Don't be a dick. Don't hurt her feelings. Don't give her a reason to be angry or cry or something.*

"The game doesn't seem to be holding your attention . . ." Her voice drops to a sultry tone, and my gut tightens. *No, no, no.*

"I need to shit." The words blurt out of my mouth so fast even I'm surprised by them. Nikki jerks back, and I climb off the bed, heading for the bathroom. Once the door is closed and locked, I pull my phone from my pocket and text Paul.

MENACE:

What the actual fuck, man? Why did you leave?

P DADDY:

I'm trying to study and having people there is distracting.

MENACE:

So get rid of her! I don't want her here either!

P DADDY:

I hope she isn't reading over your shoulder . . .

MENACE:

I'm in the bathroom. I told her I had to shit.

I cover my mouth to keep my laugh quiet. I swear I can see Paul's expression, snorting at the excuse.

P DADDY:

I'm at the library. Text Preston, he's a dick.
He'll get rid of her.

Oh, that's a damn good idea.

I pull up Preston's messages and send him a message.

OILER:

Yo, big man, I need you to get a girl out of
my dorm.

P DAWG:

So tell her to leave?

OILER:

But that's mean! You do it.

I'm pretty sure I can hear him sigh from here, but I don't have to wait long before I hear the door open and Preston's voice.

"Time to go."

I open the bathroom door, and Nikki's eyes flick to mine, wide and intimidated by Preston.

"Sorry, we've got hockey shit to do." I try to look like I feel bad, but I don't know how successful I am.

She stands and looks between us a few times before the look on her face changes to understanding.

"Oh, okay." The smile on her face says she knows something. "I get it." She winks and reaches out to touch me as she gets closer, but Preston growls, and she pulls her hand back. "Possessive, got it."

"We can talk later." She winks at me, then leaves.

"Thanks, man." I pat Preston's arm, and he grabs my wrist.

"Touch me again, I'll break your fingers."

I nod, and he releases me. Jeremy's laugh sounds from the hallway, and I smile.

"What's the deal with Curly Sue?" Jeremy appears in the doorway, leaning against it.

"I guess I flirted with her or something at the bar last night? I don't know. She's been blowing up my phone all day. Then invited herself over. Paul abandoned me, the ass." I huff and drop onto my bed.

Jeremy and Preston share a look I can't decipher before turning back to me.

"And why wouldn't you get rid of her yourself?" Jeremy asks.

"Telling her to leave would be rude," I scoff.

"Right. Of course. Silly me." Jeremy shakes his head, and Paul shows up, looking between us, then comes inside.

"Your puck bunny gone then?" He nods to me and drops his backpack on the floor.

I throw an empty water bottle from the floor at him. "She's not my anything."

"The way she was making googly eyes at you says differently." Paul toes off his shoes and sits on his bed.

"Pretty sure she thinks he's fucking me," Preston deadpans.

"Wait, what?" I turn to Preston, extremely confused. "Why?"

Paul and Jeremy crack up while I wait for an explanation.

"The way she looked between us then said '*oh*' was a dead giveaway."

Well shit.

"I guess it could be worse. Maybe this means she'll leave me alone." I shrug and hope that's the case.

My phone pings with a Snapchat notification, and I groan as I see her name.

I'm still awake when the alarm goes off at five a.m. Today is going to suck ass.

Am I the only one of us who can't stop thinking about what it felt like to have Paul against me? How badly I wanted him to kiss me? Once he got back from the library, he acted like everything was normal. What the fuck is that? He didn't ask if I wanted to watch something before bed. Didn't touch me at all. Does he regret it?

I sit up and swing my legs over to stand up. Turning off the blaring dive alarm of a submarine that Paul sleeps through every morning, I shake my head at him and pull the blanket off him. I swear he could sleep through a nuclear war.

"Fuck off," he grumbles into his pillow.

At least one of us slept, I guess.

"Time for the gym. Let's go." I flick the lights on because I'm a dick and find workout clothes. Working out is the last thing I want to do right now. Eat. I want to eat. Bury my uncertainty in carbs.

Paul bitches and moans but gets up and stumbles into the bathroom for a piss, then gets dressed.

"Why the fuck are you so awake?" He rubs his eyes and glares at me.

I shrug and grab a water bottle, seriously thinking about filling it with vodka. "I dunno. Couldn't sleep, I guess."

"Hmph" is the only response I get from him before we head out into the hallway with the rest of the team.

When we get to the gym, someone is already there on the treadmill. Since there are so many sports teams that need to use the space, we have scheduled times. But this big bastard is here anyway, like he is every damn day.

Jeremy sighs behind me, muttering "Show off" as he pushes past me to start stretching. Carmichael has obviously been here a while, which we're all used to at this point. The dude is fucking crazy about his workouts and never hesitates to tell each and every one of us how we're failing. Daily.

We all stretch while the *thump-thump* of Carmichael's feet on the treadmill hangs in the air. Everyone ignores him since no one wants to be his first victim of the day. Some guys joke, some put earbuds in, whatever we need to do to focus.

The team moves toward the treadmills and ellipticals for warmup when Coach comes in. The gruff, former NHL player is new this year, and while he's definitely a hardass, he's fair.

For the entire hour and a half we spend in the gym, Carmichael says nothing, but a few times I saw him look toward Jeremy and me and smirk before turning back to whatever he was doing. It's making me nervous.

We leave sweaty and red-faced, Jeremy and Paul with me as we head to the dining hall for breakfast.

"I hope there's cinnamon rolls. I'm fucking starving." I push past Paul to hit the line first.

"Less carbs, sugar, and butter would make you a better player," Carmichael says behind us.

"Having that stick removed from your ass would make you a better teammate," I toss back.

"Being friendly is not on my priority list."

I grab two cinnamon rolls just because he's being a dick and shove one in my mouth while I stare at him. I groan around the sweet bread and smirk when the muscle in his jaw jumps. Carpenter steps out of line behind Preston, and when he turns to see me, his face flushes bright red, and his eyes get as big as saucers, then hustles away toward the tables. That's weird.

"Your poor choices affect all of us when it makes you a shitty player." Preston's holier-than-thou tone makes me want to touch him just to rile him up.

I flip him the bird and scan my meal card at the counter, then find a table. Paul follows after me with his scrambled eggs and oatmeal.

"You know you're just encouraging him to fuck with you, right?" Paul says.

"Fuck him."

Paul snorts, "Pretty sure Jeremy has that handled."

I snap my gaze to his while he tries to hide a smile.

"What?" he asks, and I burst out laughing.

I drop my head back on my shoulders with an over-exaggerated groan. "Preston is as much fun as a broken stick stuck in the mud." I pick at my food, regretting my decision but refusing to back down now that I've made a stand. "I bet he doesn't even know how to laugh or smile."

"Maybe Jeremy has a degradation kink," Paul says so casually I choke on my food and start coughing.

"I—uh." I shake my head and try to think back to the times we've hooked up. "Okay, that's a solid maybe."

Paul looks at me with raised eyebrows. "Interesting. What about you?"

Unease has heat crawling up my neck. "What about me?"

"Do you like to be degraded?" The air around Paul shifts, and suddenly, he's looking at me like he did in the locker room when he was in his suit. It makes me want to beg, but I have never begged for sex. Not ever.

"Um." I clear the clog from my throat. "I'm not really sure."

"No?" Paul leans in until his breath brushes my cheek.

"Are you a needy little cock slut?" My body tenses, and my cock starts to thicken under the table. "Or maybe you're a good little cock sucker? Hmm? Do you need some praise with your degradation?"

Goose bumps break out along my skin on a shudder, my eyes are too wide, and my face is hot when I turn to look at him.

He winks at me with a knowing smile on his lips and sits back in his chair. The bastard. What is he playing at?

No one has ever talked to me like that. Jeremy isn't a dirty talker, and most of my other hookups were either quickies in a bathroom or with chicks. I've never considered some kind of talking kink for myself, but I know I'm going to be thinking about those words every time I jack off from here on out.

Does he really think that of me, though? I guess it's not really wrong. I use sex as a way to feel connected, to feel like I'm enough.

A lump forms in my throat, and I drop my gaze back to my plate. I'm not really hungry anymore, and now that the idea is in my head, my leg starts bouncing. Fuck. I'm such a mess.

He's not going to want to deal with my bullshit. Maybe I should just be abstinent.

I check the time on my phone and stand up. "I gotta take a shower and head to class, later."

I can feel Paul's eyes on me as I dump my tray and leave, but I don't turn around. Nothing makes sense right now, and I know if I look at him, all I'll want to do is crawl into his lap and have him play with my hair. I can't be needy.

By the time I get back to the dorm after classes and practice, I'm exhausted. I've showered, and the second I step into our room, I kick off my shoes and face-plant onto my bed. I don't want to be alone. I desperately want to be pressed against Paul, but I force myself to stand on my own. Wrapping my blanket around myself tightly, I face the wall. I wish I wasn't so fucking weak. That I didn't crave the comfort of physical touch. I hate that I need reassurance from the people around me that they don't hate me.

Tears burn my eyes, and I don't try to hold them in. There's no soul-altering sobs racking my body, just the sting of anxiety-fueled desperation pricking at my heart to drip down my face and dampen my pillow. Pain leaving a mark on the fabric that will be washed away like it never existed. If only the internal scars could be washed away as easily.

The door opens as I'm on the edge of falling asleep. I'm aware of Paul moving around the room, but I'm not awake enough to have a conversation or track his movements. My bed dips behind me, and I open my eyes, turning to see Paul sitting against my headboard with his laptop on his legs.

He looks at me for a second, then goes back to what he was doing. I scoot over a little to give him more room, and he takes it. His legs against my back are comforting. It's the reassurance I needed but didn't have to ask for.

"Did you eat dinner?" Paul's voice is quiet.

"Mmhmm."

Paul runs his fingers through my hair, and like a light switch, I'm out.

CHAPTER 7

Paul

P ractice the next morning is rough, thanks to Preston. He's not even on the ice since he's still healing up from his shoulder dislocation, but that doesn't stop him from yelling shit at us.

"You're useless if you can't keep your emotions in check!" he yells at Brendon as he and Riggs get into it. It's interesting how aggressive he gets on the ice when it's not in his nature at all once he leaves the rink. But the younger player has a lot to learn, and Brendon is not taking any prisoners today.

"Fuck off!" Brendon yells across the ice and spins on Riggs again.

"If you can't read the plays and anticipate where the puck is going to be, what the fuck are you doing out here?" Brendon's face is red with frustration and exertion. Something is going on with him, but I don't know what.

Riggs gets into Brendon's face. "Maybe the problem is your lack of accuracy!" Then he pushes Brendon. I can see it playing out before it happens, so I grab the back of Brendon's jersey and pull him backward.

"Let it go. He's a snot-nosed brat who doesn't know how to take criticism," I tell Brendon, wrapping an arm around his chest.

"I'm going to beat it into his fucking head. Smart-mouthed little shit is going to learn," Brendon growls, and I have to hide the way my body reacts to it. It's hot as fuck when he gets worked up.

Preston yells something that I don't listen to, and Brendon looks over at him.

"What do you think it'll take to ruffle his feathers?" Brendon asks, watching him tear down Riggs. I swear Carmichael gets off on pointing out everyone's flaws.

"Pretty sure Jeremy is his only weakness."

I spin Brendon around until we're facing each other and after a minute, he grabs my hand and my hip and attempts to dance with me. I laugh and follow along, glad to see him doing something that is so very him.

"You're crazy."

A big smile splits his face. "You mispronounced awesome."

Coach blows the whistle, yelling instructions at us. We line up like we're told and start running some puck-handling drills, then move into speed drills, all the while Carmichael is telling everyone how much they suck.

"I don't think you could skate any slower if we tied anvils to your fucking skates!" Carmichael yells, and I sigh.

"Why don't you fuck off?" Brendon hollers at him.

Their eyes lock with cold fury.

"Are you trying to get your ass kicked today?" I smack his helmet, and Brendon turns to glare at me.

"He's a fucking dick, and no one will call him on it because they're scared of him. Fuck him," Brendon spits.

"He's definitely not taking it easy today," Jeremy sighs.

"I didn't think he could be this much of an ass when he's not even on the ice."

We race back to the other side of the ice, in between cones, and come to a stop with the rest of the team.

"If your stamina in bed is anything like it is on the ice, I feel sorry for whoever you're fucking."

I don't know who Preston was talking to directly, but Brendon tenses, his face turning almost purple.

"Jesus," Jeremy mutters like he knows something I don't.

"Leave it alone," I grit out behind Brendon, but he's already turning toward Carmichael, anger and frustration vibrating around him.

"If it takes you that long to get your partner off, you're doing it wrong!" Brendon yells back,

What the fuck? I'm clearly missing something. I turn to Jeremy who is blushing, his eyes wide. I'm apparently the only one who doesn't know. Great.

The bastard smirks at Brendon. "How the fuck would you know? When was the last time you got someone to finish without help?"

Say what?

Jeremy groans, and before I can react, Brendon takes off toward the box where Preston is standing with the coaches. I race after him, but Carpenter steps out of line and grabs Brendon, forcing him to a stop, and I'm able to wrap my arms around him, pulling him back.

I get us turned around, and he pulls out of my grip, spinning around like he doesn't know I'm there. I'm frustrated, and I'm sure it's clear on my face when he looks at me. I don't know what's going on or how Preston and Jeremy know, but I don't. That hurts.

Under the anger in his eyes, there's something else. His normally sparkling light is dimmed by pain or insecurity, but I don't know how to fix it. I hate seeing that look on his face, knowing there's nothing I can do about it.

Coach blows the whistle again.

"If you're going to act like a bunch of toddlers fighting over the swing set, I'll damn well treat you like it!" Coach screams at us. "Oiler, off my fucking ice!"

Brendon clenches his jaw, then turns away from me, ripping his chin strap off and making his way for the shoot. He throws his stick down the hallway and storms off.

We run the drill again, Preston still yelling, but I'm not as focused as I should be. All I can picture is the hurt in Brendon's face.

I skate up to Coach so I don't have to yell. "Can I go check on Oiler? He's not himself."

The tough man looks at me for a minute, then nods. "We're almost done here anyway."

Before he can change his mind, I hustle off the ice and down the hallway to the locker room with a plan forming in my head.

Brendon and I have kissed once, but yesterday we got damn close to more. I don't think he's hooked up with anyone since Jeremy, so maybe he needs to let off some steam?

"Fuck!" Brendon hisses in the shower as the probably freezing water hits him.

"What the hell is your problem?" I ask from the doorway of the showers, and he jumps. I'm still in all my gear. I don't want to get it wet, but I will if I have to.

"Why the fuck do you care?" he bites out, and that just irritates me more.

I rip my jersey over my head and toss it aside.

"Are you trying to lose ice time?" I snap. "Our line gels so fucking well, and you're fucking it up, for what? To prove you aren't intimidated by Preston? Who the fuck cares?"

I pull my shoulder pads off and drop them to the floor, then untie my hockey pants with jerky, angry movements. Lust mixes with anger as Brendon watches me, his eyes on my body like a caress.

When I'm down to just my compression shorts, I stride toward him and flick the water to hot. I shove him against the tile and get in his face with my hand on his throat. I love that he's not much shorter than me, so we're always face to face.

"Stop acting like an idiot and letting him get to you." My voice is deeper, holding more command, and Brendon's dick thickens against my thigh. "If you really wanted to get to him, you would fuck with Jeremy, and you know it."

I roll my hips, rubbing my thigh against him, and he groans. Not letting myself think about it, with my free hand, I reach for his dick and wrap my hand around it to stroke roughly.

"Come on, give it to me," I demand. "Do you need attention? Is that why you're acting out?"

Brendon drags his lower lip between his teeth and drops his head back on the wall. Fuck, it feels so good to touch him.

"Pull my shorts down. I want your cum on me," I growl at him.

His eyes shoot open, and he reaches for the tight compression shorts. He pulls on the wet fabric until it rolls down under my ass.

"Stop."

His hands freeze on my thighs, and he runs them up my skin to my hips to hold on to.

"Fuck my thighs," I instruct as I let go of his throat. I

don't know where that came from, but I'm not questioning it. Not today.

"Switch spots and stick out your ass then." Brendon's voice is gravelly with lust, but I do what he says. My face is pushed against the wall and my ass is arched out for him. He lines his dick up with my legs and pushes in, his tip nudging at my balls. I don't even try to hold in my moan as it echoes off the tile.

"Cross your ankles, flex around me," he instructs as he grips my hips.

The water from the shower makes my skin slippery enough for him to thrust. It feels so fucking good for him to use me.

He slides his fingers between my cheeks and presses against my hole. I tense up on instinct, but it feels fucking amazing. "You want me in here?" Brendon asks with his lips against my skin.

"Yesss," I moan and reach for the back of his head while I jack myself off. "I want you to stretch me out, fuck me until I can't stand, then fill me with your cum."

Brendon's breathing hitches and he whimpers as he sprays the wall and my inner thighs with cum. His fingers dig into my skin and my own cum is added to the wall, mixing with his. I sag against the wall, and he leans heavily on me with his forehead against my shoulder.

"Shit, that was sexy." I run a finger against his tip, smearing his cum on my skin. Brendon hisses at the contact, probably sensitive after his release, but he doesn't pull away from me. I link our hands together, my palm against the back of his hand and my fingers in between his. I lift his arm to press against my heart. He's my safe place, and I just hope he knows I am for him too.

CHAPTER 8

Brendon

I open my mouth to thank him or something, but there's noise in the hallway, and I jerk back from him and move under the water. Paul pulls his shorts back up without cleaning me off him and heads to pick up his gear.

The room is quickly filled with conversation and the sounds of the team changing. It's all so normal that I easily fall back into the routine of it. When I get out of the showers, Paul is pulling on jeans with his shorts balled up on the bench.

I quickly get changed so I can get out of here, but as I'm pulling on a shirt, Jeremy sits on the bench next to my cubby.

"You okay?"

I shrug, forcing an easy smile on my face. "You know me. I'm always okay."

Paul snorts, and Jeremy glances at him quickly before looking back at me.

"What Preston said was fucked up. I'll talk to him about it."

I pat Jeremy on the shoulder when he opens his mouth to say something else.

"It's fine, man. I let him get to me today, and I knew better." I walk past him, done with this conversation. I love Jeremy like a brother. I would go to war for him, but I can't look at him right now. I know Preston is going through a lot. His dad died, he's injured, he has legal shit to deal with, processing everything, but that doesn't give him a free pass to hurt everyone around him.

Leaving the arena, I head toward the dorms. I should go to the dining hall and get dinner, but I don't want to people right now. I'm too tired.

"Hey!" The cheerful voice of my new bestie grates on my nerves, and I have to force myself to take a breath.

"How's it going?" I stop walking and wait for her to catch up.

"You know, fine." She shrugs. "I saw your practice. Did you and your boyfriend have a fight or something?"

Preston was right, I guess.

"He's not my boyfriend." The doors to the rink open behind me, and I turn to watch Paul walk away from me with Jeremy and Preston toward the dining hall. *I should have stayed with them.*

"Oh really? Hmm, I was getting a vibe." She wags her eyebrows. "It's so hot when men kiss."

"Kissing is attractive in general," I say back. "I'm heading back to my room for a nap. I'll talk to you later."

I hustle away before she can say anything else and hope she doesn't follow me. I don't have the energy today.

When I get to our dorm room, I'm disappointed when Paul isn't there, even though I knew he wouldn't be. I need to know what the fuck that was in the locker room. I'm already so fucking attached to him that I don't think I can do casual hookups too. Relationships aren't really my thing, I've never had the time or energy for one outside of hockey, but I would try for him.

I peel off my shirt and drop my pants on the floor by my bed, leaving me in just hamburger boxer briefs, then look at Paul's bed. I want to crawl into it and wrap his scent around me, but I don't want him to think I'm getting clingy or assuming things, so I crash face down onto my bed and fall asleep.

My dreams are weird, flashes of memories that I can't quite get a hold of. Something is pulling at my conscience, wanting me to wake up, but I don't know what it is. Kisses? Pressure?

Wake up. Wake up. Wake up.

I gasp awake, my head jerking off the pillow as someone presses soft kisses across my shoulders.

"Hey," Paul whispers with his lips still against my skin. "I brought you food."

My stomach lets out a loud grumble, and Paul chuckles. I drop my head back to my pillow with a smile on my face.

"I knew you loved me. You feed me." The words fall from my mouth so easily, like they always have, but do they mean something more serious now? Can I not say that anymore?

Paul's body weight presses against me, his dick hard against my ass as he groans in my ear. "Do you have any idea how sexy your ass and legs are in these?"

My eyes widen at his words and finding him hard against me. I don't know what this is or what I'm supposed to do now. I don't know how to handle this shift. Especially since I don't know the rules or what is expected of me.

"Yeah, that's cool and all, but I'm hungry." My stomach lets out another grumble, and Paul laughs. That's something at least.

"You're choosing food over orgasms?" He nips at my neck, and I shiver but lift up on my arms. Paul lets out a surprised sound and wraps his arms around my body on reflex.

"Right now, yes. Feed me."

I've been living and breathing your touch lately. If I don't come up for air, I'll drown in you.

The thought has my heart lurching, but it's true.

Paul gets off my bed and hands me the bag he brought back for me. I don't even bother to look at it before I start shoving it in my mouth. Some kind of grilled chicken salad thing, rice, extra chicken, and a chocolate chip cookie the size of my face.

While I inhale the food, Paul lays out on his bed and starts playing NHL 21 on his Xbox. Did he clean up after he got back? I don't smell his body wash, so I don't think he took a full shower, but I can't imagine he's lying there with dry cum in his pants.

That was hot as fuck, though. Somehow, he was still in control, but I was doing the fucking. I've definitely never experienced that before, but I really want to do it again.

"So you really are into guys too?" I ask with my face turned toward my food.

Without missing a beat or hesitating, Paul says, "Yeah."

I chew my food longer than needed just for something to do. "Have you done anything before? With a guy, I mean?"

"I've kissed a few but not much further than that." He shrugs like it's no big deal, but he's not pulling it off.

"What stopped you before?" *Because we did a lot more than kiss, and you had no hesitation.*

Paul's shoulders drop a little, and he shoves his hands under his legs, then shrugs. "I don't know. Just didn't feel right, I guess."

I try really hard not to smile but fail miserably. His words have happiness fluttering in my chest and heating my face.

"But it was okay with . . . me?" I hate how vulnerable my tone is, how much I'm hoping he wants to do it again.

Paul sits up and moves to face me with his feet on the floor.

"Yeah, it was . . . it was *perfect*." The last word is a whisper, but I heard it. Hope blossoms in my chest, and all I want is for him to kiss me. Tell me that I am perfect for him.

But since I can't always control the words that come out of my mouth, I have to make it weird.

"Listen, I could help a buddy out and you could use me to explore . . . things." The faked nonchalance of my tone is so obvious it's painful. I want to face-palm myself. Ugh. Why am I like this?

Paul lifts his head and meets my eyes, to which I waggle my eyebrows with a dumb-ass smile lifting my lips.

"For real?" Paul is watching me so closely it's uncomfortable.

"Yeah." I shrug. "You're comfortable with me, I'm a cuddle whore, and orgasms are awesome. It's a win-win."

Please don't break my heart.

CHAPTER 9
Paul

Reaching for Brendon, I pull him to me, crashing my lips to his. I take my frustration from the last few days out on him, all teeth and tongues and aggression, which he gives right back, climbing onto my lap. I love the way he's not fragile and doesn't back down from a fight.

I don't let the kiss go too long and pull back to rest my forehead against his, just breathing him in for a minute. Brendon slides his arms around my neck and presses our bodies together. I knew I missed his touch, but I didn't know I needed it this badly. Some part of me that I didn't know was tense relaxes. The tightness in my chest is gone, and the worry hanging heavy around my shoulders lightens.

"Lay with me for a while." I don't ask, and he doesn't argue, just nods, and we settle onto the bed. I hand him the Xbox controller, and he flips through until he finds *Star Wars: Episode IV,* then lays back against me. I run my hand through his hair, and he quickly falls asleep. My soul breathes a sigh of relief having him against me, his weight on me.

I didn't fuck this up. Thank fuck.

I watch the movie I've seen more times than I can count, letting my mind wander. What's Dad doing? Is he lonely? Would I still be here if Mom were alive? I hope we win our next game.

Brendon rolls over, pushing his face into my neck and sliding his knee between my thighs, damn near resting on my balls. Using my foot, I drag the blanket up from the bottom of the bed and cover us, then shut off the TV, and fall asleep holding my favorite person.

When I'm woken up in the morning, Brendon is sliding his hard-on against my hip and sucking on my neck.

"If you don't stop, we're going to be late to the gym," I grumble, not wanting him to stop.

"If we do it right, we'll still get cardio." The little shit smiles against my skin. "Also, I hate your fucking alarm."

I laugh and roll over him to settle in between his thighs, our hips pressed together. In the shadows of five a.m., I can barely see his pink cheeks, but the lust in his eyes is so fucking clear. I want nothing more than to bury myself inside of him or feel my body stretch around him.

The thought has me remembering that I have toys hidden under my bed and my dick throbs at the idea.

Brendon slides his hand up my chest, and he wraps his legs around my hips. I lean down and flick my tongue over his nipple. He gasps and arches into me.

"Were you serious about me experimenting with you?" My words are hesitant, quiet, in the dark of the room. Like if I whisper them, it won't hurt if he says no.

"Yes," he groans, grinding up into me.

"We gotta be quick," I groan around his nipple, biting

on the sensitive skin, then pulling as much of his flesh into my mouth as I can with hard suction.

"Fuck," he whimpers. "Not a problem."

I run my palm against his cock, reaching into his underwear and taking him in my hand. I've thought about this so many fucking times. His dick is hard in my hand, thick and heavy.

"Can I suck you?" I can't take my eyes off my hand stroking him, the flush of his skin, and the way he arches into me. The little sounds he makes in the back of his throat will be playing on repeat all fucking day in my head.

"Please," he moans, and I shift down to get him into my mouth. His skin is soft with a hint of salt when I lick across the tip. Brendon gasps, reaching for the sheets to find something to hold on to. "Please . . . fuck."

I wrap my lips around his head, bobbing a little, and watching his reactions. He grips his hair and pulls, his legs wrapping around my back.

Releasing him, I lick a line down his shaft to his balls, his neatly trimmed red hair tickling my tongue. I suck one into my mouth while stroking him in quick, hard pumps. The skin, rough on my tongue, is a new sensation, and I like it a lot more than I expected.

"Paul," Brendon pants, and I grin around his ball. "I'm gonna . . . fuck . . . I can't . . . please."

I pop his nut out of my mouth and make sure there's a hard edge to my voice when I speak again. "Be a good little slut and come for me."

His body tightens, cock throbbing, as cum erupts onto his stomach on a loud groan. I stroke him through his orgasm until he's shaking and his body relaxes, then lick my way back up his dick and suck lightly at his tip. The bitter taste of his cum is lingering on his skin, and I love it.

He hisses and jerks his hips away from me. Smiling up

at him, I move up his body, painting his skin with his cum where his shirt rode up.

"I like you messy and wrecked." I kiss his lips softly, and he groans into my mouth.

"What about you?" Brendon looks down at the tent in my pajama pants. I fucking ache, there's no denying that, but we don't have time, and I kind of like edging myself.

"Be a good boy and I'll let you make me come later." Brendon's face flames at my words, and I quickly get up and get changed, then head out of our dorm while he curses my name. For five a.m., I am way too happy, and the guys notice.

"What the fuck is wrong with your face?" Riggs, one of our young freshmen, snarls at me.

"Sorry, little man, it's grown-up shit." I clap him on the back and step onto the elevator where Carp and Willis are waiting. Jeremy forces himself next to me, and Brendon steps into the hallway, glaring daggers at me as the doors to the elevator shuts.

"What's his problem?" Jeremy asks.

"Must have woken up on the wrong side of the bed this morning." I shrug and hide my smile by taking a drink from my water bottle.

We shuffle out of the enclosed space and head toward the gym. I'm already picturing all of the ways Brendon can get me off, or torture me, and I can't fucking wait.

All through our time in the gym, Brendon fucks with me. Bending over where I get a full view of his ass. Taking his shirt off so I watch his muscles move under his skin.

By the time it's our turn for barbell squats, he's worked himself up more than he has me. I'm used to him touching me, being damn near naked around me while I had to hide my reaction. It's just another day.

"Spot me." He slaps my stomach with the back of his

hand and gets his weights set on the bar. I step up behind him and squat with him, with my arms out in case he needs help getting up. Every time he stands up, he shifts a little closer to me until he's brushing my crotch with his ass. I smirk at him in the mirror in front of us. Thankfully, no one is really paying any attention to us, so I can lean in and whisper in his ear.

"Are you trying to tell me you want me to fuck you?" His already red and sweaty face flushes darker, almost purple, and it spreads down his neck and chest.

"Maybe . . . I don't often," he grunts back, almost not able to get back up from the squat. He pushes through and gets the bar back on the rack and steps away from it. "What about you?"

I'm not embarrassed when I respond. "I've never tried."

It's Brendon's turn to smile, and it's a dangerous one. One that says he has plans that I will like. Fuck, I hate that we have classes and can't just go back to the dorm and make each other come all day.

If I'm going to play with him later, I may need to get off first so I don't look like a two-pump chump . . .

CHAPTER 10

Paul

My last class of the day is cut short thanks to a test, so I'm back in our room an hour before I expect Brendon.

All afternoon, I've been thinking about the toys I have hidden under my bed. I'm nervous, though. Nothing has been in my ass. Ever. I've never tried anal at all, actually. The high school girlfriend I had wasn't into it, and that's just not something you ask a random hookup. It just feels more personal, more intimate, somehow.

My hands are shaking as I pace the room. What if Brendon tries and I hate it? I should experiment some on my own, right? So I don't embarrass myself. If I know I don't like it, I can just tell him that instead of hating something he does to me.

Reaching for the bag under my bed where we keep the liquor, I grab the whiskey, unscrew the cap, and take a swig. It burns a bit going down, but it heats my belly. I take another swallow and put it back, then reach under my bed for the supplies.

After cleaning up in the bathroom, I lay on my bed, naked from the waist down, and just feel around. One hand stroking my dick while the other plays with my balls and presses against my taint. I'm nervous and excited about what comes next, and my cock doesn't know how to handle it. I go from raging hard to half-cocked.

Slicking up my fingers, I slide them between my cheeks and just rub my hole.

Fuck, that feels good. My eyes close, and my dick thickens.

I rub circles over the skin, getting used to the sensation, then press one finger against it. A groan vibrates from my chest, and I'm able to get my fingertip inside of me.

Holy fuck, that's weird but good. So good.

There's a slight stretching sensation, but it's not bad, just different. I pause to add more lube and slide my finger back in, this time going deeper and thrusting. It's so good. *So fucking good.*

I add a second finger and imagine what it would be like for Brendon to fuck me. It's got to be amazing. The idea of him inside my body is a foreign concept to me, but I want to feel it. I want to make him hold out as long as he possibly can, until he's shaking and whimpering and desperate to come while he uses my ass to find his own release.

Before I can switch to the plug, my orgasm hits me like a freight train. My entire body curving in around itself and stealing my breath. My hole clenches down on my fingers so hard it damn near hurts, but it leaves me panting and exhausted.

For a few minutes, I swear I see stars and have to lie there just learning how to breathe again. Holy fuck. That was amazing.

Looking at my phone, I see I don't have long before

Brendon should be back, so I hustle to grab my clothes and get to the bathroom to clean up. It takes longer than I expected, and by the time I'm leaving the bathroom, I can hear him outside the door. I dive for my bed and throw the plug and lube under my pillow and lay on top of it.

When I turn around, Brendon is looking at me with a raised eyebrow.

"Hey, man, how was class?" I ask, way too chipper. *Jesus fuck. Chill out, man.*

"You feeling okay?" He closes the door and eyes me while he drops his backpack on the floor by his bed. "You're acting weird."

"I'm not acting weird," I scoff. I'm definitely not acting normal.

He toes off his shoes, still watching me, and climbs onto the bed, pushing me back against the mattress and settling between my thighs.

"I believe I was promised an orgasm." He waggles his eyebrows and bites his lower lip.

Well, shit.

My dick is sensitive from the recent orgasm but not unwilling.

I slide my fingers into his hair and pull his mouth down to mine. Brendon groans and gives me some of his weight. It's perfect. The solid pressure of him holding me against the bed while I taste him on my lips is everything I've ever wanted. My heart soars at the connection I have to this man, how much better the touch is because I know him.

He rocks his hips against me, and I suck on his lower lip. Brendon's cock is hard against my hip while mine is barely at half-mast.

He pulls back and looks down at me with uncertainty in his eyes and tense shoulders.

"Do you not want to do this?" His voice is small and

unsure, and I hate it. I hate that I've put that thought in his head.

"It's not that I don't want to, I'm not sure I can . . . uh . . . right this minute." I stumble over my words since I'm not sure I want to tell him I was just jacking off while imagining him pounding me into the mattress. "Can we just lay here for a bit?"

"Oh, yeah. Sure." Brendon shifts and lays next to me, only our arms touching on the too small mattress. Now it's awkward. Fucking Christ.

Brendon fidgets with his fingers, popping his knuckles and rolling his wrists. It's a nervous habit I've seen him do countless times, but I don't think I've ever been the reason for it before.

Rolling onto my side, I reach for his thigh and pull it over my hip, forcing him to roll toward me.

He watches me with a carefully blank face and for once says nothing.

"I didn't say stop touching me," I murmur, gripping the back of his neck and leaning toward him. "I jacked off right before you got here." It's my turn to turn red while he smirks at me. "But making out sounds amazing."

I slide my knee between his, slotting our bodies together, and he wraps his arm around my back to hold me against him. I smile into the kiss and slide my hand down his spine to cup his ass. God, I love the feel of him.

He moans, and I shove my hand inside his underwear to feel his skin in my palm, squeezing and kneading the muscle of his ass. He thrusts his hips and rolls his body against me.

"Tell me what you're okay with," I say against his lips.

He drags his lower lip between his teeth for a second, then meets my eyes. "I like when you talk dirty to me." His face immediately flames red, and I smirk at him.

"Yeah? You like being my little needy cock whore?" I drop my voice and put some command in it. A shiver runs through him, and I lean over him.

Brendon's eyes close, and his breath shakes on the word, "Fuck."

"Hmmm," I hum along his jaw as I nip at the skin.

"No one has ever talked to me like that." He thrusts against me again, his cock hard as a rock.

"Glad to be of service." I suck on his earlobe, and he whimpers. His reactions are definitely having an effect on my dick now.

We make out for a while, grinding against each other and just getting to know each other's bodies, but we don't take it any further.

"I really need to get some homework done," I grumble against Brendon's lips.

"I do too."

We grab our stuff, and I sit up against the pillows and headboard. Brendon lays down between my legs with the back of his head against my pelvis and puts my thighs over his shoulders. It's surprisingly comfortable, so I don't argue.

As he reads his textbook and makes notes, he strokes my leg, and it's the most comfortable I've ever felt.

Brendon's phone pings, and he groans.

I snort at his reaction and watch over his head as he opens the app and clicks on Nikki's name. Twelve unopened messages.

"Why don't you just ignore her? Eventually she'll just stop, right?"

He opens the pictures of her with stupid filters on. Teddy bear, hearts, bald.

"No," he huffs. "When I ignore her, it makes her worse."

Brendon lifts the phone and takes a selfie with my legs still over his shoulders.

"Are you really going to send that?" I sit up a little as he types out "study time" on the screen.

"I'm wearing your legs as earmuffs. Maybe she'll get the message and go away." Brendon puts his phone down and lifts his book. "I doubt it, though."

"I'm not ready for everyone to know about me." My words are soft, but he hears them. Brendon turns around and sits up, his eyes locking with mine.

"There was nothing in that picture that could be identified as you. It was just leg and hip." He squeezes my leg. "I wouldn't out you. You can change your pants or something in case she shows up, if that will make you feel better."

My head buzzes with too many thoughts. The fear of being found out and being made a target. Living out in the open makes you vulnerable. I'm a hockey player. I know I can take a hit and stay standing, but that doesn't mean I want to be judged for who I'm dating or for who I find attractive. Homophobia runs rampant in sports. As soon as a player comes out, no one cares about how they play, only their sex life. It's bullshit and not the way I want my life to go.

I nod and settle back on the pillow while I suck on the inside of my lip. Brendon leans over me, his hands on the mattress on either side of my hips, and he kisses me softly. He sucks on my bottom lip and presses his mouth against mine again.

"Do you trust me?" he whispers against my lips.

"Yes," I answer without hesitation.

He smiles and kisses me again; it's a light pressure, soft, and sweet. More comforting than anything else.

"I wouldn't do anything to hurt you on purpose." He pulls back enough to meet my eyes.

"I know."

CHAPTER 11

Brendon

F rom the second my skates hit the ice, I know
something is wrong.

Dread sits heavy in my stomach, and a weight
pulls hard on my shoulders, but it isn't until the Minnesota
lineup is announced that I start to understand why. I didn't
look at the list of players this time. Hockey is a small
community, and we know a lot of the players either
personally or in passing.

The announcers call out "Chad Fenwick," and nausea
rolls through me. Fuck. I played with him when I was
teenager, before I joined the Lumberjacks. A shiver runs
through me, and my skin breaks out in a cold sweat that
has nothing to do with the ice under my feet. I would like
to believe that he doesn't recognize my face or name, but
I'm not that lucky.

Memories try to invade my mind, making my hands
tremble and my stomach roll, but I can't let him fuck with
my head. I'm not the same kid I was when we were on the
same team.

The game starts, and I'm on the bench waiting for my

shift, watching my old teammate across the ice. His eyes meet mine, and he sneers, leaning toward one of his teammates and says something to him. They laugh, both looking in my direction, and my stomach clenches.

"What's up with you?" Paul nudges me with his shoulder, and I straighten up, looking back at the ice to watch the game. I can't show him that I'm a victim.

"Nothing."

Coach calls for a shift change, and we head out on the ice. Like a bat out of hell, Johnson, Albrooke, and I take off, racing for the puck. I slam into Fenwick, and he grins at me.

"Surprised I didn't hear your dumb-ass sounds across the ice. You still squawk?"

Goddamn it.

A tingling starts in my chest as embarrassment and shame heat my blood.

My body moves across the ice, but my head isn't in it. I don't know what I'm doing, too lost in overthinking everything I've ever said. Minnesota gets a goal, and we head off the ice for a shift change. Have we been out here long enough to call a line change? I'm in a daze as I follow my teammates to the bench, barely recognizing that I handed my hockey stick to the assistant. My body moves on muscle memory alone at this point, not needing any direction from my brain. I feel dizzy and heavy, like I have a spotlight on me. Has Chad or any of his lackeys told anyone what happened that day? Does anyone else know about the abuse and the tears and humiliation?

"Dude, what the hell is wrong with you?" Paul leans over to look me in the face. "Are you sick or something. You look pale." He pulls a glove off and touches my face.

"What's the deal, Oiler? Why's Johnson babying you?"

Coach leans over my shoulder, his eyes roaming over my face.

"I'm fine." I shrug them both off and reach for a water bottle just to give myself something to do.

Coach pats my helmet and walks away, but Paul isn't giving up.

"You may be able to fool everyone else, but you can't fool me," he grits out quietly before putting his glove back on and sitting up.

Right now, his irritation is the least of my worries. Maybe this is the final straw and he'll walk away from me.

For the rest of the game I'm not on the ice with Fenwick, so I can breathe. He's probably been a bully his whole life. Has he hurt anyone else? I have to assume he has. Someone like that wouldn't be a one and done.

That fucker is just trying to get in my head, and I've let him.

I crack my neck and try to get my head on straight.

Paul gets a shot on goal with an assist from me and lights up the lamp, Riggs somehow manages a breakaway in the third, and it isn't until the end of the game that I notice a coach on the Minnesota bench staring at me.

Coach Craig Williams.

I'm frozen in place, eyes locked with the man who allowed me to be belittled for years. I can feel the blood draining from my face, the air in my lungs being sucked out by some invisible vacuum, and I could swear I was sixteen again. Weak. Vulnerable. Humiliated.

He can't be here. Mom said he was coaching for Michigan. Did she tell me the wrong school? I purposefully didn't look it up because I knew I would obsess over it and count down the days until I had to see him again. Not to mention, Minnesota's coach is some dude named John. What the fuck is he doing here?

Someone pushes on my back, and I stumble, turning my head to see Jeremy with a big grin on his face. He wraps his arm around my shoulders in excitement. Our entire team is on the ice, celebrating our win while I stand here stuck in my past.

"Come on!" He pats my back and ushers me toward the line of our guys so we can shake hands with the opposing team. I don't want to do this. I don't want Fenwick to touch me even through the gloves.

As the handshakes start, and the mumbling of "Good game" surrounds us, Fenwick's sneering face fills my vision.

"Squawk for me, birdy," he says, holding on to my hand while the guys around him laugh.

My body trembles and saliva pools in my mouth a second before nausea rolls through me, and I lean over and puke on the ice. I brace my hands on my knees as everything I've had to eat or drink since the start of the game is splashed at my feet.

Fucking hell.

My face is sweaty but not from heat, and my hands are so shaky anyone who touches me will be able to feel it. I'm not okay. Laughter fills my ears, and I'm not sure if it's in my head or outside of it.

"Oiler!" Coach hollers as he comes toward me. Paul and Jeremy flank me as we head toward the shoot to get off the ice and head to the locker room. "Go see medical. Did you hit your head? Food poisoning? What's going on with you?"

"I'm fine, Coach."

He doesn't look like he believes me, but he lets me head down the hallway anyway.

I knew I would have to face them at some point, but I didn't think it would be together. Not only did Williams not stop Chad from fucking with me, I'm pretty sure he encouraged it.

When we get to medical, Dr. Butler is there and waiting for me.

"Thank you, boys. I can take it from here." He shoos Paul and Jeremy, leaving me alone with the man. He's a good guy from what I can tell. Doesn't take any shit, but he's friendly and approachable.

"What brings you to my office, Mr. Oiler?" He gives me a quick glance over, probably checking for blood.

"I threw up on the ice."

"Did you hit your head during the game?" He pushes on my neck, takes my helmet off and feels around in my sweaty hair, and flicks a pen light between my eyes.

"No."

"Eat anything weird? How does your stomach feel now? Any other symptoms?" He motions for me to lay down and lifts my jersey when I do, pushing on my abdomen.

"No, I'm fine." *If by fine I mean on the edge of a nervous fucking breakdown because I'm a big baby and seeing my old bully has turned me back into a freak, then yeah. I'm fine.*

"Hmm. Well, take it easy on your stomach tonight and check in with me in the morning." He helps me sit up, and I head to the locker room to get changed.

The team is rowdy after the win, which I expected, but it's overwhelming to my busy mind. I flinch when someone yells and head to my cubby to strip down. Paul sees me and comes over in just his compression shorts. It's sexy as fuck to see him like this, despite the bruise forming on his arm from a hit he took in the second period, but my head is too busy to let my body respond.

He puts his hand on my shoulder, and I jerk out from under it without thinking about it. His hand hovers there in the air for a second before he drops it back to his side, confusion, hurt, and concern on his face. No one here knows what really happened on that team. I thought I was over it, that I had moved on, but apparently not.

"What did the doctor say?"

"That I'm fine," I snap the same words I've said a dozen times tonight and pull my jersey off. I wrap that irritation around me like a shield to stop my hands from trembling. Frustration is so much easier than fear. I don't have time to be sucked down into that headspace right now. It has to wait.

Someone pats my back, and I quickly shrug it off. Jeremy steps into view with confusion on his face, and I have to grit my teeth together so I don't go off. Why can't they all just fuck off and leave me alone? I just want to be left alone!

I pull on my suit without showering, which gets some raised eyebrows, but no one asks about it, thank fuck. I can't shower in here. I need the privacy and safety of my own bathroom with a locking door. Once I'm dressed, I quickly exit and damn near run back to the dorms. My lungs burn and my legs protest the effort after the game, but I force my body to move anyway. I need to get to safety.

With every step I take, I feel like I'm being watched. As if people all around me are whispering and laughing about me. *Make it stop.* I just need it all to stop.

Someone tries to talk to me in the hallway, but I ignore them and burst into my dorm room like my ass is on fire, slamming the door behind me and leaning against it. I check under the beds, in the closets, and the bathroom to make sure I'm alone, then pull out the rum from under Paul's bed and chug as much as I can stand. On my empty stomach, it doesn't take long for the alcohol to hit me, but instead of the happy drunk I usually am, tears start falling down my face in chest-rattling sobs.

Freak. Weak. Birdy.

I manage to get mostly undressed and head into the bathroom with one sock and my underwear still on. I give zero fucks. The warm water has my eyes closing as it rinses the day and the game from my skin. Finally, I'm warm, no one is touching me, and I can't hear anyone talking about me. Peace. I found peace.

After passing out drunk, my stomach isn't happy with me this morning—neither is Paul, if I'm being honest—but I'm pushing through. Doc cleared me to play, and when my skates hit the ice for warmups, an anxiety I haven't felt in a long time settles on my shoulders. I'm actually afraid of what will happen this game. Will I have to see Coach Williams? Will Fenwick get under my skin again and fuck up my head?

Paul and Jeremy are watching me like they would an animal at the zoo, like they don't know what to do with me or if I'm dangerous. My skin is too tight, the pressure on my chest too heavy, and I can feel every pair of eyes on me. I know it's stupid and not accurate logically, but that doesn't mean anything to the panic.

Will Jeremy and Paul laugh at the stupid nicknames too? Will they start making fun of me for things I've worked so fucking hard to mask?

Shaking my head, I force myself into character. These guys expect me to act like a dumbass, and I'll throw everything off if I don't. I was already weird yesterday. I can't risk being off today. But now I don't know what's too much or too loud or too weird. I'm second-guessing everything.

As we stand in the hallway waiting for the pregame to start, I slap sticks with Paul and Jeremy, then shove my stick between my legs and ride it like a horse. Why? No idea. But I hear the laughter of the crowd, and it makes me feel worse. I should be used to being laughed at. I'm always doing shit that makes the crowd laugh, but it doesn't feel right today. Doing weird shit is what I'm known for, and it happens more and more when I'm stressed.

Paul slides up next to me, pulling my helmet to his and slaps the back of my head.

"We got this."

After introductions, the game starts, and our assistant coach offers water and snacks to those of us on the bench. Willis eats a banana before he gets on the ice, Riggs eats a damn Snickers bar, and I'm offered a Payday.

"Fuck yeah! I love Paydays!" I grab the candy bar and rip it open with my teeth since my gloves are useless right now. I shove the salted peanut-covered caramel candy bar into my mouth and groan.

"Jesus, Oiler, you gonna deep throat that thing?" Matthews, one of our D men, laughs.

"You wish," I toss back around a mouthful of candy. "You know you're jealous of this nut in my mouth." I send him a wink. Paul snorts to hide his laughter, and Matthews just shakes his head at me. They're all used to me by now and don't really take me seriously. If they hear the shit Chad says, will that change? Will I become the outcast again?

"Switch!" Coach bellows, and the first line comes off the ice while the second line rushes out.

I have one bite left and surprise Paul by shoving it into his mouth. His teeth graze my fingers, and my dick stirs.

He lifts an eyebrow at me as he chews and swallows the salty-sweet treat but doesn't say anything.

"Nuts are good for you. Protein." With a big smile, I turn back to watch the game. It takes every bit of my self-control to not look at the bench on the other side of the ice. To not track the movement of the man who haunted me like a nightmare for years.

We're finally called to the ice, and I race for the puck in our attack zone, Johnson and Albrooke right behind me. I get the puck and fling it to Johnson, only to be slammed into the boards. Hard. I swear I felt a rib pop, but I don't let the pain stop me.

Swinging my gaze to the guy who hit me, I see Fenwick's smiling face behind some guy I don't know.

"Nice to meet you, birdy," the player who slammed me says before taking off.

What the actual fuck?

Does their entire team know?

Shoving off the wall, I find the puck and speed toward it, but I'm once again hit, this time shoulder chucked by some big D man.

Fuck these guys.

"Oiler!" Carmichael yells at me as I pass him in the stands.

"Shut the fuck up!" I snap back at him but keep moving down the bench. I'm not in the mood for his shit.

"Is it just me or are they going after you more than normal?" Albrooke leans over and asks me.

"Kinda seems that way." I shrug him off.

For the rest of the game, every chance they get, I'm slammed, tripped, and shoved. My ribs fucking ache, and every breath comes with a shot of electricity straight through me, but I don't let it stop me. I won't let them see me break.

CHAPTER 12

Paul

What the fuck is going on with Brendon? He's acting weird, jerking away from touch, and got drunk the night before a game. I check the dining hall after the game but don't see him. Running into Jeremy leaving the rink, we walk together.

"What was that with Brendon?" he asks me.

"I have no fucking idea." And that makes me nervous.

Over the years, I've been able to piece together that some kind of trauma happened, but I don't know what it was or when it happened. Did something trigger a memory?

"I haven't seen you guys in a while. Movie marathon tomorrow?"

"Sure." I hear myself say the word, but I'm not really paying attention to what he said. I'm too worried about Brendon and at this point, I'm not sure how Jeremy and Brendon's relationship is, so I don't want to say anything.

"I'm going to crash. Later." I open my dorm and find Brendon getting dressed to go out.

"Hey, where you going?" I try to sound casual, but I'm kind of hurt he didn't ask if I wanted to hang out or join him. I can't remember the last time he didn't.

"Frat party," he says, and I turn around to look at him.

"Since when do you go to frat parties?" I unbutton my shirt while I watch him pull a clean T-shirt over his head. He's got a massive bruise forming on his side that looks bad. "Holy shit, did you have that looked at?" I grab his shirt and lift it to see the mark. I trail my fingers over the darkening flesh carefully, following the edges over his ribs and around to his back. "You could have a cracked rib."

"I'm fine." He pulls the shirt from my hand and steps around me, careful not to touch me.

"What the hell is going on with you?" I demand. Since when does he not want to touch me? Did I do something? Is this his way to say he doesn't want to mess around anymore?

"Nothing. I'm fine," he snaps as he pulls on his shoes.

"Bullshit!" I step into his space and pull his face up to look at me. He flinches but doesn't pull away. "There's something going on. Talk to me."

Brendon wraps his hand around my wrist and pulls my hand from his face and pushes me away from him.

"Don't touch me." The even, almost cold tone of his voice is a knife in the heart.

Then he's gone, and I'm staring at the door as it closes behind him.

What the fuck just happened?

CHAPTER 13

Brendon

I don't know how many shots I've had, but I feel fucking good. My body moves to the beat of the music blaring through the house. I don't remember which one because I don't care, and it doesn't matter.

Nothing matters but the hum in my veins and the blank space in my head. No past, no future, just this moment and the next.

My head is clear. The fear of earlier, the feeling of being trapped and abused is gone thanks to the liquor, and I can enjoy the sway of bodies. In here, I can get lost in the movement.

A warm body presses up against my back, a hand on my hip, and I smile. It's not the man I want touching me, he's not comfortable in public yet, but that's okay for now.

The stranger grinds against my ass, his hand sliding under my shirt, and it steals my breath. I shouldn't let him touch me like this, but I'm damn near desperate for someone to *want* me. Paul talks a big game but hasn't done anything more than we've been doing. Kissing, handjobs, a couple of blowies, but nothing more. Orgasms are great but damn it, I want to fuck.

A smaller, curvier body slides against my front, and I pop my eyes open. The girl is a curly blonde, smiling up at me like I hung the damn moon. Fucking Nikki. I've been avoiding her the last week, but I should have figured she would find me here.

Reaching for the side of my neck, she presses her mouth to mine. She moans, but it doesn't feel right. It's probably better for people to see me or Paul with someone, especially since I'm so touchy with him, but I hate this. She's a pretty girl, a bit intense, but she's not Paul. I want Paul. I crave the way he gives me orders and uses me to feel good. He makes the constant buzzing in my head stop.

He deserves better than me. I'm a mess, annoying, need reassurance all the damn time, moody, and loud. He's not even here, and I miss him. How lame is that? I live with him but having him gone for an hour is too much?

I pull back from her lips and kiss her forehead, hoping she doesn't get pissed off. She sways with me and whoever is still against my back. It feels good to be touched, but it's not right. It's not who I want.

Fuck.

Why am I so weak?

My happy mood fades, the comfort of touch morphs into too much, it's too hot, and the music hurts my ears. I need to get out of here.

Pushing my way through the crowd without a word to anyone, I get blocked and pushed around while the walls close in and the panic rises. I need to get out. It's too loud. Too hot. Too much.

Get out. Get out. Get out.

My breathing is coming too fast as my pulse spikes, the alcohol that was making me happy and loose now makes me paranoid and edgy. My body is vibrating under my skin, and I just want to scream to make it all stop.

Pain slices through me in an instant, stealing my breath and shutting down my brain as quick as a blink. Someone elbowed me in the nasty bruise that has turned purple from tonight's game, but the panic is gone.

What the fuck?

Just like that, the overwhelming stimulation is quiet, and I can almost breathe again. I cover my side in case I get bumped again, and I make it outside to the cool winter air and suck in a deep breath. The sun is down, but the night isn't dark like back home. We're too close to the city to see the stars, and that makes my chest ache. I miss the stars. We lived on the outskirts of Muskegon, where the city lights didn't wash out the night sky. Sometimes we even saw the aurora borealis. It was rare but beautiful. Something about it made me feel tiny, like when people stand at the edge of the ocean.

Leaning against a tree that has lost all its leaves, I lift my face to the sky and close my eyes, just breathing in the night air.

Do I really want to be here? In this big city, at this big college, working toward the unknown? I miss home. My family. The familiar streets.

Nothing out here is familiar or comforting. I just want to go home.

A tear slips from the corner of my eye, and I let it fall. Maybe it would be better for me to just transfer home. I'm sure I could get into a college there and play hockey.

I slide down the trunk of the tree, the rough bark scratching at my back as my shirt rides up, but I don't care. The bite of pain clears my head a little.

I'm so damn tired. Tired of fighting myself. Tired of not being enough. Tired of wanting things I can't have.

I thought I was over that shit with Chad, had moved on. Since I have sex regularly, cuddle and freely touch Paul, I thought I was past it, but tonight proves I'm just as weak as I was when it happened. Paul deserves better than me and my baggage.

I close my eyes again and rest my head on the tree, quickly falling asleep.

My eyes pop open with vomit shooting out of my mouth. I empty my stomach on the grass under a tree, gasping for breath and trying to remember where I am and how I got here. Why am I sleeping outside? It's still dark, and I have no idea how long I've been out here, but I'm freezing.

Once my stomach stops trying to force its way out of my mouth, I sit back and look around with one eye half opened. My head is throbbing like someone is using it as a bass drum. Fuuuck.

Slowly, I make it to my feet and head toward the dorms. The cold air prickling at my goose bump-covered skin. Did I have a jacket or hoodie? I don't know.

I stumble my way across campus, the longest fucking walk of my life, and thank whoever is listening that I have my keycard to get into the dorms. The warmth of the dorm building makes me shiver more.

When I get to the door, I pat my pockets and grumble when I don't find my keys. Fuck. Paul will be pissed if I wake him up. I try the door, hoping to get lucky and almost sag in relief when it opens, but that relief is quickly gone when I see Paul standing in the middle of our room, arms crossed, and angry.

I close the door and lean back against it. The alcohol is still in my system, making my head a little fuzzy still.

"Where the fuck have you been?" Paul's tone is quiet. It's so much worse than yelling.

"The party." I shrug and reach for a hoodie hanging on the back of my desk chair. Not only am I cold but I feel vulnerable, like I need a shield to protect me from my best friend. I hate that feeling. All I want is to be wrapped around him, safe.

Why can't he just hug me? I don't think he's ever looked at me like he is now, in this moment. Like he hates me. He's been frustrated with me, sure, we've argued, but he's never been this angry at me. It's soul-crushing.

"Why? I called you and you didn't answer," Paul demands, his frustration wrapped around him like a cloud, suffocating me. He strides forward and stands so fucking close I can feel his breath on my face.

"I didn't hear it," I snap, too tired and exposed to de-escalate the situation.

I shove him back, but he grabs my hoodie and pulls me flush against him.

"When I call or text, I need you to respond," he grits out, looking me in the eye. His fierce green eyes vibrate with emotion that I can't read. The look on his face changes when he looks me over. Did I puke on myself or something? "Why are you putting more clothes on?"

His touch is too much, and I shove him away from me. The panic from earlier overtakes me, and I'm left with the need to scream.

"Don't touch me!" The words are loud in my head, but I don't know if I managed to say them out loud. Immediately, the hands that were on me are gone, and I almost sob with relief. I'm vaguely aware of tears streaming down my face, and my body burns. The band around my ribs constricts, and I can't breathe.

Backing up away from him, the only thing I can focus on is being alone. Alone is safer.

"Go away," I snap, my body vibrating with the war in my head spinning out of control. "You're acting like a jealous boyfriend."

Hurt splashes across his face, and I want to punch myself for it. I'm garbage. I deserve to be alone where I can't fuck up anyone else. My damage is hurting those around me now.

"Spoiler alert, I basically am your boyfriend." Paul's shoulders tighten as he prepares for me to hurt him badly. "Do you not want to do this anymore? Whatever this is?"

It would be so easy to lie to him and tell him yes so he goes away. I just need a fucking minute to get my head together, but he won't stop.

I stumble back, hitting a solid surface and slide down into a ball on the floor. Wrapping my arms around my knees, I bury my face in my legs and rock back and forth.

You're okay. Breathe.

"Brendon." *That's Paul.*

Paul won't hurt you.

His anger has faded, and I know if I look up at him, it'll be pity in his fucking face. God, I'm such a fucking mess. Who the fuck is going to want to deal with this shit?

Something brushes the back of my hand, and I flinch. There's a shuffling sound, and I peek up over my knees to see Paul sitting on the floor with his legs on either side of mine like a barricade while he watches me.

"You're okay." His eyes meet mine, filled with determination and pain while I'm falling the fuck apart. I hate myself for how weak I am.

"I don't—" My words are cracked and pitiful, but he hears them. "I don't want to stop."

A flittering memory from last night flashes in my head. Nikki kissed me. Fuck.

"Wait." Paul tenses at my words. "Nikki was there. I think she kissed me."

He grits his teeth, the muscle in his jaw jumping, but he nods. I can see his need to touch me simmering below the surface, but he holds back.

"You're mine. No one touches you but me. Do you understand?" Paul's voice is warm but hard like he's trying to keep himself under control.

I nod and drop my forehead back to my arms so I don't have to see him anymore.

CHAPTER 14
Paul

"Brendon," I breathe his name like a plea. "Can I touch you?"

Not being able to touch him is killing me. It's so weird for him to not want it. It scares me.

I barely hear the whimpered "Please," but I move slowly. When he flinched away from me, it broke my heart, and I'm not sure I can handle him doing it again.

His breathing is coming faster, like he's fighting to hold on to the emotions boiling inside of him, but it's cracking. Slowly, I reach for his hand. The same way I would a scared animal. I don't want him to push me away, but I half expect him to.

Lifting his hand, I open his fist and press his palm against my cheek, his red-rimmed, glassy eyes peek over his arms to watch me, and I hold his gaze. I hold his hand against my face, nuzzling his palm as he lifts his head. A tear trails down his face, and when I brush it away with my thumb, he breaks. Brendon lets out a sob and crashes into me, wrapping his arms and legs around me, and burying his face in my neck while he cries.

My best friend, the love of my fucking life, is in pain and fighting himself.

I hold him against me while he lets out the emotions threatening to choke him. I don't say anything, I don't have to. Not right now. He's falling apart, and I'll be here to pick up the pieces when he's ready.

We sit there for long minutes as he gets it out of his system, letting go of the pain he's carrying. Hurt I hope he'll let me shoulder the burden of.

Once he slows down, the muscles of his back relaxing and his sobs quietening, I whisper against his skin.

"You're okay. I've got you." I kiss his hair, his neck, all the parts of him I can reach.

"Can you lay with me?" His voice is so small, like a child who's afraid of being rejected.

"Of course." I smile at the request. I will never turn him down when he needs me.

I stand and offer him a hand up, which he takes.

Brendon reaches for my shirt and pulls it up. I lift my arms so he can get it off and do the same to him. Being skin to skin is so fucking intimate. It's comfort and love and peace.

I kiss his forehead, and he reaches for my pants with a blush on his cheeks that's cute as fuck.

"What do you need right now?" I watch him as he moves, looking for what he doesn't want to say out loud.

"Cuddles." The word is almost aggressive, like he's afraid I'll make fun of him for it.

"Okay." I hook my fingers under his chin and lift his face to mine. I wait until his eyes meet mine, then I brush my lips against his in a careful, lingering kiss. "Come on."

I grab his hand and pull back my blankets to climb in. Brendon drops his pants in a heap on the floor, hurries to turn off the lights in his hockey underwear, then slides in next to me. His cheek is on my chest with my arm around him and his thigh between mine. I run my hand through his hair, and he settles.

"Do you want to watch something?"

He shakes his head and drags his stubbly face against my skin. "I'm sorry."

His words are so quiet I almost think I imagined them.

"Sorry? For what?"

"I'm not easy to deal with. I know that. I'm sorry."

My hand tightens in his hair, and I pull his head back until I can see him.

"No." My tone is harsh, but I don't care. "You are not hard to deal with. Whatever the fuck that means."

A tear slides down his face, and I hate whoever made him feel like he's too much.

"You're my favorite person. You're *my* person. There's nothing about you I would change. You hear me?" I don't let him dip his head back down until he nods. "What's this about?"

"Nothing," he whispers against my chest.

"Bullshit." I run my fingers through his hair again. "If you don't want to talk about it, say that, but don't lie to me."

He doesn't respond for a long time, and I don't try to force him to talk. My boy has a busy mind, and sometimes it takes him a while to work through all the thoughts.

"Whatever it is, you know I won't judge you, right?"

He nods against my chest, his rough cheek scratching my bare skin.

"I was bullied on the team before I met you."

My heart hurts for him. Kids are assholes. They always have been and probably always will be. Brendon is such a soft-hearted guy that I'm sure it hurt. People assume that because he's a hockey player, he doesn't have feelings or whatever, but it's not true.

"They were assholes," I say against his forehead.

"Coach Williams is Chad Fenwick's stepdad, so he got away with everything. At the time, I would make this weird sound sometimes, so Chad started calling me birdy." His voice is thick like he's trying not to cry again, and it makes me want to find Chad so I can introduce him to my fist. "The rest of the team followed suit. Then they started mocking me and fucking with me."

"I'm sorry." I curl onto my side so I can hold him better. "That never should have happened."

Brendon rolls over and pulls my arm around him so his back is to my chest, like he doesn't want to look at me while he talks.

"It got worse as time went on." His voice is so quiet I almost have to strain to hear him. "When calling me names and mocking me didn't get a reaction anymore, they started shoving me or tripping me. I would leave practice with scrapes and bruises that I would tell my mom were just hockey injuries."

Fear settles into my gut like ice. I'm afraid of where this is going.

"I told the coach about it, but he told me to suck it up, boys will be boys, stop being a pussy." Brendon's chest tenses under my hand, and I rub big circles on his skin.

Anger burns my veins that he wasn't helped. He reached out to the person who was supposed to help him, and they did nothing. Coaches are there to help shape the players, protect them, aid them. This guy failed on all accounts.

"I started dreading going to practices and games. He and his friends would corner me once everyone was gone and fuck with me. It got worse and worse until they finally went too far. They shoved a bar of soap into my mouth and held it so I couldn't spit it out. I choked on it, almost threw up a few times."

His voice is almost devoid of emotion now, like he's telling me about the weather. There's no attachment to the words. My throat aches with the sorrow I feel for him. He was a victim, and no one cared.

"Someone punched me, but I'm not sure who. I fell and Chad told me if I was going to act like a bitch, I would be used like one."

My gut clenches, and I rest my forehead against the back of his head as tears flow from my eyes.

"They laughed as I choked and begged him to stop. But it just made them worse."

"Brendon," I choke out his name. Cupping the side of his face, I turn him toward me, needing to see him. "None of that was your fault. That coach was a piece of shit and should not be allowed to be around kids."

My boy, the love of my fucking life, looks at me like he's a child. Hurt and uncertainty and humiliation clear in his sad brown eyes.

"What they did does not make you less. They're fucked up, not you." I hold his face in my hands, making him look at me. "Do you understand?"

"I've never told anyone any of that," he whispers.

"No one? Not your mom? Or a therapist?" How has he been carrying this around in him alone?

He shakes his head, and I rest my forehead on his.

"This changes nothing for me, okay?"

Brendon shudders, then kisses me softly. I follow his lead, letting him take this where he needs it to go, but he doesn't deepen it. Just takes comfort from me. It makes my heart soar to know he reaches for me when he needs something. It's everything because he is everything. My everything.

"Can you turn the TV on?" he mumbles, pushing me onto my back so he can lay on me.

"Of course." I get everything turned on and flip through the options before choosing *Letterkenny*. I can feel Brendon smile against my chest, then his whole body relaxes as I run my fingers through his hair. In no time, he's sleeping, but it takes me a while to shut my brain off. The story he told me plays on repeat in my head. It makes me want to hurt someone and wrap Brendon in a bubble so no one can get to him but me. If I ever get a second alone with Chad, I'm going to make him pay for what he's done.

CHAPTER 15
Paul

I am definitely concerned about Brendon. He's shut down, doesn't ramble the way he normally does, hasn't been hanging around the dorm. It's been a few days since he stumbled home smelling like booze and confided in me. He's never done this before, so I'm at a loss of how to handle it. Do I let him process and give him space, or do I show up and show him that I'm not scared of his emotions? Since he won't fucking talk to me, I don't know what he needs right now.

I thought I saw him at one point today, grabbed his arm to stop him from walking away from me, but it was some football player. Damn near got a fist in my face for that.

After class, I know I have a bit before he's done for the day. When I get to our room, there's a brown teddy bear in a Darby U hockey jersey sitting on my bed. What the fuck is this?

I put my backpack down and pick up the stuffed animal. A note sits on my blanket under it.

For when you need a cuddle and I'm not around!
    -Nikki

Seriously? *Ugh.* I toss the bear on Brendon's bed with the note and start deep cleaning to keep my head busy. I don't know what I was expecting today to be, but being avoided by the boy I'm head over heels for was not it. I was hoping we could get dinner, cuddle, have an orgasm or three—you know, romantic shit. Instead, I'm tearing apart my fucking dorm room to keep my mind from spiraling.

Once I've cleaned out my desk and reorganized my closet, I start pulling all the shit out from under my bed. The box that has the toys I bought makes me stop. I kind of forgot about these.

My dick twitches at the idea of this box. Hmm . . .

Putting the box on my bed, I shove everything else back under it and head to the bathroom with the lube and plug. Since I've never done this before and don't know how messy it could get, the shower seems like a good place to *play.* Sitting on the closed toilet lid, I do a search for anal prep on my phone and am overwhelmed with the number of videos, articles, and pictures.

My brain hurts, and that dude has two forearms in his ass. Jesus.

I put my phone down and decide to just wing it. It can't be too hard.

I strip off my clothes, turn the water on, and put the supplies inside the shower before stepping in. Excited, nervous energy races along my skin, tickling my stomach and making my dick ache. I do a quick rinse and slick up my fingers. The black silicone plug isn't too big, but I definitely think I need to work up to it.

I rub my finger around the skin and breathe carefully. It's a strange sensation, being touched here, but it's not bad. Once I'm able to relax, I push a finger in and lean against the shower wall. Goose bumps erupt on my skin at the unfamiliar sensations.

Thrusting the finger a few times, going a little deeper each time, I groan. One finger becomes two, and I'm pushing back on them. Fuck, it's so good. I haven't touched my dick, but the desire is strong. Pulling my fingers from my body, I feel strangely empty. It's not something I'm used to, and I can only imagine how much *more* it'll be after having sex, but the idea is exciting.

Grabbing the plug, I make sure it's coated in lube and slide it between my cheeks. I push against my hole to get a feel for it and groan. The anticipation is an erotic dance in my abdomen that I want to chase for the rest of my life. Pushing it in, I hiss at the stretch but whimper when it's fully seated inside of me. My hands tremble, and my knees try to give out, but I catch myself on the wall.

Holy. Fuck.

Electric tingles zap across my skin until even the water is almost too much. I reach for my cock and my body tenses, squeezing around the toy, and my eyes roll back into my skull. Why hasn't anyone told me how fucking good this feels?

If Brendon doesn't fuck me soon, I'll revolt.

With my hand around my dick and the water streaming down my back, I imagine Brendon behind me. His fingers digging into my hips, my hand in his hair to keep him pressed to me, and my ass slapping against him while he fucks me.

My breathing turns ragged in the steam, and I shiver as arousal pools in my groin. Cum shoots across the tub and shower wall while my ass clenches so fucking hard I cry out in agonizing pleasure.

My orgasm goes on forever, draining all the energy in my body until I'm weak and panting. It takes several minutes for me to be able to stand without leaning on the wall and remove the plug. I get it rinsed off and clean myself again before turning off the water and grabbing a towel. Sleep pulls at my eyelids, and I crash face first onto my bed in nothing but a towel and pass out.

Someone slaps my bare ass *hard*, and I jerk up on my hands to glare at Jeremy who has a shit-eating grin on his face.

"What the fuck, dude?" I start to sit up and realize I'm naked. Fuck. The towel I had on apparently came untied. I guess it's better that he found me ass up instead of the other way.

"Time for practice. Let's go."

I grumble and rub my hand over my face.

"I'm coming." I sit up and cover my lap with the towel, then look around the room but don't see any evidence of Brendon. "You see Brendon today?"

Jeremy lifts an eyebrow at me and looks at our friend's bed before answering. "No, I haven't. Not since the gym this morning. Why?" He moves to the bed and picks up the bear, then reads the note. He shows me the message with a questioning brow.

"He's got himself a fan," I grumble with a huff, then answer his question. "I don't know. He's been weird."

"Like weirder than normal?" Jeremy shoves his hands in his pockets and leans against the desk.

"Yeah." Fuck it, I don't care if Jeremy sees my ass. He's seen it before.

I get up and start pulling on clothes.

"He went to a frat party." I shove my arms through my shirt. "Have you ever heard him mention he wanted to go to one?"

"Uh, no. He's never said anything to me about it."

I grab my socks and shoes, then sit on the bed to pull them on.

"How was it? Was he crazy?" Jeremy asks.

"I didn't go." I shrug like it doesn't bother me, but it does. It stings. "He didn't want me to."

It's quiet in the room as that sinks in. When I stand, Jeremy is looking at me like he doesn't believe the words that just came out of my mouth.

"What? Did you guys get into a fight or something?"

We leave the room and head downstairs, continuing our conversation.

"No." I don't want to tell Jeremy the story he told me. I can't break that trust, but I don't know who else to talk to. Jeremy is the only one here that knows him.

"Weird."

The cold air of the rink blasts us as we step through the door and hurry to the locker room to get our gear on. The locker room is loud with the chatter of our teammates. It's such a familiar sound that I barely notice it anymore. Hockey and locker rooms have been a huge part of my life for so long that I don't know what life looks like without it.

I love that my grandparents care about hockey. They used to come to all my home games and travel if it was close enough. They have team gear from all the different ones I was a part of over the years. They're my biggest supporters, and I don't know where I would be without them believing in me, but I wish Dad gave a shit. I don't remember if he used to come to games when I was little or not, but I definitely don't have any memories of him

123

coming. What will it take to make him proud? To get his attention?

When I get to my cubby, Brendon is already pulling on his skates. There's an awkward vibe around him, but I'm not sure why. Did I do something? Did Nikki do something?

Jeremy walks past him and pats his shoulder. "Hey, man, plans after practice?"

"I've got homework," Brendon mumbles back without looking up, then grabs his stuff and heads out to the ice. *What the fuck was that?*

"Okay, yeah, he's being weird." Jeremy watches him leave with a concerned expression on his face.

Out on the ice, we do some drills, Carmichael telling us how lazy and slow we all are, while Brendon puts on that dumb-ass smile and starts screwing around. All while not looking at me. It's one of the first practices Carmichael has been back on the ice for. He can't do scrimmages or any full contact drills, but he can do everything else as long as he's careful.

"All the pizza and cheeseburgers are really paying off, huh?" Carmichael yells at Brendon.

Brendon opens his arms in a hug and widens his eyes. "Were you not hugged as a child? Do you need a cuddle?" He skates toward Carmichael who is giving him a death glare. "Come on, buddy. Bring it in."

"Touch me and I'll use your skull as a urinal." The rigid set of his shoulders and cold tone of his voice is slightly terrifying, but it makes Brendon smile wider. Is he trying to get his ass kicked?

Everyone has turned to watch the exchange, and Jeremy just sighs. Why does Brendon love messing with Preston so much?

"I'm not kidding, Oiler." Carmichael stands his ground. "I'll drop your ass to the ice."

Brendon doesn't stop, and Preston moves so fast I barely catch it when he hooks his stick behind Brendon's knee and pulls. Brendon drops to the ice laughing, and Coach finally blows the whistle for us to clear out.

Jeremy skates over to him and offers Brendon a hand up, which he takes. Brendon drapes an arm over Jeremy's shoulder for about half a second before Carmichael yanks his boyfriend away. Brendon laughs as the three of them make their way down the hallway with me following behind. When did I become a lost fucking puppy begging for attention?

We get changed, and Brendon continues to avoid me.

Jeremy and Preston are talking quietly for a few minutes before Jeremy bumps my shoulder. "Dinner?"

I glance at Preston with a suspicious look. "Do you have plans?"

Jeremy laughs and wags his eyebrows. "I'll make it up to him."

I glance at Brendon for a second, then nod. He said he had homework to do, but since he hasn't been in the room, I don't know where he's going to do that.

I hate that he's keeping shit from me. I'm his best friend. Why doesn't he trust me? I guess dating your best friend is a bad idea after all . . .

A while later, Jeremy and I have grabbed food from the dining hall and are sitting in my dorm room watching *Doctor Strange*. I'm not really hungry, so I'm picking at my food.

"What's up?" Jeremy nods at my lack of eaten dinner.

I take a deep breath and let the words tumble from my lips that I've never said before.

"Brendon and I are kind of together."

125

It's quiet for so long I look up to see Jeremy smiling at me.

"I fucking knew it!" He points a finger at me. "I fucking *knew* it!"

"Shut up," I grumble, picking at my food.

"How long? I mean, you guys have basically been a couple for years," Jeremy scoffs like he wasn't fucking Brendon for two years.

"It's new, but he's been weird, and I don't know what to do." I shrug and toss my stuff back in the white paper bag it came in. "He's never avoided me like this."

"I'm sure whatever's going on with him has nothing to do with you." Jeremy pats my knee. "Did you guys get into a fight?"

"No. I'm not entirely sure what happened. He confided something to me, but I'm struggling to connect the dots."

I lay back against my pillow and stare at his bed, wishing he was here. Is he hurting again and too embarrassed to show me? Is he mad I saw him break down? Why can't he let me love him?

Picking up my phone, I text him while Jeremy turns back to the movie on my TV.

P DADDY:

Where are you?

He gets the message almost instantly but doesn't open it. Is he really doing homework? He hates the library, says it's too quiet and it makes his brain buzz. Where else would he go? Is he avoiding Nikki, or did she find him again and is talking his ear off?

CHAPTER 16
Brendon

F uck, it's cold in here, but at least I'm alone. Nikki is driving me nuts, hanging out outside the rink waiting for practice to end or outside the gym in the morning. I swear she knows my class schedule too, so she just pops up.

I shiver in my hoodie, cursing her and myself for this stupid idea. I may have grown up in ice rinks, but I'm usually *on* the ice working up a sweat, not alone in the stands.

I can see my breath as I huddle against the wall with my hood pulled up over my head and my hands inside the sleeves while awkwardly gripping my pen. The lights shut off, and I'm shrouded in darkness.

Uh-oh.

"Hello?" I sit up and look around. My voice echoes in the empty space.

The sound of a lock turning is barely audible from where I'm at, but I definitely heard it. I am well and truly fucked.

I drop back against the brick wall with a huff. How

long have I even been in here? Too damn long, apparently. Yesterday I didn't get locked in here. Why was today different?

Pulling out my phone, I check the time and see that I've been in here for three hours. Yesterday I was here for two. Ugh. *Why am I so dumb?*

A text pops up from Paul, but I don't open it. I don't know what to say to him. It's not fair to Paul that I've taken my shit out on him. Logically, I know that, but I don't know how to admit that when talking about it makes me want to vomit. I hate that seeing Chad and Williams pushed me so far over the edge after all these years that I ran full speed into a bottle. I needed to forget how damaged I am.

Emotions knot in my throat, making it hard to swallow or breathe. My body is tensing, preparing for the onslaught of fear to take over.

Closing my eyes, I push my head against the wall and rub a hand over the bruise hard enough to hurt.

I hiss, and my face tightens with the pain, but the spiral in my head stops, and I'm able to breathe.

My phone goes off again, this time a call from Paul. I sigh, my shoulders dropping in defeat, but I don't answer it. I can't. I'm humiliated that he knows my deepest shame, and I don't know how to move past it.

I just want to curl up in his lap and let him hold me. Tell me he loves me and won't get tired of me being a space cadet. But acknowledging that I'm annoying, pointing out my flaws, is not in my best interest.

His anger hurts, yet that's what I seem to be good at lately, pissing him off. In the years we've been friends, we've argued a few times, but he's never been angry at me. Not like he has lately. I'm fucking this thing up, and it's barely started. Why am I pushing so hard against the thing

I want the most? I love him so much it hurts, but why am I so afraid of him? Why do I keep hurting him?

I shove my phone in my backpack and put my books away since I can't see enough to get any work done anyway. Curling up around my bag, I lay on the metal bench and prepare for a long-ass night.

I could probably call Coach to come let me out, but that makes me look like an idiot, and I don't need any more help there.

Making myself as small as I can to keep my body heat in, I use my backpack as a pillow and try to sleep. It's damn near impossible to sleep while shivering, and my bladder is demanding attention. Shit. Are there motion-activated cameras in here? Will I set off some alarm if I go piss?

Only one way to find out.

Grabbing my bag, I carefully make my way down the bleachers to the bathroom. No alarms start screaming, so I empty my bladder and leave the bathroom. Maybe there's another door that's open that I can leave through.

As I'm wandering through the arena, there's something calming about being in here alone. I'm safe. And when I stand at the entrance to the ice and look out over the rink, I'm hit with a sense of peace. So many people have played in here. Scouts coming to see players in action, injuries, blood, sweat, and tears. If this building could talk, there would be so many stories that have been forgotten over the years. Wins and losses, overcoming adversary, and heroic comebacks.

It's this feeling that kept me playing during the worst years of my life. Despite the pain and humiliation waiting for me off the ice, I couldn't give this up.

A door squeaking open echoes, and I spin around to see if I can find where it came from. I hurry down the hallways, looking for movement, light, or any kind of sound. Rounding a corner, I run face first into Coach, and my scream of surprise echoes down the hallway.

"What the hell are you doing in here, Oiler?!" he demands, red-faced and looking pissed off.

I put a hand on the wall and one on my hip as I try to calm my racing heart. "I got locked in doing homework in the stands." That's a completely normal thing, right? Totally not weird.

"And you didn't call anyone because . . ." He trails off, waiting for an explanation.

"Well." I shuffle my feet and shove my hands into my hoodie pocket. "I didn't want to look like a dumbass."

Coach blinks at me for a long moment. "Well, thank God you don't look like an idiot."

Yeah, I deserved that.

He tells me which door he unlocked and tells me to get lost, so I hurry away from him and breathe a sigh of relief at the warmer air outside. It's Valentine's Day in Denver, Colorado. Not exactly tropical, but it's warmer than inside.

I'm still shivering as I hustle to the dorms. All I want is a hot shower and sleep.

My stomach clenches painfully.

Okay, and food.

And cuddles. You want to be held.

Fuck off, voice.

Nerves flutter in my chest when I pull open the door to the dorm building and wait for the elevator. I hope Paul isn't out looking for me.

The ride up is quick, and when the doors open on the third floor, I'm half expecting him to be standing there with his arms crossed and a glare on his beautiful face. Instead, I find Nikki.

Fuck.

"Hey, can't really talk right—"

"I brought you dinner. Did you get the gift I left on your bed?" She shoves a white grocery bag at me that I grab on instinct and look up at her, confused.

"What?"

"The gift. I left it on your bed." She cocks her head to the side like she's wondering if I understand English. "Hmm, maybe your roommate took it? He seems like the jealous type."

"I haven't been back in hours, and he wouldn't take something that wasn't his." Now I'm getting mad. She doesn't know him, or me for that matter. How dare she talk about him like she does? "I have to go." I push past her down the hallway but stop outside our door. Is Paul inside? Is he pissed? Is he going to yell at me again or treat me like I'm breakable? I take a deep breath and reach for the handle, but the door opens before I can grab it. Jeremy stops short and smiles at me.

"Hey, man, where have you been?" He puts his hand on my arm, and Paul's head pops up over his shoulder as he gets off the bed.

"I, uh . . . got locked in the ice rink." A shudder runs through me again, and I huddle in my hoodie, wishing Paul would just wrap his damn arms around me and hold me tight.

Jeremy chuckles since it's exactly something that would happen to me and pats my shoulder on his way past to his own room. I stand awkwardly in the doorway while Paul stares at me.

"Are you going to come in or . . ."

Forcing myself to swallow past the lump in my throat, I close the door behind me and drop my backpack on the floor.

"You're avoiding me."

He's not pulling any punches today. Not letting me hide. I both love it and hate it when he does this. It means I've been too in my head lately, and he's going to make me face at least some of it. But it hurts, and after being locked in the dark recesses of my head for days, I snap. "You're not my keeper!"

"You're right, I'm not your fucking keeper. I'm trying to be your friend. You won't talk to anyone, disappear for hours, and are just acting weird. I'm concerned about you." By the end of his rant, Paul is yelling and crowding me against the door.

I shove against him, but he barely budges. "Just fuck off! I didn't ask you to save me!"

"I love you. You don't have to ask!" His angry red face is in mine.

"Stop acting like you're a knight in shining fucking armor. Mind your own business!" I shove him again, this time managing to get him to back up enough for me to get past him and into the bathroom. I close the door in his face and hate myself for the hurt I see there. I'm going to be his ruin.

Stripping out of my clothes, finally not shivering anymore thanks to the heat of anger, I turn the water all the way to hot and punish myself with the burn. My pale skin immediately turns pink, and I hiss at the sting.

If only the trembling in my soul was as easy to get rid of as the shaking in my hands.

With my palms on the wall of the shower, I lift my face to the boiling water and force myself to take the pain. It's nothing less than I deserve for hurting him. Maybe the heat of the water will wash away some of the fucked-up parts of me. Make me normal. Make me easier to love.

Love.

My head snaps up right as the word hits my brain. Paul

said he loves me. Did he mean *love* love or just like a friend love? Excitement and fear mix, neither one knowing which way to go. The "what ifs" arguing both sides of the case and coming to the same conclusion.

There's no way he could really love me.

The weight of it pulls on me until my knees give out, and I fall in a heap on the shower floor. Tears pour from my eyes, mixing with the scalding water until I can't tell which is which anymore. I'm so damn tired of holding it all in, of carrying it around with me everywhere I go, never able to get a lungful of air. Faking smiles and laughs so no one looks too closely while on the inside I'm falling apart. I hate that I hide it all so well that no one knows, but all I want is for someone to notice, but at the same time, if anyone did notice, I would tell them I'm fine because I don't want to be a burden.

Forcing my body to move, I reach for the body wash but freeze when a find a black silicone butt plug and lube sitting on the shelf. For a second, my mind goes blank. Almost like I can't process what I'm seeing.

Lust flares in my body, despite the inner turmoil, and I'm so desperate to feel something else I grab onto it with both hands. The image of Paul using it, stretching his hole and coming, has my own dick throbbing. Will he let me lose myself in him? Just for a minute?

The last thing I should do is touch him. I know that. I'm going to give him whiplash with this back-and-forth bullshit, but I fucking need him. It makes me weak to need him as badly as I do. It's definitely not fair to him. I get him, but what does he get? A fucked-up friend who uses him.

I dry off quickly, take the plug and lube, and leave the bathroom naked and on a mission.

Paul's head snaps toward me and eyes widen when he

sees me, his gaze drags over my body and snags on the plug in my hand. His cheeks turn pink, and his throat bobs as he swallows.

I lift the toy before I speak. "Something you wanna talk about?"

"Not really," he says, sitting up and swinging his legs over the edge of the bed. "Come here."

Goose bumps break out all over my body at his tone, and I move without thinking.

Please take me out of my head. I need you.

I stand between his knees and let out a calming breath, tossing the supplies on the bed.

"What do you need, Brendon?" Paul puts his hands on his knees, leaning forward to barely brush his nose up my stomach. I shiver, a little gasp escaping my mouth, and my head drops back.

"I need to come." The words fall from my lips with no thought. "I need to fuck."

Paul cups the back of my thighs, pulling me closer to him so he can leave open-mouthed kisses on my skin while ignoring my cock bobbing between us.

"We're going to talk about this after, got it?" His voice leaves no room for misunderstanding or argument.

"Fine, just make me stop thinking first." My words are a needy whimper. Reaching for him, I cup the back of his head and slam my mouth against his, then lean a knee on the bed. I can't have nice and slow. It gives me too much time to think. I need to get lost in him.

Paul runs his hands across my ass, kneading the muscles, and lightly scratching my skin as my hips settle between his spread thighs.

He pulls back enough for our eyes to lock. "I want you to fuck me."

Nothing in this moment matters but him. There's no world outside of this bed.

Shifting back on the mattress, he lays back against the pillows, and I pull his pants and underwear off, dropping them somewhere on the floor. He's hard, thick, and veined.

And I want a taste.

Dragging my hands up his thighs with my eyes locked on his, I lick up the underside of his dick. Paul grabs a handful of my hair and pulls my mouth back to his as his nostrils flare and his pupils blow wide with arousal.

"Flip," he commands, and my body moves to lay down without thought, taking his spot on the pillows.

His scent surrounds me, comforting and sexy. He's taken on that commanding presence that I can't take my eyes off of. I've never been drawn to dominant guys before, but it's different with Paul. I'm safe with him.

He straddles my hips and leans over me.

"Prep my hole," he demands against my mouth, and I pat around the bed for the bottle of lube. Once I find it, I get my fingers slick, reach between us, and slide my fingers between his cheeks. Paul whimpers into our kiss when I find the puckered flesh and swirl my fingertip around it.

God damn, that's sexy as fuck. I throb, my hips arching up to find friction.

I press one finger in, and he's surprisingly relaxed.

"How long has it been since you used the plug?" I pant, watching his face as I thrust my fingers in and out of his body.

"Few hours." He bites his lip and pulls my mouth back to his. "Fuck. I need you."

My dick aches at the very idea of pushing into his body.

"I don't want to hurt you." I slide another finger in and have to admit that he's still pretty damn stretched. I'm leaking precum onto my stomach, and when Paul sits up, he swipes his thumb through it, then sucks it from his skin.

"You're a needy little fuck stick, aren't you?" Paul growls as he grinds his ass over my dick. The roll of his body, the flexing of his muscles, is almost as arousing as the pressure on my cock.

My hips jerk up off the bed at the sensation. "Please," I whimper, his words pushing me closer to the edge of no return. "I need—"

"You need to take what you're given." Paul stops moving, giving me the much-needed break to catch my breath, and grabs the lube. The cold liquid slides down my shaft, and he strokes me to make sure I'm all slick before lining his hole up and pushing against it.

My hands clench and release at my sides, wanting to help, but if the look on his face is worth anything, it means he won't let me. He's running this show, and I just have to lay here and enjoy it.

"Push out a little," I tell him, and the head of my dick is sucked inside, surrounded by the heat of his body. My eyes cross and roll back into my head. "So fucking good," I moan.

Paul sinks down slowly with a groan until he's once again sitting on my hips. I watch him adjust, the flush on his face and chest such a fucking turn-on.

"I want to touch you," I whimper. My hands balling into fists, then relaxing with the urge to reach for him.

"Too bad."

He leans forward again, one hand grips my bicep and the other is high on my chest by my collarbone, letting me take his weight as he rocks his hips. With every rock forward, he lifts a little more, testing the feeling until he's riding me hard. We're sweaty bodies, grunts and moans, chasing mindless pleasure. I'm lost in him, in the sensations, in the pressure. The constant buzz in my head gloriously quiet for once.

"Stroke me, I'm going to mark you with my cum before you fill me with yours."

I whimper but do what he's told me and wrap my palm around him, jerking him off to the same rhythm of his hips. I'm almost there. My hips flex on instinct to meet his rolling hips.

"Fuck, please." All my attention is focused on my groin, on my need to come inside the man I love. Probably the only man I'll ever love.

"Come on then, big bad hockey player. Give it to me." Paul picks up his pace, filling my ears with his panting breath and the slapping of our bodies meeting.

Sweat breaks out on my skin, and my muscles tremble. I'm already so fucking close to the edge, but I can't quite get there. I clench my eyes closed and arch my back, grinding up into Paul while my body shakes against my will.

"Tell me you love me," I beg, lost in the sensations where the mental walls I keep up are nothing but dust.

There's a pause before I feel Paul's breath on my cheek. The hand on my arm moves to grip the back of my neck.

"I love you, Brendon." His words sound off, but my lust-addled brain doesn't know why. "Come for me. Show me how much you love me."

Lights spark behind my eyes as my orgasm explodes through me. Hot cum splatters on my stomach and chest and over my hand. There's a ringing in my ears, and my entire body goes from tense to weak in a matter of seconds. My arms and legs are limp on the mattress as air heaves in and out of my lungs. Paul wraps his arms under my body and presses his face into my neck, holding me tightly and kissing my neck.

CHAPTER 17
Paul

My hands are steady by some miracle, but my body feels like it's vibrating. What the fuck was that? Did he hear how much truth was in my words?

The urge to cry is so damn strong because I love him so much it hurts. It aches. Knowing he doesn't love me back and may never is a bitter pill to swallow.

Brendon's body is limp under me, sated and relaxed for the first time in days, and I don't want to let him go. Something in his head is twisted, and every part of me wants to fix it, but I don't know how. I don't know what happened or how to put the pieces of him back together. It's like someone handed me a puzzle but put a blindfold over my eyes. I can feel the edges but can't see how they fit together.

It hurts to know he's in so much pain. Does he not trust me with the truth? All I want is for him to be okay.

We need to talk. I can't keep living like this. Never knowing what version of him will walk into our room or if he's coming back at all. It's exhausting.

Forcing myself to let him go, I sit up. His now soft dick slides out of me, leaving me feeling empty, and I climb off the bed to get a washcloth. After getting one wet and cleaning myself off, I head back to the bed and find Brendon sitting up and running a hand through his hair.

I stand between his knees and wipe his chest off. Once he's clean, I toss the cloth toward the bathroom, and he leans his forehead against my abdomen with his hands on my hips.

"I know you want to talk, but I'm so tired." His voice is small, and it hurts my heart. I run my hand over his head, dragging my short nails against the back of his head. He shudders and moans, wrapping his arms around my legs in a hug. Brendon normally has a big personality, he takes up space in the room, and loves life. The fact that he's shut down right now is physically painful.

I reach for his chin and lift his face so I can see him.

"I don't know what's going on with you right now, but stop shutting me out." I drag my thumb along his bottom lip. "I'm supposed to be the one you aren't afraid to come to when you need something."

A tear falls from the corner of his eye, and I brush it away.

"I don't know how to do this," Brendon whispers.

"Do what? Lean on me?" This feels like so much more than just friendship. I want everything with him, but I don't think he does.

Brendon closes his eyes and sighs. "I've never had a real relationship before."

"What do you mean?" I brush my thumb across his cheek and watch him struggle to find the words. *Tell me what you want and it's yours. I'll give you everything.*

My heart is pounding; can he hear it? It's deafening in my ears.

Brendon's shoulders tense and a blush crawls up his chest to his neck. "Can we not do this right now? I'm tired."

He probably is tired, but I'm not letting him pass out before he talks to me. I can't do this shit with him anymore. We're figuring it out right now.

"No, I'm not waiting anymore." My tone is sure, solid. "I'm done with you avoiding me." I trace his bottom lip with my finger again. "Do you not want to be together? Is that what's stressing you out? This isn't working and you want to break it off but don't know how?"

His head is shaking no before I've even finished the questions.

"No, that's not it at all." He tightens his arms around my legs and pulls me against him so his chin is resting on my stomach. "I'm not easy to deal with, P Man. I'm annoying and loud and too much." His voice cracks, and he looks like he's in pain as he looks at me.

I tighten my hand in the back of his hair.

"Listen very closely," I demand with my eyes locked on his. Brendon tenses but waits.

"That's bullshit." He tries to shake his head, but I don't let him. "Whoever made you believe that is wrong. You are exactly the way you are supposed to be. You aren't annoying or too much. Not to me, not to Jeremy, not to the rest of the guys on our team."

Another tear trails down his face, and this time, I lean down and kiss him. The soft press of our lips doesn't hide how his trembles. My poor boy is scared, and I hate that for him.

"I love you," I whisper against his mouth.

A sob tears from Brendon, and he wraps his arms around my neck, leans back, and pulls me down on top of him. He breaks the kiss and leans his forehead against my cheek while I hold him. How many times have people put an exception on their love? How many people have told him he would be easier to love if he changed something? I hate all of them.

"I love you too." His words are packed with emotion, both sorrow and joy. My throat tightens too with the happiness of hearing the words I never expected to. For years I've been hoping but never thought it would actually happen. I never thought it would be true.

It warms my heart but fills my gut with ice. I can't be like my father. Do I love Brendon like he loved my mom? Can I risk falling into myself like he did if I lose him?

I shift a little, getting comfortable, and he rolls into me to keep his entire body against mine. He's so needy for physical comfort, and I will never complain about it. I need to be needed. I need to know I'm enough.

"I don't want to change who you are. Ever. Be loud, do weird shit, flirt, get excited about things," I tell him as I rub his back.

"Okay." His voice is breathy, and I smile.

I press a kiss to his forehead and pull his face into the crook of my neck.

We lay in the quiet for a few minutes, Brendon nuzzling my skin and sniffling every once in a while.

I'm starting to fall asleep, comfortable and warm, when Brendon pops his head up.

"Fuck! I'm the worst!" he almost yells, startling me.

"What?" I sit up, looking around for whatever has him stressed out.

"That was your first time, wasn't it? Are you okay? I didn't hurt you, right?" The anxiety painted on his face is so fierce it takes me a second to realize what he's talking about.

"Yeah." I chuckle. "I'm fine."

"Why are you laughing?" He sits up, and his face morphs into disgruntled.

"I thought something was seriously wrong." I reach for his hand, and my chest tightens. I don't know how much my dad loved my mom, but I know that if I lose Brendon, it will be the end of me.

"I'm a selfish dick, that's what wrong."

I smile at him and open my mouth to respond when his stomach growls, making me laugh.

"We should get dinner." I kiss him quickly and slide off the bed.

"Ugh! Pants are the worst, though!" Brendon whines, but he gets dressed.

I find my clothes and pull them on. Brendon moves behind me and wraps his arms around my waist. His breath on my neck sends shivers down my spine.

"Thank you." His whispered words are so quiet I almost don't hear them.

I reach over my shoulder to cup the back of his head and turn my face toward him to press a kiss to his lips.

"I've got you." *Always and forever.*

CHAPTER 18
Paul

Something is moving against me, my dick achingly hard, and someone is groaning quietly. I'm pressed against a warm body that smells like Tide laundry soap, team shower body wash, and warm skin. Familiar and warm. I don't know what time it is, but I also don't give a shit.

I take his mouth in an aggressive kiss, making him take me, and pushing my body weight against him. I push him onto his back and straddle his hips. Reaching for his hands, I pin them next to his head, and he arches into me. His cock throbs, and he pushes his hips against me.

"Someone likes being restrained." I nip at his ear, and he groans. It's so much hotter than I expected it to be. There's something enticing about having this strong, athletic man whimpering under me that is going to quickly become addictive.

"Only by you." Brendon's breathy, sleep-rough words are a shot of adrenaline to my system.

I push my ass against the hard ridge of his dick with more pressure, and he groans a throaty sound for me.

"Hmm, do you like being teased?" I drag my lips along his scruffy jaw. I want to devour his mouth while we take pleasure from each other's bodies until we're weak and sated.

"You're a real ass, you know that?" Brendon whines when I slide my ass against him again.

I chuckle and bite at the skin of his neck. "I do have a pretty nice ass."

A shudder runs through him, and I bite him again, loving his reaction.

"You're so responsive." I drag one hand down his chest and pinch his nipple when I find it. He arches off the bed with a strangled moan and grabs the back of my neck with his now free hand, yanking my lips to his in an aggressive kiss.

I nip at his lip, and he opens for me, my tongue sliding into his mouth to explore him. His approval vibrates through his chest, and I let myself sink onto him.

He threads his fingers through the hand I have on the bed. It makes my heart lurch. I can't keep my emotions out of this. If he pulls away and puts me back in the friend zone, it'll break my heart.

"Pull my cock out," I growl against his lips. His free hand struggles to do what I've demanded, but he manages to reach inside my boxer briefs. The heat of his palm and the grip of his fingers around me make me moan. "I'm going to fuck your fist, mark you with my cum."

"Yes, please," he whimpers.

Reaching for the lube I have stashed under the bed, I dribble some in his palm until we're both so fucking slick.

I take his mouth again, thrusting into his hand and grinding my ass against his dick at the same time. It feels so fucking good to have him desperate beneath me and his air filling my lungs.

"I'm so close," Brendon moans, his grip on my dick tightening.

"Don't fucking come yet." I squeeze his throat, choking off a whimper and riding him harder, chasing my own release.

I shudder as my orgasm crashes over me, sending electric pulses of pleasure through my body and curving my shoulders forward. I'm breathing so hard it takes me a minute to realize Brendon is almost sobbing with his need to come.

"Good boy," I breathe out and push his hand away to wrap my own around him. His hips jerk, thrusting into my hand as I sit up and use my free hand to paint my cum on his skin and top lip.

"Taste me while you come."

He licks me from his skin, and I lean forward to press on his chest, but he grabs my hand and sucks on two of my fingers as he explodes beneath me. His cum mixes with mine, and it's the hottest thing I've ever seen. I can't tell whose is whose, and I love it.

Brendon sags on the mattress, panting and sweaty.

"Not a bad way to start the day." I chuckle, and he flips me off.

"You're an asshole."

I lean down to kiss him, getting a hint of myself on his tongue, then bite his lower lip.

"Come on, I didn't make you wait that long."

I kiss him again and climb off him, needing to piss. Putting my dick away, I head to the bathroom. Brendon grabs a shirt off the floor and starts cleaning himself up.

I do my business and wash my hands as someone knocks on the door. I freeze for a second, hoping Brendon is decent.

The door opens, and I hear Brendon say, "Are we having a no pants day? 'Cause I'm down for it."

"No, I need you to trace this bite mark." That's Jeremy's voice. What the hell did he just say? Since I'm in here, I brush my teeth quickly to make sure I don't have cum breath.

"Like, the individual teeth or, like, the circle it makes?" Brendon asks, and I am thoroughly confused.

"Each tooth," Jeremy instructs as I open the door.

"Now I feel weird being the only one with pants on," Brendon complains around a pen cap he has in his mouth.

"Why don't you have pants on?" I ask Jeremy.

"I needed someone to trace this and didn't want to wait too long." Jeremy shrugs like that sentence makes sense.

"And why is Brendon drawing on your neck?" I cross my arms and cock my head at the two of them.

"I'm going to get it tattooed." I must have a strange look on my face because Jeremy looks at me and starts laughing.

"Fuck yes!" Brendon shouts. "That sounds like a terrible idea, and I'm one hundred percent on board for this." He caps the pen and slaps Jeremy's shoulder. "You should put pants on, though."

"Hang on." I hold up my hands and step closer to the disaster duo. "Why are you going to tattoo whatever that is on your neck?"

"It's Preston's teeth." Jeremy shrugs. "To show him I'm in this relationship all the way."

"Are the two of you sharing a brain now?" I ask, looking between the two of them. "You could just, I don't know, tell him that?"

Brendon and Jeremy look at each other and shake their heads. "Nah, this is better," Jeremy says.

"You guys are idiots." I huff. "Do you have an appointment already or what?"

"No, I figured we could find a place and get it done." Jeremy shrugs again. "It shouldn't take that long." He moves to the door. "I'm going to get dressed."

Since I can't leave these two unsupervised, I head to my dresser.

"I'm obviously driving." I pull open my dresser and start digging for clothes. "I want it on record that this is a stupid idea, and I will not be taking any responsibility."

"Duly noted and ignored." Brendon claps me on the shoulder, and Jeremy leaves.

In just a few minutes, we're climbing into my car while Jeremy googles tattoo shops.

"There's one over on Ashland Drive; it's like four miles from us," he says and turns on the directions so we can find it.

"I want a neck tattoo," Brendon says, and I am not surprised. "Will you bite me so I can match Jeremy?" He looks at me, and I can feel my face heat with a blush. I do a lot of shit for Brendon. No one is surprised if he sits on my lap or steals my drink from my hand anymore, but bite him? In public?

"What? You want me to bite you?" I sputter as we pull into the parking lot of the shop.

"Well, I mean, if Jeremy did it and Preston found out, he would murder both of us. So, if you do it, you'll be saving our lives," Brendon explains, and damn it, he's got a good point, but still.

"Okay, I'm going in," Jeremy announces and gets out of the car.

We follow while Brendon begs me to do it. It's not that I'm against biting him. Seeing my cum on him was hot as fuck. I'm sure seeing my teeth on him will be too, but that's not something we can explain away when people ask about it. I know he won't make up some story about it; he'll flat out tell people it was me. But when he looks at me with those big puppy dog eyes and a pouty lip, I know I'm fucked.

The place has black-and-white checkered tile floor, light gray walls with artwork all over the place, and very bright lighting. There's a table and chairs set up around the room and what looks like a red room divider in the back in case someone needs privacy.

A beautiful woman with green hair and loads of tattoos talks to Jeremy while I try to hold strong against Brendon.

"Come on, I'll make it worth your while." Brendon wags his eyebrows at me, and I glare at him.

"It's a horrible idea. Why do you want this?"

The smile drops from his face, and it turns serious. "Because you're my person."

I huff but nod. "Fine, if you really want to do this, I'll do it."

A huge smile brightens his face, and it's everything I've wanted to see for days. He jumps up and down, then walks to the counter to talk to the same woman Jeremy talked to.

Brendon attempts to flirt with her, but she is completely not interested, and I drop down into a seat, hating that he's flirting with her. He can't openly flirt with me, and it's my fault. I don't think he would care all that much if everyone knew, but I'm just not ready yet. So, this is my punishment, I guess.

A short, thin man with long brown hair pulled back in a ponytail and full sleeve tattoos calls Jeremy back, and Brendon comes to sit with a clipboard and paperwork.

It doesn't take long for him to fill it out, and he's so excited he can't sit still, so he's looking at all the art on the walls, flipping through the artists' books, checking his phone, then comes back to me.

He stands between my knees and puts his hand on my shoulder. "Bite me."

There's a ridge in his jeans that tells me he's turned on by the idea, and I'm not sure which part does it for him. My teeth on his skin? Being in public?

"Kneel." The word is deep and commanding. Brendon drops to his knees and sits back with a pink blush on his cheeks that I love. Not taking my eyes off his or thinking too hard about it, I slide my hand into the back of his hair and hold it tight to pull his head to the side, then lean forward and drag my nose along his bared neck. His breathing shudders and goose bumps break out on his skin before I sink my teeth into the exposed flesh. I don't bite him hard, just enough to leave an impression, and he whimpers.

Brendon shifts, running his hand over his dick as I release him, and sits back. I'm achingly hard and want to shove my cock down his fucking throat, right here in the waiting room.

Brendon stands, adjusting himself, and I do the same, then we head back to where Jeremy is getting tattooed.

The tattoo artist finishes up and wipes his skin off with some kind of cleaner. It's a simple mark on Jeremy's skin that Preston is going to shit a brick over.

Brendon lopes across the space like a puppy and drops down into the seat Jeremy just got out of.

"Me next!"

The tattoo artist raises an eyebrow but shrugs.

"Okay then." He sanitizes everything and gets set up again. "I don't know who bit you, but they need to do it again. This has faded too fast. Unless you want me to just wing it."

"No!" I snap, but when everyone turns to look at me, my face heats. Fuck. That was possessive as fuck. *Take a chill pill, caveman.*

Jeremy heads to the mirror they have on the wall to look at his ink, and I head to Brendon. Leaning over him, I bite him a lot harder this time. Brendon lets out a pitiful, aroused sound, and shifts in his seat. When I stand, his face is bright red and he's pulling on his jeans, probably to give his dick more room. The tattoo artist sighs, and I move back to lean against the wall with my arms crossed.

The entire thing takes only a few minutes, and when he gets up out of the chair to look in the mirror, he gives me a look that can only mean one thing. Sex.

With a smug look on his face, we head to the counter for him to pay and get care instructions. I listen to her and take the paper she hands him since I know he's going to lose it and forget what she said.

"I'm hungry. Let's get some lunch." Brendon smacks my stomach with the back of his hand, and we climb back into the car while Jeremy buries his face in his phone.

The three of us fuck around for a while, getting lunch and finding an arcade to waste time at before heading back to the dorms. There are some dumbasses with cameras standing around, but they don't bother us as we enter the building. Thankfully, the reporters are dying down and not following Preston around everywhere anymore.

"Man, I'm ready for a nap." Brendon yawns and stretches.

"You're ready to get fucked," I mutter, and Jeremy laughs. The elevator opens on our floor, and we head down the hallway toward Jeremy and Preston's room. I, for one, am not going to miss Preston seeing that fucking tattoo for the first time.

"Uh, whatcha doing?" Jeremy stops at his door and turns to stare at us.

"Movies and naps," Brendon says like the answer should be obvious. I don't know if he's serious or not, but I am definitely not cuddling with Jeremy.

"I'm not going to die today." I back away with my hands raised.

Jeremy opens the door and stops as all hell breaks loose. Inside is his mom and grandma. Mrs. Albrooke appears to be recording, and I hear Jeremy's sister say, "Nice hickies," as Brendon yells and pushes Jeremy out of the way to get to the woman. Mrs. Albrooke gives him a one-armed hug as Grandma Brown hugs Jeremy.

"How did you get in here?" he asks his grandma.

"Oh my God, what is on your neck?" Stacy's squeal through the phone has both the older women turning to look at Jeremy's neck while he mumbles "Fuck," then laughter erupts from the phone.

"What the hell is that, Jeremy?!" Mrs. Albrooke demands, and I snort. I'm betting he didn't think about his parents finding it.

"It's Preston's teeth," Brendon tells her helpfully. "Look, I've got one too!" He turns his head to show her, and she glances at him.

"Why did Preston bite you? Oh no, you guys aren't doing orgies or something, are you?" Jeremy's mom's face falls like she's in physical pain.

I burst out laughing, doubled over, and Brendon starts smiling like this is the best day of his life while Jeremy pales.

"Orgies? What the fuck, Mom?"

"Don't cuss at your mother," Mr. Albrooke says through the phone.

"Why would you get that tattooed on your skin?" His

153

mom is horrified, but Stacy, Jordan, and Keith are all yelling to get a better look at it when the door opens. Preston and Lily walk in, and Jeremy turns on his boyfriend.

"Did you know they were coming?" he demands, staring wide-eyed at the big man.

"Of course. I made plans for them to be here to meet Lily." He's confused, and Jeremy looks like he's ready to have a mental breakdown.

Grandma walks over and gives Preston a hug, his smile softening when he looks at her, and carefully wraps his arms around her. That's weird as fuck and makes me uncomfortable. Since when does Preston look like that at anyone? Has he been possessed?

"Mrs. Albrooke, can you make taco salad?" Brendon pleads, sticking his bottom lip out.

"Are you having sex with Preston too?" she asks Brendon, who pales when he looks at Preston.

"Absolutely not!" Brendon all but yells, and I snort, trying to hide my laugh. The idea is hilarious.

"What the hell kind of a question is that?" Preston asks, clearly confused.

"They both have your teeth marks tattooed on their necks! What are we supposed to think?" Mrs. Albrooke all but yells, frazzled.

"Excuse me?" Preston grabs Jeremy's face and jerks it to one side, then the other. "What the hell is that?" he demands.

"I got a tattoo of your teeth marks." Jeremy's face is so bright red it looks like he has a sunburn. "Look, it seemed a lot more romantic in my head and didn't involve my mother being here when you found out!"

Preston blinks, then starts laughing. "You're insane."

He's definitely possessed. I don't think I've ever seen

him smile, much less laugh.

"I think you meant an idiot," I pipe up, shaking my head at the lot of them.

"What the hell is on Brendon's neck then?" Preston points at a very nervous Brendon. "That had better not be mine or Jeremy's teeth."

I step in front of Brendon. "They're mine."

"Yeah, nobody touched your fuck boy," Brendon says.

"What did you call him?" Grandma asks.

Preston's sister Lily gets introduced, and Preston mumbles, "Fuck it," before taking Jeremy's hand.

"Jeremy, I love you more than I ever thought possible. My life is not complete without you. *I* am not complete without you." He drops to one knee, and everyone falls into stunned silence. "Will you marry me?"

"Dude!" Brendon yells, grabbing onto me and shaking me in his excitement for our friend.

"These bands aren't perfect. Like us, they've been struck and dented, but the flaws in the metal make them unique and strong."

My throat catches with emotion. These two have been through the wringer the last few months, and I'm so glad they have each other, but I'm also jealous as fuck.

Jeremy drops to his knees and kisses Preston with tears in his eyes.

"Is that a yes?" he asks with his lips against Jeremy's.

"Yes," Jeremy croaks. "I love you so fucking much."

They wrap their arms around each other in a tight hug, and it's so fucking sweet. Preston isn't one to show emotion, ever, so seeing this is heavy. I feel honored to be a witness to it. It gives us a peek into what Jeremy gets with him.

They talk for a few minutes, and Jeremy's mom and grandma are sniffing back tears.

"Of course I will marry you and fight with you and love you and build a life with you. You're never getting rid of me," Jeremy says.

We all cheer and crowd them, wrapping them in a hug. This is the coolest thing I've been a part of.

"You're a part of the Albrooke family now, and we won't ever let you go," Mrs. Albrooke says, kissing Preston's cheek, and a pang of sadness hits me square in the chest. My dad doesn't care about what's happening in my life. My grandparents do, but I doubt my dad would even answer the phone if I called him to tell him I got engaged. I always wanted parents like the Albrookes, ones that cared too much.

"I'm taking your name when we get married," Preston says with the utmost seriousness, sliding the ring onto Jeremy's finger. "I don't want to be a Carmichael anymore. Make me an Albrooke."

Brendon looks at me with an expression I can't read. It's soft but sad somehow? He reaches for my hand and squeezes it. A knot forms in my throat, and I wish I was able to kiss him right now, right here, but I'm not ready. And I don't know what this is between us.

Preston starts getting antsy and shrugs everyone off, so we step back and give him room. We all know he's not a hugger, except for Jeremy and Grandma apparently, so I'm surprised he let us do a group hug in the first place.

I push Brendon toward the door and tell them we'll see them later.

"But . . . but . . . taco salad," Brendon whines.

"Mrs. Albrooke isn't making you taco salad in the dorms." I give him a stern look and push him down the hallway, then into our room. Once the door is closed, I shove him toward the bathroom. "Besides, I'm tired. It's nap time and you need a shower."

CHAPTER 19

Brendon

The tattoo on my neck is itchy as fuck. I swear I'm going to scratch it off.

"Leave it." Paul's command has my fingertips freezing on my neck where I was rubbing the skin. I'm trying to be gentle with it, but *fuck*, it's driving me nuts.

"I can't!" I snap back, clenching my hands into fists. "Why doesn't anyone tell you how much this shit itches?"

Paul looks at me like I'm a dumbass. "They do; you just don't pay attention."

Ouch.

"If it's itchy, put some lotion on it."

"Ugh!" I drop my head back on my shoulders, and Jeremy chuckles. "What are you laughing at? Why isn't yours itchy?"

"Because someone makes sure it's taken care of." Preston's tone is a little condescending, but I scoff anyway, trying not to look at Paul.

"Gotta make sure it heals so you can leave new imprints on it, right?" I wag my eyebrows at Preston, half hoping he'll swing at me to distract me.

When he just looks at me like he's bored, I smile. "I should bite him, and we can compare the marks."

I'm smacked upside the back of my head, and I turn to glare at Paul.

"Don't be an idiot."

"Good hustle out there today, boys!" Coach hollers through the locker room as we get changed after practice.

I'm pulling on my shoes when my phone goes off with a social media tag.

Paul, Preston, and Jeremy head out, so I follow along behind them while I check the notification on Instagram.

DarbyUFan4Life posted a picture from the stands during practice. Most of them are of me, though. That's kinda cool. I'm not a star player, so having someone notice me is pretty awesome.

I like the post and shove my phone in my pocket with a little extra pep in my step.

Jeremy and Preston are holding hands, and while I love it for them, I hate that I can't. I mean, I could, but not with Paul.

Are we at the casual hand-holding stage? I tattooed his teeth on my neck. That should say something, right? Or is that just being brushed off as me being extra and over the top?

The idea hurts. I hope he knows it's more than that.

Back at the dorms, Jeremy and Preston head out with their families, so Paul and I grab our homework and settle on his bed.

I'm halfway through my business class homework when my phone goes off with a Snapchat notification, and I groan. Paul snorts as I pick it up and open the app. Nikki has sent me a picture of herself in the library with stars around her head and her eyes crossed with the caption "studying has me like."

I type out a quick "me too" and toss my phone, hoping that's the end of it.

Of course, it's not.

> NIKKI:
>
> Where are you? I don't see you.

> BRENDON:
>
> In my room, it's almost lights out.

Please please please don't show up.

> NIKKI:
>
> Oh! I can head over there if you want a study partner! We can quiz each other!

FUCK.

> BRENDON:
>
> I'm studying with my roommate.

She sends back a bunch of crying emojis, and I want to throw my phone out the window.

> NIKKI:
>
> I wish he liked me.

Insert eye roll here.

I sigh and look up at Paul who's watching me with an expression on his face I can't quite read.

"What?"

He looks at my phone, then back up to me. "Your new bestie need something?"

I scoff. "She's not my bestie, and I think she just needs a friend." I shrug and put my phone down to focus on my homework again.

I'm staring at my textbook but not actually absorbing any of it. There's too much going on in my head. My eyes are unfocused as I brush my finger over the raised scab on my neck. It's possessive and comforting to have a permanent mark on me from him. Even if he was hesitant to do it, I needed it. I still do.

"Stop messing with it," Paul mutters, and my eyes snap back into focus as I turn my head to look at him.

The desire to ask him what this all means is so damn strong it's almost suffocating, but I can't. The words are stuck in my throat, and I can't keep my head on anything else.

I close my book harder than I mean to and drop it onto my desk on top of the other shit that's stacked there and climb into bed. I can feel Paul's gaze on me, but I don't say anything. With my back to him, I cover myself and force my eyes closed.

The voices in my head tell me I'm an idiot, that getting that tattoo is a surefire way to put distance between us, that he's only messing around with me, and I'm not his long term.

Paul moves around the room, turns off the light, then stops somewhere near the beds.

"Are you hiding under the blanket so you can scratch the tattoo?" His question almost makes me laugh. It's definitely something I would do.

"No." My voice is a croak, and my bed dips as Paul climbs in behind me. He slides up to spoon me, wrapping his arm around my waist over the blanket.

"What's going on in that head?" He doesn't sound judgmental, only curious.

"Do you hate the tattoo?"

His answer is immediate. "No."

"What do you want me to tell the team when they ask?" We both know they will ask.

"Whatever you want." I can feel Paul shrug behind me, so I turn to face him.

"You don't care if I tell them it's you?" I lift an eyebrow at him.

"No, I don't care." He shakes his head and lifts my chin to turn my head. Paul leans in and softly kisses the tender spot on my neck, making me shiver.

"You're my person, remember?" His lips against my ear have goose bumps breaking out along my skin.

"Are we together? In an exclusive relationship, or are you just figuring your shit out?" I hate how small my voice is, how needy I am for assurance.

Paul rests his head on my pillow, watching me. "An exclusive relationship?" He smirks at me. "Is that a fancy way of saying boyfriends?"

I can't help the little smile that turns up the corners of my lips. "Maybe."

Paul chuckles quietly. "I would be okay with that, but I'm not ready for everyone to know yet."

Hope blossoms in my chest, lighting me up inside. "Okay, I get that." I lean forward and kiss him quickly. "But you're mine, right?"

He smiles into the kiss. "Right."

Scooting over, I pull Paul farther onto the bed, then push him onto his back so I can lay on him. It takes some moving around to get him under the blanket, and I realize he still has his jeans on.

"You cannot sleep in jeans." I scrunch up my face in disgust.

He rolls his eyes and reaches for the button.

"It's pretty sexy seeing you get naked in my bed, though," I tell him as he shimmies out of his pants.

"I'm not getting naked," he tells me, kicking the

offending material onto the floor, and pulls me against him. "Not today."

I lay my head on his chest and breathe a sigh of relief at his heartbeat in my ear.

"But you do want to get naked with me again, right? Like, experiment more?" *Please, for the love of God, tell me you want to fuck again.*

"Oh yeah, definitely." Paul runs his hand through my hair and pulls my head back so I'm looking up at him. "I want to know how good it feels to be inside you."

My dick hardens against his thigh, and he chuckles darkly while my face heats.

"How good it feels to push into you, tight and hot."

My ass clenches at the idea. It's been a long time since I bottomed, but holy fuck yes, please.

I slide my knee between his and shift to climb over him, but his grip in my hair tightens.

"Go to sleep, Brendon."

"Uh. But. What?" I blink up at him, sure I didn't hear him correctly. "You're kidding, right?"

"No, go to sleep." He raises that damn eyebrow at me, giving me the no-nonsense look I both hate and love.

"But—"

"Sleep." He puts my head back on his chest and wraps his arms around me.

I close my eyes and grumble into him, "I hate you."

CHAPTER 20
Brendon

I've barely made it back to our room after morning workout when there's a knock on the door. I grumble, wanting nothing more than to take these stupid pants off, but open the door to find Nikki smiling at me expectantly. *Fucking Christ.*

"Hey, what's up?" I try to hide my disappointment and lean against the door. She strides in like she owns the place and sits on Paul's bed.

"Come on in, make yourself comfortable." I close the door and sit on my bed.

"Where's Darby Bear?" She looks around the room with a raised eyebrow and suspicion, then turns to me.

"Huh?" What the fuck is a Darby bear? I look around too, like I know what the fuck I'm looking for.

"The bear I left on your bed." She says it like that's helpful. When was she in here?

Bear . . . bear . . . bear . . . there was a bear . . . somewhere . . .

"Riiiight . . ." I turn around to look at my bed, running

163

it through my head where the stupid thing could be. I look at my bed but don't see anything.

"I put it right here." I turn to look at her, and she's pointing to a spot on Paul's bed.

"That's not my bed." I point to Paul's bed where she's sitting.

"Is it not?" Nikki cocks her head. "Every time I've come in here, you're sitting on it."

"He has the TV, so I sit over there a lot, but it's not mine." *So get off my boyfriend's bed.*

She climbs off the bed like it's disgusting, and I turn back to mine. On the other side of my pillow I see a brown fuzzy leg and reach for it.

"Here it is." I show her. and she takes it from me, placing it on the bedside table. *Am I a child?*

Don't answer that.

"You should make your bed." She puts her hands on her hips and shakes her head at me, then does just that, straightening out my blanket and fluffing my pillow.

I shrug and scratch the back of my head. "I don't see the point of making my bed when I'm just going to get back into it."

"Do you wash your laundry? By that logic, you shouldn't bother to do that either."

Okay, she has a point there.

The door opens again, Paul's voice entering before we can see his face.

"Hey, bay——" He clears his throat, and I smirk at him over Nikki's head. "Hello, Nikki."

The smile that was on his face falls into an expressionless mask. He doesn't like her, and that is hilarious to me. She's never done anything to warrant that kind of response. I think he's a little jealous.

"Don't you have class?" He looks at me with a pointed

look. Pulling out my phone, I swear and grab my backpack. I want to kiss him before I head out, but I can't with Nikki here. Ugh. "Later."

Nikki, of course, follows me out of the room and into the elevator.

"Is he gay or something?" Nikki's question catches me off guard, and my head snaps to the side to stare at her.

"What?"

"He looks at you like he either wants to eat you or murder you." She shrugs.

"He's my best friend." I cross my arms and beg this elevator not to stop on every floor so I can get the fuck out of here, but today is not my lucky day.

"That doesn't answer my question." She doesn't lower her voice at all, despite there being more people in the car.

"No, he's not. Not that it's any of your business," I snap a little harsher than I meant to, and the people in front of us turn to look at me.

Nikki turns to watch me, and a smile curls the corner of her lips that makes me uncomfortable.

When we finally reach the main floor, I push my way out and don't feel all that bad about leaving her behind. I have to protect him.

I find a seat in the back of the lecture hall, and my phone buzzes in my pocket.

P DADDY:

That's a really cute teddy bear. Are you going to cuddle with it tonight instead of with me?

MENACE:

Instead of? No. He's going to join us. He's part of our throuple now.

P DADDY:

If it touches me, I'll light it on fire. It's tainted.

MENACE:

I've got a taint you can play with . . .

I snort to myself and put my phone away as class starts. It vibrates in my pocket, but I try to force myself to focus on taking notes instead of sexting with my very hot boyfriend. *I wonder if he would send me a dick pic . . .*

It takes all my force of will not to fall asleep in class. I have no idea what he talked about or what our next homework assignment is. I'm totally fucked.

When he excuses us, I stand and stretch, turning my body to get that full-body pull, and jump when Nikki is standing behind me.

"Jesus, dude." I pull my arms in to protect my chest like she's going to hit me. The chick is weird, doesn't blink enough, and I swear has ninja training. I'm going to tie a bell on her shoes or something.

"Yes, Jesus was a man." She cocks her head, looking at me like she's confused.

"What?"

"Jesus in Spanish is also a male name."

Is she having a stroke or something? What the fuck is she talking about?

"Right. Cool. Thanks for that. I gotta go." I grab my bag and head toward the door, but she follows me.

Outside in the hallway, Paul's smiling face greets me. He opens his mouth, but I open my eyes as wide as I can and make a slashing motion by my chest where Nikki won't see it. His smile falls, and he lifts an eyebrow at me.

"Lunch?" Paul asks, still looking very confused, but his soft, worn jeans that cup his thighs so perfectly are damn distracting. He always looks too good, put together even in just jeans and a hoodie and backward ball cap. The dude is sexy as fuck, and it's rude. Glancing down at myself, I'm in baggy black sweatpants and a purple Darby Hockey hoodie. I run my hand through my hair, feeling a little self-conscious next to him.

My stomach grumbles loudly as I stop in front of him, and Nikki steps up next to me. Once again, Paul slides a blank expression over his face, but this time it bugs me. It's so abnormal for him. I want his smile.

"Yeah, I think Carpenter said something about a team lunch?" I try to use our best friend mind powers to tell Paul I'm making it up but trying to make an excuse for Nikki to fuck off, but he looks at me like I've grown another head. Great.

"Right . . ." He nods slowly and pulls his phone from his pocket and turns on the screen. "We gotta hustle or I'll be late to my next class." He puts his phone away and nods at Nikki, then takes my arm and spins me around, marching me down the hallway.

"She just showed up in my class and started talking about Jesus," I whisper to Paul. "She's kinda weird."

"You're an idiot." Paul huffs and shakes his head.

Once we get out of the building, he lets go of me, and we walk normally toward the dining hall.

"Well, you're the one who loves me, so what does that say about you?" I pinch his cheek, and he jabs his fingers into my armpit, making me scream. "Asshole."

Paul chuckles but grabs my arm and wraps it around his shoulders. I try to hide my smile but fail miserably since he mutters, "Shut up."

"Aww, does someone need a hug?" I tease him, pinching his ribs and wanting nothing more than to interlace our fingers, kiss him right here in front of everyone. But I won't. While I don't care if everyone knows, I know he's not ready, and I respect that. It's taken me a long time to get to this point, and with Jeremy and Preston out to the team, I'm more comfortable officially coming out. Will anyone be surprised? Probably not.

As we get to the dining hall, a group of people come out and hold the door for us. Scanning the tables, Carp is sitting with the guy who showed us where to get good cinnamon rolls, Willis, and another guy I don't know, but if I had to guess, also a jock.

Paul and I grab food and head to the table with our teammates. I drop my tray next to Carppy, and he gives me a nod.

"Hey, guys, how's it going?"

"Brendon has a stalker," Paul says casually, and everyone turns to look at him.

"What?" Carp asks.

I shake my head and start to argue, but Paul puts his hand over my mouth and continues. No one looks surprised by this.

"Yeah, this little puck bunny pops up in his classes, shows up at our dorm, brings him shit. It's creepy."

I lick Paul's palm, and he jerks his hand away from me with a glare.

"She is not stalking me." I shove a bite of my chicken into my mouth. "She's a little intense, I'll give you that. But she's not dangerous or anything."

"The girl is weird," Paul argues.

I pat his cheek condescendingly. "Don't worry, buddy, she won't take best friend status."

"She's following you?" Willis asks.

"I think she has classes near mine." I shrug, shoving another bite into my mouth.

"Listen, if you're jealous of my teddy bear, you can snuggle him too," I tell Paul with a pat on his arm.

"Teddy bear?" the friend of Carp asks. *What the hell was his name . . .*

"Yeah, I found it on my bed," Paul tells them. "With a note that said something about cuddling it when she's not around."

"I didn't see a note," I say around a mouthful of food.

"Why did you let her put it on my bed?" Paul glares at me.

"I didn't even know about the bear until this morning."

Everyone at the table freezes and stares at me like I've said something really weird.

"What?"

"So, wait," Carp starts. "Neither of you let her in the room, but the bear was in there?"

Oh.

"How did she get in?" Willis asks.

"Ding ding ding!" the cute dark-haired guy sitting next to Carp says. "What do we have for him, Johnny?"

"Who's Johnny?" I ask, and he laughs. But seriously, who's Johnny?

"Does she have a key to your room?" Carp tosses out.

"I don't think so? How would she have gotten that?" I shove more food in my mouth and groan when the salty, crispy fries hit my tongue. These would be better with cheese and bacon, but fuck, they're so good.

"Do you guys make sure to lock the door when you leave?" Carp looks at me, and he's not wrong for the assumption.

"Sometimes I forget," I mumble around my fries, and he sighs.

"Well, we have to go to Vegas tomorrow, so make sure your door is locked."

Carp and his friend share a look, and it's so quick I almost missed it, but they are so fucking, and I can't wait to tell someone, so I pull out my phone and type out a message to Paul.

MENACE:

Cap is doing the dude he's sitting next to.

Paul's phone vibrates on the table, and he looks at it confused but picks it up.

P DADDY:

Nick? How do you know that?

Nick! That's his name. Paul is so much better with names than me.

MENACE:

They had a LOOK.

Paul sighs and shakes his head, then shoves his phone in his pocket. Jerk.

CHAPTER 21

Paul

The bus ride to UNLV is long as fuck, especially with Brendon next to me touching me at every fucking opportunity. Coach gives out room assignments, we get our bags, and head to drop our shit off before we all head out to find food. I remembered to bring a bag of snacks for Brendon, but I want real food. I'm on the fourth floor with Louis, the first line left winger, Jeremy and Brendon are together on the third floor, while Preston is on the fifth floor with Willis. Someone is switching rooms, and it's probably Willis and Jeremy.

In the elevator, they switch keys, and I smirk. Called it.

I'm disappointed not to be rooming with Brendon, but it is what it is. I'm sure Willis will beg me to change rooms with him by tomorrow. My boyfriend will go out of his way to annoy his roommate until he snaps, and I honestly can't wait.

Louis gets the door open, and I follow him in, dropping my bags on the bed closest to the door since he took the other.

"You going out for food?" he asks, rearranging his bags

the way he wants them.

"Yeah, if I don't get something in my stomach, I'm going to punch someone."

He chuckles but nods. "I feel ya, but I don't want to sit ever again. My ass is numb from the damn bus ride."

"No shit. Why does Coach hate us so much? It would have been so much easier to fly." I grab clothes and get changed quickly so I don't smell like bus and B.O. anymore. "You coming out?"

My phone buzzes with a picture message from Brendon. Carefully shifting so Louis won't be able to see my screen, just in case, I open the message and snort at Brendon's dick being hugged by that fucking bear.

P DADDY:

I'm sure your stalker would love to know how you're using that bear.

MENACE:

Since you aren't available for dick touching, I'll have to use him.

Why am I a little jealous of a stuffed animal?

P DADDY:

Don't get cum on it, it'll show.

MENACE:

Sigh. You ruin all my fun.

I pocket my phone and blush when I find Louis watching me with a knowing look on his face.

"What?"

His smile widens. "Got yourself a girlfriend?"

I'm already tired of that question.

"Nope." I pop the p and slide my shoes back on. "I'm heading out."

I go to the stairs and stop halfway between the fourth and fifth floors, then text Brendon to come meet me.

I hear the door above me open and close a few minutes later, echoing in the stairwell.

"Are you luring me out to murder me?" Brendon's voice bounces along the walls as he makes his way down to me.

"Nah, only to take advantage of you," I call back and head up to meet him on the staircase. I don't waste any time when I get in arm's length, just grab him and pull him against me. "You're such a fucking tease," I growl before taking his mouth in a hard, rough kiss. Backing him up against the wall, I lift his arms above his head and hold them there. Brendon wraps one leg around mine and arches into me with a whimper.

My dick is hard in my jeans, rubbing against his, and all I want to do is make us both come. I don't know how much time we have in here, but fuck it, I need him. Releasing his hands, he grabs my face while I open his shorts and pull his underwear down to under his balls and wrap my hand around him. He groans into my mouth, panting and desperate to come.

"Are you going to come for me?" I cup his balls and gently squeeze while pumping him hard.

"Please." Fuck, I love it when he begs.

I drop to my knees and take his head into my mouth, the salty taste of precum and the musk of his skin a heady combination. Since I don't have much experience giving blowjobs, I can't take much of him in my mouth, but he never complains. I use my hand to help me, squeezing and rotating around him, and I swear his knees almost give out.

"Fuck. Please. I need to come," he whines, and I hum around him. Brendon's hips jerk up off the wall, and hot cum fills my mouth. I choke, my gag reflex kicking in hard, and I turn to the side, spitting cum and saliva onto the stair, coughing and trying not to throw up while Brendon spurts more cum on my cheek.

"Fuck. Sorry." Brendon groans. "Are you okay?" His words are airy as he tries to catch his breath, and he slides down the wall. I'm wheezing, coughing, and trying not to laugh because this is the most ridiculous thing I've probably ever done. Here I am kneeling on a hotel staircase, cum on my face, coughing, hoping nothing got on my clothes. I can only imagine what the employees will think when this is found.

Brendon cups my cheek and turns my face back to his. His cheeks are bright red, and even though his body is relaxed from the orgasm, there's a tension to him.

"Are you okay? I'm so sorry. I should have warned you." He wipes the mess off my face with concern in his eyes.

"Stop, it's fine." I hold on to his wrist and lean forward to kiss him. "I'm fine. And I had plenty of warning. I'm just not used to it and panicked for a second."

"Let me make it up to you." Brendon reaches for my pants, but I stop him. Apparently, almost asphyxiating on spunk takes my hard-on away.

"Stand up."

Brendon looks at me for a second, then does as he's told. I lean forward and suck his now soft cock into my mouth, cleaning him up, and he shudders.

"I can't let you leave here a mess." I smirk and pull his underwear back up over his hips. "Let's get some dinner."

I stand and press my body against him, taking his mouth in a deep, slow kiss. My tongue dances with his, enjoying the feel of him and the way he melts for me. Brendon wraps his arms around my neck and sinks into me.

Brendon is one of those people who came into my life and changed it. We connected immediately like kindred spirits. In a matter of weeks, I couldn't imagine my life without him. In less than six months, I knew I loved him. I tried to ignore it, pretend it wasn't true, but there's no one else for me. He's my sun, and I revolve around him.

Resting my forehead against his, I slow our kiss until we're just standing here sharing air and heartbeats.

"I love you," I whisper in the silence, watching his brown eyes shimmer.

"I . . . have an idea." Mischief brightens his face, and uncertainty tightens my gut. This is not going to go well.

"What?"

"Let's get married."

My head blanks out with white noise, and I blink at him.

"What?" I ask again. There's no way I heard him correctly.

"Let's get married." A huge smile splits his face, and when it's directed at me like this, it's so damn hard to think straight. "We're in Vegas. We can go down to one of the hundreds of chapels and get married. We don't have to tell anyone if you don't want to, but then you'll be mine and I'll be yours. Officially."

Nerves tremble in my stomach at the idea. Do I want him to be mine in every fucking way possible? Yes. One hundred percent yes.

But marriage?

We've barely started this relationship, but I want this so badly I can taste it.

"Yes," I blurt out. "Let's do it." I don't want to think about it or pick it apart or wonder about the consequences. As much as it scares me, I want this. I want him and damn what anyone thinks.

Brendon's face lights up like a kid on Christmas. He jumps up and wraps his legs around me with a huge smile on his lips. I lift my face to him, and he kisses me with my hands on his ass and his entire body wrapped around me. For the first time in a long fucking time, I'm at peace and just fucking happy. This is my boy, my man, mine. Even if we have to keep it a secret for a while, he's still mine.

"Aww, how are you gonna carry me over the threshold if we aren't sharing a room?" Brendon pouts with his lip out.

"That's your biggest concern?" I laugh. Fuck, I'm happy. This boy is about to be mine. We can conquer anything as long as we're together.

"It's tradition, Pauly," Brendon says very matter-of-factly.

"Well, we also aren't sharing a room, so we can't consummate the marriage until we get back. I'll just have to carry you over the threshold of our dorm room." I nip at his lip and smirk when he grinds his dick against my stomach.

"Fuuuuck." Brendon rolls his body and runs his fingers into the hair on the back of my head. "That's so long."

"But it'll be worth it." I kiss him again and let him slide down my body to stand on his own. "Let's get dinner before Jeremy comes looking for us."

Brendon throws his head back with an exaggerated groan but follows me out of the stairwell.

We're heading down the hallway toward the elevator like nothing has happened when Jeremy and Preston step out of the elevator.

"There you are," Jeremy says. "Where were you?"

Brendon and I say the same thing at the same time, "Jacking off," then laugh.

Jeremy rolls his eyes, and Preston sighs.

CHAPTER 22

Brendon

Preston and Jeremy are leading the way down the street toward some restaurant that I already forgot the name of but apparently has good chicken. I don't know.

"Let's ditch them and grab burgers on the way back," I whisper to Paul before checking the time on my phone and doing a quick search for places to get married near me. The amount of red dots is mind-blowing. "We have time."

"We can't just disappear." Paul eyes our friends. "What are we going to tell them?"

"I have a stomachache." I shrug.

He looks between them and me, then nods.

"Hey, guys." I groan and stop walking, holding my stomach. "I don't feel good. I'm going to go back."

Jeremy and Preston turn around with concerned expressions, but Preston holds his arm up to keep Jeremy from getting too close.

"What's wrong?" Preston asks with suspicion.

"My stomach." I moan again.

"Probably all that candy on the bus." Paul shakes his

head and puts his hand on my shoulder. "I'll take him back and just Uber Eats some dinner."

"We can bring you back something," Jeremy offers, but Paul waves it away.

"That's all right. Thanks, man." Paul turns me back toward the hotel. "You guys go ahead. We'll be fine."

I amble along, groaning and complaining for a few more minutes until we turn a corner and no one will see us.

"Don't go into acting; that was atrocious." Paul rolls his eyes at me.

I pull out my phone and find the closest place we can get married.

"Five-minute walk that way." I point down the street the way we're going, shove my phone in Paul's pocket, then jump up onto his back.

"What the fuck?" he yells but catches me and holds on to my legs.

"Hi-ho, Silver, away!" I yell, shoving one fist in the air while wrapping my other around his chest.

With a sigh, he starts walking in the direction I pointed, and my phone gives directions from his pocket, which makes me laugh.

"In a hundred feet, turn left," the animated female voice says from his hoodie pocket.

"I think your dick is talking." I nip at his neck and lick his ear. Paul shudders and tries to hide a moan, but I hear it and smile into his skin. "We need to find a way to switch rooms."

Paul's stomach grumbles, and I pat it. "Don't worry, buddy, I'll feed you soon."

"With what? Cum?" Paul scoffs, but honestly, it's not a bad plan . . .

"I mean, it has calories and, like, protein or

something." I shrug. "There's worse things you could put in your face hole."

"I've already put your dick in my face hole today," Paul says over his shoulder to me as he turns us to face the mock chapel.

The building is covered in red and pink lights, has a steeple, and what looks like wood doors with stained-glass windows like those super old churches. But there's also neon rose, ribbons, and wedding rings. It's a really classy place.

"You really want to do this?" Paul asks while letting me down. I stand shoulder to shoulder with him, staring up at the sign that reads FREE ELVIS PICTURE WITH WEDDING PACKAGE.

"It's perfect."

"You're wearing slides and basketball shorts, none of our family or friends are here, and there's an Elvis impersonator." Paul ticks off each item on his fingers, and disappointment settles in my stomach.

"It's okay if you don't want to do this. It was a crazy idea." I shrug and try to keep the hurt from my voice. I want him to be mine. Only mine. Is that too much to ask? He's said he loves me the way I am, that I'm not annoying or too much.

Tears sting my eyes, but I refuse to let them fall. I clench my jaw to give myself something to focus on and cross my arms to pinch my inner arm where he won't see. Pain makes the spiral stop.

Paul grabs my chin and turns me to face him, cupping my cheeks in his palms.

"I want nothing more than to make you mine in every way I possibly can," he breathes, pressing our foreheads together. "But I don't want you to look back and regret the way we did it. I can wait if you want to do it the traditional way."

A painful knot is in my throat, and no amount of clearing my throat will get rid of it.

"What part of me is traditional?" A tear falls down my cheek that he brushes away, and I give him a shy smile.

He laughs and kisses me quickly. "You do have my teeth marks tattooed on your neck."

"It was really my way of proposing." I chuckle and wrap my arm around his waist, glad to have the tension broken. "Surprised you didn't realize that."

He kisses me again, just a soft press of his lips on mine, before the smile falls again and that serious expression takes over. My poor Pauly is always so serious.

"And you're okay keeping it quiet for now?" He brushes his thumbs over my cheeks. "I'm not ashamed or embarrassed of you, but I'm not ready to come out yet. To have to explain myself to everyone."

"I'll wait as long as I have to. You're worth it." I turn my face and kiss his palm so he smiles at me again.

"Let's do this."

When we get inside, there is a line of couples waiting to fill out paperwork with a woman with very fake blonde hair, a skintight red plastic dress, and those super tall clear plastic shoes that strippers wear.

I want to be her best friend. I can only imagine the stories she has to tell.

One couple is a man and woman, him in a lime green Speedo while she's in a white-and-red striped string bikini top and denim shorts so short I'm betting her flaps are out. Both are covered in tattoos that were probably drawn by a toddler, and I'm betting neither of them have been sober in a decade. They are all over each other, and I'm pretty sure I just saw her nipple.

Vegas is amazing.

I slide my hand into Paul's hoodie pocket, and he slides his in from the other side, holding my hand and sending me a knowing smirk. While I can't imagine any of our teammates coming in here, I'm still hesitant to hold hands with him in here.

Out on the street, he kissed me. He made that move, not me. If someone saw us, that would be on him, and we would deal with it, but I don't want to be the reason he's outed before he's ready.

Our relationship has moved really fast, I know that, but at the same time it's been so slow. We've known each other for years, have been roommates for months. We know all the bad and good parts of each other and love each other anyway.

Despite it all.

And I have his teeth tattooed on my neck. If that doesn't say I'm committed to this, I don't know what does.

The lady calls us up—Ashley, according to her name tag—and looks between us.

"You marrying each other or just filling out the paperwork for the lucky lady?" She snaps her bubble gum, but I don't get any judgment from her either way. I'm sure she's seen it all.

"Each other," Paul says, and she hands over the paperwork for us to fill out, checks our IDs, and processes the payment.

"Do you have a witness, or do you need one?" She clicks something on her computer.

"Uh." We look at each other. We didn't think of that. "We'll need one," we say together.

"No problem." She inputs something into the computer, checks the paperwork, then hands us an "unofficial" marriage certificate to use until we get the real one in the mail, and gives us the one for the officiate and witness to sign.

Holy shit. This is really real.

Excitement swirls in my stomach, and the urge to do something weird is so fucking strong, but I don't want to embarrass him, so I hold it in.

"Chapel two." She points over her shoulder. "Elvis will be with you in about fifteen minutes along with a witness. Congratulations."

Paul grabs the papers and my hand, leading me inside the room with a big smile on his face and love shining from his eyes.

With the door closed, he turns on me and pulls me into a deep, demanding kiss.

"I love you," he whimpers against my lips before fucking my mouth with his tongue. It's urgent and erotic, a sensual dance that is driven by instincts and hormones. It's intoxicating, and I want so much more. I'm hard and aching in a matter of seconds, and it doesn't matter that I came an hour ago. I want him again. Here. Now. He grinds his cock against me, desperate, needy sounds coming from him.

I would give anything to be in a private room right now with him, let him take everything he needs from me until he's weak and sated. He can have every part of me. I have no walls anymore, nothing to hide. Not from him. Never from him, never again.

"All right, let's get this done." The gruff voice of a man who is done with life and has been smoking a pack a day for twenty years scares us, and we jump apart, panting. Both of us hard as fuck, and my shorts offer no protection. I turn my back and tuck my dick into my waistband while Paul pulls his hoodie down farther.

"Up at the altar. Come on, boys." He waves toward the

front of the room where there's a raised step and an arch with very fake, old flowers I think are supposed to be roses. Maybe. And white Christmas lights, to give it that romantic vibe. I think.

It doesn't matter. It's terrible, and I love it.

There are old church pews in the audience, and as I walk past, there are some suspicious stains on some of them. I guess we aren't the only ones who got a little carried away in here. I try to hide my laugh at the idea but end up snorting into my hand, and my body shakes.

Paul turns a very confused face to me. "What the hell is wrong with you?" he whispers.

"Pretty sure there's cum stains on those benches," I say out of the corner of my mouth as we take our spots on the floor that have been worn away from all the people who have stood here before us. Paul's face twists into disgust, and he eyes the benches in question like they've personally offended him.

The door opens again, and a woman dressed very similar to Ashley strides in. It's honestly impressive that they can walk in those shoes. I would probably fall and break my nose or something.

She takes the papers from Paul, and our officiant, who looks nothing like Elvis, sighs and starts the vows while Paul takes both my hands in his.

"Do you take, uh . . ." He trails off, and the woman says "Paul" from the front pew.

"Right, Paul. Do you take Paul to be your husband, to have and to hold, through sickness and health, good times and bad, forever and ever, amen?"

"Amen," I say on instinct, and Paul laughs. "Wait, yes. Shit. I do."

He chuckles, and the officiant starts again.

"And do you take—"

"Brandon," the woman says.

"Brendon," Paul corrects.

"Brendon to be your husband to have and to hold, through sickness and health, good times and bad, forever and ever, amen?"

"I do." Paul's eyes are locked on mine as he says the words, and my smile is so big my fucking cheeks hurt.

"By the power vested in me by the state of Nevada, I now pronounce you husband and husband. You may kiss your husband." The man could not sound any more bored, but I don't give a shit. Paul is mine. Legally. Officially. No one can take him from me.

I jump on him, wrapping my legs around his waist and my arms around his neck, and kiss the fuck out of him.

"You're mine," he says quietly against my lips.

"Forever and ever, amen." I beam at him.

"Sign here, please." The woman's no-nonsense words break into our bubble, and I drop my feet to the floor. Paul takes the pen and signs, then hands it to me to do the same.

"Smile." She lifts one of those old Polaroid cameras that spits out the picture at the bottom, and we stand next to the worst Elvis impersonator on Earth but with the biggest grins on our faces.

She takes the picture and hands it to us with our temporary certificate.

CHAPTER 23

Paul

I 'm *giddy*.

I've never associated that word with myself before and it's . . . amazing. I'm *married*. Brendon is officially mine, and I want everyone in the entire world to know. Right. Now.

We're walking down the street, Brendon talking a mile a minute in his excitement, but I can't take my eyes off the Polaroid picture we were handed. The happiness on my *husband's* face.

A grin takes over my own face, and I grab a fistful of his shirt, shoving him back against the wall of whatever building we're standing next to, and plant my lips on his. It doesn't matter that we're in public and anyone could see us. I don't know how close we are to the hotel and to our teammates. In this moment, I need him, and I will not wait another second.

My lips crash onto Brendon's while he's still talking, and I take advantage of his open lips, thrusting my tongue into his mouth like I'm fucking it. Tasting every inch, every millimeter, of him. I need him branded into my brain, into my flesh, into me. He's *mine*. Forever.

Brendon's hands grab my ass and pull my hips to his, and he grinds against me. I groan into him, desperate to feel everything right this second.

I'm lost in him. In this second of time that's standing still. Wrapped around the man I've loved for years and never thought I could actually have, I've found peace. The part of me that has been broken since my mom died heals. The scar still shiny and fragile, but it's there, knitting me back together.

The urge to cry hits the back of my throat and burns my eyes, so I lean my forehead against Brendon and just breathe. Wrapping my arms around his neck to keep him as close as possible, we just exist in this together.

His lips brush against my cheek, placing soft, sweet kisses along my skin.

"You okay, P Man?"

"I love you," I whisper, opening my eyes to meet his. "So much it scares me."

Even in the dim light, I can see his brown eyes sparkle at me and the freckles dotting his cheeks.

"We'll be okay. Come hell or hot water." The sincerity in his voice almost has me miss *what* he said.

"Hot water?" My face scrunches up in confusion.

"Yeah, hell or hot water. It's a saying."

I can't stop the laugh or the smile that turns up my lips.

"It's hell or *high* water, babe." I give him a quick kiss, then step back.

"I don't think so." Brendon shakes his head. "It's hell, the water would be hot."

I sigh and grab his hand so we can find food before having to be back in the hotel.

"Whatever you say."

Brendon links our fingers and lifts our hands to his mouth, then bites my hand.

"Hey!" I yell at the unexpected sharp pain. "No biting."

A knowing, sultry look transforms his face. "And we don't lick people, right?"

Heat floods my body at the mental image of Brendon licking me, taking my cock into his mouth and sucking on me. Fuck. My dick thickens in my jeans, and I have to adjust myself. Brendon snickers, and I glare at him.

"Bastard," I grumble at him but continue down the street.

There's a McDonald's close to the hotel, so we stop and get a bag of burgers before heading back.

We stand together outside, looking up at the building with a bag of cheeseburgers in my hand.

"I don't want to go in there." Brendon sighs.

"We could sit in the stairwell again." I shrug, not wanting to leave him either.

"Or you could come to my room, and I'll see if I can annoy Willis until he takes your room key and fucks off."

I laugh but shake my head. "As amusing as that sounds, I don't want to share you yet."

Brendon gives me a shy smile and we enter, going to the elevator and getting off on the fourth floor and heading to the opposite staircase as last time. The door closing echoes, but we drop onto the top step, and I put the bag between us.

"This is going to be hard to keep a secret," Brendon says quietly before taking a massive bite of his burger.

I unwrap the yellow paper and crumble it up into a ball. "Why?"

I watch Brendon's throat work as he swallows before he answers. "Because you deserve more than that." He turns his head to look at me, and it warms my heart. Brendon is such a good man. I got lucky having him as my best friend but even more so to have him love me.

"I'll get myself figured out and we can tell people." I squeeze his hand, and he lifts mine to his lips, pressing a soft kiss to the back of it. "You deserve to not be a secret too. I'm not ashamed of you. You know that, right?"

Brendon nods. "I know. It's weird to come out. To feel like you have to announce to everyone what you like in bed." He shakes his head. "Can you imagine if everyone had to do that?" He changes his tone, mimicking a woman. "I just want everyone to know that I like being humiliated and gangbanged. I didn't choose this life, it chose me. This is the real me."

I laugh, picturing a sassy girl telling her parents and can't contain myself.

"It's fucking stupid." Brendon shakes his head. "And why do straight people then think they can ask follow-up questions?" This time he lowers his voice and sounds like a stereotypical dumb jock. "But, like, which one of you is the girl?"

I pick at the bun, eating little pieces before I reply. "That's one of the big things holding me back. That and people thinking less of me. I don't want who I love to change people's opinion of me." My shoulders slump, and I lean my forearms on my knees. "I know I shouldn't care what other people think of me, but it's hard."

Brendon moves the bag and slides over until he's touching me from shoulder to knee. "We shouldn't care what other people think, but we all do." He lays his head on my shoulder and sighs. "But if someone you've known a while judges you for it, they weren't your person. You'll find better ones who won't care or judge."

"Change is scary."

"It is, but I'll be there, and honestly, if anyone is a real dick, we'll sic Preston on them."

We both laugh, and for some reason, it makes me feel better to picture Preston punching some homophobic asshole because he ran his mouth to me. Not that I couldn't handle it myself, but knowing Preston would probably have my back helps. Jeremy will only be pissed that we didn't invite him to the wedding, but not that there was one.

For a few minutes we sit in comfortable silence, just eating and throwing the balled-up wrappers at each other with easy smiles. We're just us.

Brendon pulls out his phone, checks the time, and sighs.

"I don't want to go back to my room without you."

Reaching for his chin, I turn his face toward me and kiss him softly, lingering. With our lips still exploring, Brendon moves and pushes my knees apart. He puts a hand on the back of my neck and intensifies our kiss. I think it's the first time he's taken over, taken what he needed instead of letting me tell him what he'll get. It makes me smile, knowing he's comfortable making his needs known. His hips meet mine, rubbing us together, rolling his hips, and panting against me.

"I want to suck you off," Brendon says against my mouth and moves both hands to my pants, but I grab his wrists.

"Hey, hey, hey," I say as I lean my forehead against his. "We don't have time."

Brendon groans and shoves his face into my chest. "I'm going to go annoy Willis until he demands you change rooms."

I can't help but chuckle and run my hand down his back. "We'll survive a few days."

"Says you," he grumbles into my shirt.

"Hey, you got off, like, three hours ago. You'll live."

Brendon pops up off my shirt with an intense expression. "When you jack off next, send me pictures or like a video of you coming." He bites his lip and grinds against me. "Fuck, that would be hot." Brendon nips at my bottom lip, rolling his body against mine. "Go do it right now, please? I want it."

I've never done anything like that, but it's turning me on how badly he wants it. It'll be weird, but I'll do it for him.

"Yeah?" I watch his face, watch the lust turn his skin pink and blow his pupils wide. "Will you send me some too?"

"Fuck yeah, I will. Goddamn. Go right now. I'm hard as a fucking rock."

I reach between us and grip his cock through his shorts. He whimpers, and thrusts into my grip. I love watching him start to lose control. When he gives into sensation and just takes from me.

"You're so sexy when you want to come. Don't keep quiet, I want to hear your sounds." My lips brush his ear, and he shudders, leaning harder into me and chasing the high of orgasm.

"Please," he whimpers and grips onto me hard enough to leave red marks on my skin but not bruises. A part of me wants the bruises too. He has my mark tattooed on him; I want it too. I want rings to show everyone he's mine and I'm his, but it's my own fault we don't.

I'll get there, and hopefully, it won't take me too long.

What are you going to do if he dies? Or leaves?

That stupid voice in my head ruins everything. The excitement I had just a second ago is gone and filled with fear. I can't lose him. It will kill me.

I wrap my arms around Brendon and just hold him against me while I kiss him.

"I love you," Brendon says with his lips still on mine.

A door opens below us, echoing off the walls, and we freeze, staring at each other with pounding hearts.

"Paul? Brendon?" Jeremy's voice has us both relaxing. Brendon moves to sit next to me on the step.

"What?" we say at the same time and smile at each other.

"They're checking rooms, hurry up!" The door bangs shut again, and I sigh.

"Good night, *husband,*" Brendon says, wagging his eyebrows at me.

A big smile splits my face. "Good night, husband."

I kiss him, then we gather our trash and head to our own rooms.

CHAPTER 24

Paul

I t's been a week since Vegas. Since I married the love of my life. But I'm still scared he's going to leave and take my heart with him. I will be a ghost of who I am if I lose him. Despite him wanting to have sex and expecting it when we got back from the Vegas game, I haven't been able to. It's so intimate. Something is telling me to hold back, not to consummate the marriage. Like it won't hurt as much if he changes his mind now.

We've been avoiding Brendon's new bestie, Nikki. I swear she just hangs out in the hallway waiting for the door to open. She posts pictures on Instagram and shit, tagging Brendon and putting shit like #bestie in the caption. Sometimes I'm not even sure how she's getting the pictures because the angles are so weird. Other times, she gets him coming out of a class or practice or during games. It's annoying as fuck.

Games are almost over since we aren't doing post-season games, and finals are coming up. We're not going to the Frozen Four, so we're able to relax after this.

I snagged Brendon after his class to have lunch with me today since it's one of the few days a week we can.

When we get to the dining hall, we find Jeremy in line for food too and sit at a table together. There's a sense of normalcy to it that I crave. This is normal, no surprises, just us hanging out.

"Where's Daddy Preston?" Brendon asks much louder than he should have.

Jeremy laughs and shakes his head. "He's in class. I swear you have the memory of Swiss cheese.

"Are we going to the heroes party next week?" Jeremy asks before shoving a huge bite of chicken into his mouth. The fraternities are throwing a street party for International Woman's Day and have themed it heroes.

"Oh shit, that's next week, huh?" Brendon pulls his phone, probably looking at the date. "Shenanigans, obviously," he says while shoving a bite of his lunch into his mouth. He reaches across the table to snag a crouton from my plate too. I stab the back of his hand with my fork, but he manages to keep a hold of it and shove it in his mouth.

He gives me a big grin, and he chews.

"You're a menace." I move my plate farther from him, and Jeremy snags a tomato this time. "The fuck?!"

Both of them laugh while I grumble and pull my plate off the table to clutch it against my chest.

"Fuck both of you."

Jeremy and Brendon both waggle their eyebrows at me, then crack up.

"Idiots, the both of you." I shove a bite of my salad into my mouth and glare at them.

"Obviously, I want to get drunk. Are they doing a theme?" Jeremy asks, bringing the conversation back around.

"It's called heroes, what do you think it's themed?" I look at Jeremy like the moron he is.

"I don't care, I want to wear a costume," Brendon agrees, pointing his fork at Jeremy.

Jeremy starts laughing and slides his hand down his face. "I obviously need more sleep."

"Is the dorm having a party?" I ask, hoping I can keep both of them close to home. Chasing drunk jocks across campus is not fun, and I'm not sure how much Preston will put up with before disappearing with Jeremy.

"Probably, but the frat houses will be a fuck-ton more fun." Brendon wags his eyebrows again.

"Since when are you into frat parties?" Jeremy asks the same question I'm thinking.

"Dude. Have you ever been to one? They take drinking to another level."

I shake my head at him, knowing how it worked out for him last time. I guess it was fun while he was doing it?

"Should we do a theme? Like we're all superheroes?" Jeremy and his love of Marvel movies makes me laugh.

"I'll be Batman, Brendon can be Robin." I smile wide at Jeremy who scoffs.

"DC? Are you serious right now?"

Brendon's foot hooks around my ankle under the table and pulls so he can wrap both legs around mine. He pulls out his phone and types out a message to someone while I argue with Jeremy over what makes a superhero (apparently having cool toys to save Gotham doesn't make Batman a superhero), and my phone buzzes in my pocket.

I pull it from my hoodie pocket and see Brendon's name on the screen.

MENACE:

I've always wanted to fuck Batman.

I try to hide the smile that itches to stretch across my face, but Jeremy calls me on it.

"Someone send you a titty pic or something?" Jeremy asks.

"What?" I look up at him, confused.

"Why are you smiling at your phone?" Jeremy nods toward my lap.

"Titty pic was your first guess?" I put my phone back in my pocket.

"I was hoping Brendon wasn't sending dick pics at the table." Jeremy shrugs and finishes his food.

Brendon moves like he's going to pull his dick out right here in the dining hall, but I slap his arm, and he stops with a big grin on his face.

"If you pull your dick out in here and Preston finds out, he will murder you, and I won't be able to stop him," I tell him, and Jeremy snickers.

"That's true," Willis says as he walks past our table.

"It was just a message from Grandma. Apparently, Drumstick is being a broody bitch again."

We finish our food and put our trays away. Jeremy and Brendon run from the dining hall and start pretending to do karate on the lawn, then end up rolling around on the grass like a couple of dumbasses.

It makes me happy to see him being his goofy self. I love all the parts of him, all the different versions that exist in him, but this one reminds me to laugh and have fun. I stand at the edge of the cement pathway and watch my best friends wrestle and laugh while yelling insults at each other.

Carpenter stops next to me and crosses his arms, bumping his shoulder into mine. "They really are children, aren't they?" he huffs and shakes his head.

"Yeah sometimes." I watch as Brendon gets Jeremy in a

head lock and wraps his legs around Jeremy's hips. Jeremy taps out and screams a high-pitched sound.

"Does that make you Daddy?" Carp smirks and laughs to himself.

"I mean . . ." I sigh and shake my head when Jeremy charges at Brendon, knocking him to the ground and tickling our redheaded friend until he shrieks.

Our captain claps my shoulder. "Good luck, man."

The sun is setting, and the lights around campus come on. Jeremy and Brendon run toward me, covered in grass.

I hold up my hands to slow them down. "No!"

Jeremy grabs my hands, and Brendon jumps onto my back, wrapping arms and legs around me to stay on. I grip onto Jeremy to stay standing while Brendon laughs like a crazy person.

"What the hell, dude?!" I hook my arms under his knees to hold him, and my phone starts buzzing with an incoming call. Without asking, Jeremy reaches inside my pocket and answers the video call.

"Grandma!" Jeremy shouts, turning to get me and Brendon behind him.

"My boys!" Grandma smiles. "What trouble are you getting into today?"

"Uh, all of it?" Brendon says, biting my ear.

Nothing like trying not to get aroused in front of your grandmother. Thanks a lot, ass.

"I like it." She nods.

"Do not encourage him!" I beg.

He raises one fist in the air and cheers.

"How are you, Grandma? Tell me everything." Jeremy takes my phone and walks away.

"You really are a menace." I turn to look into the smiling face of the boy I love.

"Yeah, but you like me this way." He shrugs with a

beautiful smile on his face. The darkness that still lingers is in the background, but in this moment, he's happy. "Giddy up, P Daddy!"

I roll my eyes at the name but brace myself and take off toward the dorms as fast as I can while Brendon hoots and hollers. One of his arms is around my chest, and his chin is on top of my head. This carefree, laughing side of him is everything. I would do anything to make him happy.

Does he know that?

CHAPTER 25

Brendon

I t's party time, and I am *rocking* this Robin costume. I
even got my hair cut. It looks like shit, but I'll buzz
the sides down to the skin after this so the top is long
and floppy still.

The body-hugging suit shows off the muscles I work
hard to maintain for hockey, and I'm looking sexy as fuck. I
add the mask to my face and turn to find Paul staring at
me from the bathroom door.

"Fuck." Paul adjusts his dick in his costume that hides
nothing, and I put my fists at my hips. "Are you sure you
want to go, 'cause I'm sure we could find *something* to do
around here . . ." He trails off, dragging his eyes over me
again.

The heat in his gaze is tempting. Really tempting. We
only fucked once and just used hands and mouths to get
off since then.

I want to fuck, to be inside of him and let him
command my body while calming my head, but some part
of me is hesitant. Something about it is vulnerable and
emotionally raw, and it scares me.

A hand on my cheek makes me blink, and I look at Paul who's now standing in front of me.

"Where did you just go?"

I force a smile to my lips and shake my head before taking his mouth. The kiss is full of heat, tongues and teeth and groans. Paul holds my face in both his hands, angling the kiss the way he wants, and deepens it. I hold on to his hips, rubbing my aching cock against his.

"I need you," I pant against his lips.

"Then stay with me; you can have me." One of his hands cups my ass cheek and squeezes. I groan at the contact, loving the way he touches me.

I open my mouth to agree, when there's a knock on the door and the handle turns. We jump apart, quickly adjusting ourselves, and face Jeremy in his Superman costume. You would think we would be used to it, but we get jumpy every time someone knocks.

"Come on, my merry band of hooligans!" he calls, thrusting one fist in the air and running down the hallway. His cape billows behind him, and I mirror his pose.

"Come now, Batman, there is fuckery a foot!" I yell over my shoulder and run down the hallway toward the elevator.

When we step out of the dorm, the campus is crawling with people, and there's a feeling in the air of fun and shenanigans.

We make our way to the frat houses and look around. Looks like they're basically having a block party. All the houses are decorated, the street is blocked off and decorated, and there's people everywhere. Each house has a different theme. One is Barbie, one is superheroes, one looks like a Ren fair, and so on.

Hot breath caresses my neck before lips move against my ear. "Remember, flirting is okay, but no touching."

A smile takes over my face, and I lift my phone to take a selfie with Paul and Jeremy before we get shit-faced. Preston is meeting us here for whatever reason. I don't know. He's not my problem.

I stick my tongue out, Jeremy cheeses hard, and Paul just lifts an eyebrow trying to look unamused.

"This damn costume doesn't have pockets!" I growl. "How do chicks do this?!"

Paul huffs and takes my phone. "You're just going to lose it."

He's not wrong. I head in the direction of a table with what looks like Jell-O shots. I pay for three and grab blue ones.

Jeremy takes it, but Paul shakes his head. "Someone has to stay mostly sober."

I shrug and toss back both mine and his. I'm not wasting perfectly good vodka.

"What flavor was that?" Jeremy asks with a disgusted look, scrunching up his face.

"I don't know. Blue." I toss the cups in the trash and move on. Looks like every house has their own drink station set up, and everyone has a different drink. I am about to be wasted.

The sun has barely set and there's already people puking in the street and in bushes. Amateurs.

There's candy all over the place, bottles and cans and cups littering the ground, and music blasting from the houses. Games are set up, people are fucking in the shadows, and I think this is debauchery at its finest.

CHAPTER 26

Paul

I don't know when I took on the role of fun police with Jeremy and Brendon, but it feels like it's just always been that way. They decide to do dumb shit, and I follow along to make sure they don't get hurt or kicked off the hockey team. Unfortunately, in a situation like tonight, I can't keep them both at arm's length, so after Brendon has had four drinks, he disappears. Jeremy is bobbing for boob squishies in water for some reason, and I'm kind of surprised Brendon isn't right here with him. Seriously, where is Preston?

A drenched-faced Jeremy lifts a dripping foam boob with a triumphant smile on his face. "I did it!"

He shoves the boob down the front of his suit and giggles like a schoolgirl at the round spot on his chest.

Jeremy looks at me, and I shake my head.

"Dude, have a beer and lighten up. Get laid or something." He smacks my stomach and walks off. If I'm being honest, he's the better one to leave alone. Only the devil knows where Brendon is and what he's getting himself into.

I scan the street again and catch a flash of short red hair. Hustling toward it, I find Brendon dancing with a chick dressed like Barbie and a Ken doll is grinding against his ass.

Does this cross the flirt but don't touch rule? I'm not entirely sure. Part of me likes watching him enjoy himself. It's erotic, the way his body moves while sandwiched between them. His hands on her waist, guiding her to arch the way he wants while the man behind him does the same. If I were dancing with him, I wouldn't get to see it like this.

Opening my camera app, I record him for a few minutes. The knowing smile on his face and the carnal sway of his body.

His head turns, and our eyes lock. The smile turns into a smirk, and he grinds into the guy harder. It's sexier than I expected, to be teased like this. No one knows we're married, not even Jeremy and Preston. It's no one's business what we're doing in the privacy of our room, but it also means that I can't walk up to him right now and own his mouth the way I want to.

The bastard knows it too.

It's like he's edging me, and if I'm being honest with myself, I kind of love it. The buildup of sexual tension that will at some point burst into mind-numbing pleasure. It has to give in at some point, right?

I'm not sure why Brendon seems hesitant to have sex, but he also doesn't seem to want to talk about it. Orgasms are great in any form, but I kind of expected to fuck more once we got the first time out of the way.

I stop recording and lean against the house with my arms crossed. Brendon leans down like he's going to kiss the girl's neck while keeping eye contact with me. I lift an eyebrow and square my shoulders. He smiles like he's won a prize and pulls back.

Jackass.

I'm going to make him pay for that later. He better not be wasted when we get back.

I wave him over, and he excuses himself from his dance partners and gallops toward me like a damn horse.

"What's up, Pauly boy?" He wags his eyebrows at me with a shit-eating grin splitting his lips.

"Don't get too drunk. You owe me tonight."

Brendon steps in a little closer, and his demeanor changes from excitement to sex.

"Yeah? You gonna give me your ass?" he asks quietly, and my eyebrows rise in surprise for a minute.

"Maybe." I drag my eyes down his body, desperately wishing I could feel him against me right now.

Brendon snorts and slides his hands around my back, then down my back to cup my ass under the cape. I quickly scan the area, but no one is paying us any attention. I hate that I feel the need to hide this, to hide him, but I'm not ready.

"I promise to make it feel good." His lips brush my skin, sending goose bumps across my body.

"I want to suck you so bad right now," I growl.

Brendon nips at my neck quickly and steps back. "Follow me."

He turns and heads into the darkness behind one of the houses. The backyards are decorated, but there's shadows past where the lights shine. Behind a tool shed, I push his back against the wall and take his mouth in a hot, demanding kiss. He moans for me, opening quickly to let me own him. I'm hard in a matter of seconds, grinding against him. The slick fabric of the costumes making it so fucking easy to slide.

"Fuck," he whimpers when I wrap my hand around him through the material.

"You wanna come, Little Menace?" I nip at the skin of his neck, careful not to leave any marks.

"Please," Brendon begs as his fingers flex on my arms.

I pull on the Velcro keeping the costume closed and pull it down his body, surprised when I find a red jockstrap.

Brendon bites his lip and smiles at me when I groan. I reach out a trembling hand and feel my way around his bare hip and ass cheek.

"Fuck my throat, baby. Come in my mouth so I'm full of you."

Brendon shivers, and I drop to my knees in the grass. Lifting the pouch, his balls and cock are released. I run my nose along the crease between his thigh and groin, inhaling the musky smell of him. The short red hairs tickle my skin, and I stick my tongue out to taste him. Brendon runs his hand into my hair and tugs just enough to tell me he's impatient. I smirk up at him and lick a line up the underside of his cock.

"Mmmm," I groan before sucking the head into my mouth.

"Fuck," he mewls, his hips bucking off the wall. "Please. I need to come."

Wrapping a hand around his dick, I stroke him in tandem to working him over with my tongue. I switch between sucking on him and lapping at him like a fucking ice cream cone. He thrusts into my mouth, his hand stills in my hair, and I love watching him from my position. Looking up his body, seeing him roll his hips and the clenching of his muscles as he fucks into me.

"Your cum is mine. You understand me?" Saliva drips down my chin, and I scoop some up with my fingers and watch him closely as I find his crack. He widens his feet, and I swirl the wetness around his hole.

He groans and shudders, his breathing getting heavy.

I get more saliva and push the tip of my finger into his hole, and he comes without warning.

"Shit fuck shit," he breathes out, almost panicked sounding as the bitter taste of his cum fills my mouth. I choke on it, some falling from my lips before I manage to swallow it. "I'm sorry," Brendon pants, and I chuckle, wiping the mess from my face with my hand onto the grass.

"It's okay." I lick my lips and wipe my face to remove any lingering cum and saliva. "That was hot as fuck."

I stand and help him back into his costume, patting his now soft dick, and he hisses. Once he's dressed again, I lean into him and run my nose along his.

"I like the way you taste."

There's a strange look on his face that I can't read.

"What?"

He chews on his lip for a second. "I like when you cum on me, mark me with it."

I smirk at him. "Good. I want to come on your face, your chest. Everywhere."

Someone laughs loudly, and we jump at the unexpected sound.

"We've been back here a while," I say and adjust myself to hopefully hide my hard-on a little. "Stay out of trouble. You owe me an orgasm." I grip his jaw and kiss him quickly, then step out of the shadows. He damn near cackles as I walk away from him to find Jeremy. Hopefully, he hasn't found too much trouble either.

I find Carpenter, and we grab beers as we watch the bad decisions being made around us. Over the sounds of the different movie scores playing, it's mostly laughter we can hear. A shout every once in a while, or a moan that carries on the wind, but we both know that the coaches for all the active sports teams will be hard on players tomorrow while everyone is hungover. I wish them all the best of luck.

Jeremy steps up next to us eating a full-sized KitKat. "Sup?"

"You're going to give yourself a stomachache." I shake my head at him. "Your roomie gonna rub your belly for you?" *Like I do for Brendon . . .*

Carp points to Jeremy's crotch. "What the fuck is that?"

I look too and snort at the squishy boob that looks like he shoved it into his underwear.

Jeremy looks down too and curses. "The stupid thing won't stay. I need a bra."

Carp sighs heavily and takes a drink of his beer while Jeremy shimmies around trying to get it to fall down one pant leg.

"It's stuck," he complains. "Get it, Paul."

"Excuse me?" I meet his gaze. "You want me to shove my hand up your pants to grab your boob?"

"That is the most ridiculous sentence I think I've ever heard." Carp laughs.

"Come on! I look like I've got an infected nut or something!" Jeremy argues.

"Did you swap brains with Oiler?" Carp asks.

"I swear to fuck," I mumble under my breath and hand Jeremy my beer to hold. He takes it, and I squat down. Pushing his pant leg up as much as I can, I force my hand into the fabric and feel around for the boob. "How did this shit become my job? Where's Preston?"

I've barely gotten my fingers on the foam toy when Jeremy crashes into me, bending my wrist at a weird angle and jerking my shoulder while dumping my beer down my back. My elbow hits something hard, and Jeremy ends up sprawled on top of me with his legs on either side of my head.

"What the fuck?!" I holler, trying to get my arm out of Jeremy's pants.

"Hey there, buddy . . ." Brendon's voice filters through the pain and surprise, and I sag onto the ground. "Whatcha doing there?"

"Get the fuck off me!" I smack Jeremy's ass hard, and Brendon giggles. No shit, giggles!

"Can you let go of my nuts, please?" Jeremy whimpers in pain, and I immediately release whatever I was holding.

"My bad."

"That's not what you said yesterday," Brendon singsongs. Jesus, he's so drunk.

My face heats as Jeremy stifles a laugh, and Carp raises an eyebrow at me.

"Shut the fuck up, Brendon," I grit out through clenched teeth. "Get off!"

He laughs again, dropping his head onto Jeremy. "I already did."

I'm going to strangle him.

Carp sighs again and puts his beer down, then lifts Brendon off Jeremy who stands so I can pull my arm from his damn pants.

Brendon is leaning into our captain, laughing so hard he can't stand up straight. Bastard. Jeremy is blushing and rubbing his junk while pointedly not looking at me.

"Are you two done causing trouble now?" I huff out, rubbing my shoulder.

"It's still early!" Jeremy whines, fixing his pant leg and finally getting the boob free.

Brendon reaches down and snags the squishy before Jeremy can and steals it.

"Dude! Give me my boob back!" Jeremy hollers, rushing Brendon who holds it up above his head.

"I grabbed it! It's mine!"

Jeremy jabs Brendon in the armpit with his fingers, causing Brendon to scream and drop his arm so Jeremy can grab the squishy, but Brendon won't let go, so Jeremy bites him.

"I swear you two are toddlers."

Carpenter laughs and slaps me on the back, which makes a wet sound thanks to the beer.

"Yeah, I'm out, guys. I'm not wearing a beer-soaked costume the rest of the night."

Brendon and Jeremy stop fighting over the boob for a minute to look at me.

"Just take it off then." Brendon shrugs like that's the obvious answer.

"I'm not walking around in just my underwear."

"But you have such a cute butt," Brendon argues. "The world deserves to enjoy it."

"You three are the strangest trio I've ever met." Carpenter laughs and walks off. "Good luck!"

Fucker.

"You want my costume?" Brendon offers, pulling on the fabric until the Velcro rips open.

"No!" I say quickly, knowing what he has on underneath. No one gets to see him in that jockstrap but me. No. One.

"Aww, are you trying to protect my virtue?" He pats my cheek, and Jeremy snorts.

"Little late for that, isn't it?" Jeremy smacks Brendon's ass, and a growl emanates from my throat without my meaning to. Brendon drags his teeth over his bottom lip while Jeremy turns around with a confused look on his face.

"Is there a dog here or something? Did you hear that?"

I swear alcohol lowers his IQ to a negative number.

"You guys shouldn't be left here without supervision, and I need to change." I snap my fingers, trying to get their attention, and redirect the conversation.

"So go change and come back!" Brendon pinches my cheek. "We'll be fine." He leans in so Jeremy can't hear his next words. "But make sure you don't get rid of that costume; we'll need it later."

"Then why don't you just come with me now?" I pin him with a look, and his cheeks turn pink.

"I gotta get myself a boob." The seriousness of that statement is impressive.

I huff out a deep sigh and concede. "Fine, I'll be back in twenty minutes." I hand him his phone. "Don't lose this!"

"Yes, Daddy." Brendon rolls his eyes and takes the device, then grabs Jeremy and disappears into the crowd.

I'm going to kill him.

After rushing back to the dorms to change and wipe off some of the beer, I'm back at the block party that's even busier now than when I left. Finding my dumbasses in this mess is going to be a challenge.

I check the bob for boobs station and don't see them, so I wander around, following the bright lights that they surely hopped to. A few of the guys from the team are shot-gunning shots, Riggs, our youngest player, is doing a chocolate-eating contest and already looks ready to puke, but no Brendon or Jeremy.

The longer I look, the more concerned I become. Do I actually think they'll get themselves in real trouble? Kind of? Streaking is not out of the question for Brendon, and if he does it, Jeremy will probably join in. Pass out in a corner somewhere? Definitely. But I don't think they'll break windows or anything like that.

But with as drunk as they both are, I can easily see Brendon making out with some random person. That thought flares jealousy in my gut. He's mine. I'm not sharing him. Watching him flirt is one thing, but actually touching? Kissing? No, dammit.

I've made a round, weaving in and out of partiers and stepping around vomit, and don't see either of them.

I don't think he would actually hook up with anyone, but it's always a fear. I trust him, but I don't trust that I'm enough.

Not being enough is a theme in my life. I wasn't enough to make my dad stay present after Mom died. My girlfriend in high school bounced the day before senior year started because she found someone else. I've lost more friends than I can count over the years. It will kill me if Brendon decides to walk away too.

I start checking the backyards, getting frustrated when I can't find either of them and stomp my way to the next one. Rounding a corner, I finally find Brendon being pulled into a house by a girl in a pink wig.

What the fuck?

My heart sinks as the door closes and he disappears inside. Do I follow them inside and see for sure what is happening or let my imagination play out? If he fucks her or gets his dick sucked, is that a mental image I really want? Would he really do that, though? Even drunk, it's hard to imagine.

I want to know the truth.

With a weight on my shoulders, I make my way to the back door and enter. It's dark in here, of course, but it doesn't take me long to find the back of Brendon's red head in the kitchen. He's leaned his ass against the counter, and I can just make out the top of the girl's head as she bobs on his dick.

Fuck this.

Anger and betrayal have me spinning on my heel to leave the house, slamming the door on my way out. Tears prickle the backs of my eyes, and there's a sharp pain in my chest that I can't rub away. It's piercing like a spear straight into my heart and electrified. Even though I saw it, I can't wrap my head around it. I thought I meant more to him than this.

It's agony, being disposable. Especially when you love someone with everything you are. How am I supposed to go back to just being friends? Bury my feelings in a lead-lined coffin? Pretend like I didn't see anything and see what he does? I can't.

My chest and shoulders are tight with the urge to cry, but I refuse to let myself out here in public. Once I'm safe in my dorm room, all bets are off, but for now I have to keep it together.

Why can't you just let me love you the way you deserve? Are you as scared of this as I am?

I'm back around the front of the house when I stop and lean against it. Closing my eyes, I take a deep breath and hold it, forcing my mind to clear.

If someone asked me if I thought Brendon would cheat on me, the answer would be a resounding no. Did I see Brendon, my Brendon, or someone who looks like him in the dark?

Spinning back around, I run back to the kitchen, barging through the back door, yelling his name. The girl screams and jumps, grabbing onto the man's legs for balance.

"Get the fuck off him!" I demand, pushing her back

when she stands up. Turning to him, I grab his costume and realize it's not Brendon.

My eyes track over this man's face, like I can't believe what I'm seeing. From the back, he looks exactly like Brendon, even from the side, but the relief coursing through me almost takes my knees out.

The guy shoves me back, and I mumble an apology before leaving the house and replaying the scene over and over in my head.

Blindly, I stumble across campus and somehow make it back to the dorm where I strip out of my clothes and hiss at the pain in my shoulder from the movement. That's going to be a bitch tomorrow. I find the bottle of pain reliever and swallow them, then drop onto my bed.

Where the fuck is my husband?

CHAPTER 27
Brendon

I feel like shit. My costume is soaked down the front from trying to bob for dicks, since they ran out of boobs, and it's cold. Jeremy also dunked me in the bucket, which led to a dick squishy war. There are dicks everywhere.

My head is spinning, and I keep running into shit. I don't know where Jeremy or Paul went, and I have vomit on my shoes, I think. Is it mine?

I taste my mouth, and I don't think I've thrown up . . .

The noise has died down, but is that because I left the party zone or because the party is over?

Where's my phone?

I stumble my way around, I think I'm on campus still, and kind of hope to find my dorm. My stomach hurts, and I want to cuddle with Paul, and my head is pounding.

Is that the dining hall?

Am I going the right way?

I'll find it eventually.

I just want to go to bed. The alcohol is wearing off,

giving me the hangover of all hangovers. I need Paul to cuddle me, play with my hair, and let me lay on him.

"Hey, man, you good?" An arm drops around my shoulders, and I turn to find Willis, one of our D men.

"Hey, buddy. Where are the dorms? I'm tired." I pat his stomach and lean my head on his shoulder.

He chuckles and turns me around. "You just missed the door, come on."

"You're such a nice boy." I pat his cheek while he leads me to the door of the building I was walking past.

"Yeah, sure, dude, whatever you say."

He opens the door and leads me inside. I lean against him while we wait for the elevator. My energy is quickly leaving me, and my stomach is super not happy. Shit.

The ding of the doors opening has me jerking open my eyes that I didn't realize I had closed. Willis keeps a hand on me as we step inside, and he hits the three for me. I relax against the wall for the quick ride, and my teammate walks me to my room. I try the handle, and it opens. I cheer and pat Willis on the arm.

"Thanks, partner."

He laughs and shakes his head while I enter the dark room and close the door behind me.

I pull on the neck of my costume but get caught and end up falling on my face on the floor.

"Paaaaaaaul," I whine, my face still on the dingy carpet. "Help me."

There's a rustling and a huff.

"Paaaaaaaaul," I whine again.

"What are you doing?" he grumbles.

I roll over onto my back and try again but can't figure out why the stupid thing isn't coming off.

"I neeeeeeed you," I call. Fuck, I need him so much. So much more than I should. It's scary how much I need him. He's my husband, but sometimes it still doesn't feel real. "Please." There's a lump in my throat that hurts to talk around. He could walk away, get tired of me and my antics.

I grip the edges of my costume and pull hard, ripping it until I can finally get my arms free and slither out of it. When I'm in just my jock and socks, my stomach rolls, and I hustle to the bathroom on all fours, barely making it in time to throw up in the toilet.

The room spins, and sweat breaks out along my forehead and back while I empty the contents of my stomach into the porcelain bowl.

I'm gasping for breath on the linoleum floor, leaning on the toilet when a damp cloth is placed on my face. Paul wipes my mouth and gives me a cup. I swish my mouth out with the water, then lean against him.

"All done?" His voice is quiet in the dark space that smells like both of us. I nod, and he flushes, then helps me to my feet. "Come on, time to sleep."

"Can I sleep with you?" I sound pathetic, but I don't care. I don't feel good, and I just want the comfort of him next to me. We sleep together most nights, but tonight, I need him to tell me it's okay. I need him to tell me he doesn't hate me, he isn't mad at me, he isn't tired of me.

"Of course." He kisses the top of my head and leads me to his bed. He pulls back the blanket and lays down so I can lay on his bare chest. The warmth of his body calms my mind and loosens the knot in my throat. I close my eyes, and I'm out before he's pulled the blankets up over us.

The dive alarm of Paul's goddamn phone starts screaming at an unholy hour. I want to shove ice picks in my ears to make the sound stop. There are already drums being played by hyperactive toddlers in my head along with a band that's synching tighter and tighter until I want to scream.

"Rise and shine," Paul's sleep-roughened voice rumbles in my ear, and he rubs his hand down my back to rest on my bare ass. *Why is my ass bare? Am I naked?*

"Turn it off," I grumble, dropping my arm over my head to protect myself from the obnoxious noise. "Why do you hate me?"

"Time for the gym, come on." Paul pushes me off him and climbs off the bed. When I sit up, the pain in my skull intensifies, and I groan. "Meds and water are next to you."

Cracking an eye open, I see the two pills and water bottle sitting on the bedside table and take both. Thank fuck one of us was smart enough to think about that.

The light in the bathroom flicks on, and I flinch as pain shoots through my brain.

"Fuuuck," I groan, covering my eyes with my hands and leaning my elbows on my knees.

"You should get up and move, finish the water bottle. You're dehydrated," Paul says as the scrape of his dresser drawers being opened sounds.

I get to my feet and sway a bit. When I crack my eyes open again to see where I'm going, I see Paul watching me with a weird expression. If I wasn't in so much pain, I might be able to figure it out, but I can't right now.

I stumble to the dresser and pull open my drawer to find some shorts.

"May want to change out of the jockstrap." Paul's words have me looking down at myself. Shit. That would explain the naked ass.

I find underwear and push my jock to the floor. As I step out, I start to fall over, but Paul grabs me, and I sag into him.

"Thank you," I pant, already exhausted.

His lips brush the back of my neck, then he helps me get the compression boxers on that I use for workouts. It takes a ridiculous amount of energy to get them over my ass, and by the time they're up, my stomach is rolling. I run for the bathroom and throw up the meds and water, then dry heave. My muscles ache, and I lean my head on my crossed arms on the toilet seat. Fuck. Me.

By some miracle I make it to the gym only a few minutes late. Paul found some stale-ass crackers in our room, and I got more meds down with water. So far, it's holding, but I'm sweaty from the exertion of getting here.

By the time the meds kick in and the band around my head loosens, I realize I am not the only one hurting this morning.

Carmichael is of course showing us all up. Paul appears to be fine—but he's babying his shoulder a bit for some reason—along with Carp, but everyone else is sluggish. I don't feel so bad now.

Coach comes into the gym while we're rotating through our stations for leg day and huffs.

"Tonight's practice will not be easy. If you're going to act like a bunch of jackasses, learn how to take care of yourself so you're not hungover the next day," the gruff man snaps. He's clearly unimpressed with us. "Hydrate. Vitamins. Pain meds before passing out. And learn your goddamn limits!"

He storms from the gym, the door slamming against the wall on his way out, and a bunch of us flinch at the noise.

We fucked up, and we all know it.

I'm at the leg press, forcing my way through my second set when Jeremy comes over. He's pale with dark circles under his eyes and looks like he's about to fall over.

"Okay, we may have gone a little overboard last night."

219

He leans against the machine when Preston comes over and snorts behind him.

"No shit," I complain. There's a loud clang as I let the weights fall. "I feel like a newborn kitten. I'm not even using the weight I normally do."

I grab my towel and wipe the sweat off my face, weak and exhausted. I just want to go back to bed, but I have classes after this.

We all switch machines, and I see Jeremy try to talk to Paul, but Paul is stretching his arm. He's clearly upset about something and in pain, but I have no idea what is going on. Did I do something?

After an hour and a half of bullshitting my way through my workout, I force myself to shower and change before heading to the dining hall for food. I'm not really hungry, but if I don't eat now, I'll regret it later.

Jeremy and Preston are waiting for me when I leave the locker room fucking around on their phones.

"What did you do to Paul?" Jeremy asks before looking up.

"What are you talking about?" I cross my arms and wait for him to pay attention.

"He's mad about something. What did you do?"

We start walking toward the dining hall, and I have a sinking feeling in my stomach. *I have no fucking idea.*

"Why do you think I did something?" I ask defensively. If Paul is mad about something, there's a ninety percent chance it was something I did or said. That's just a fact.

Jeremy gives me an "are you serious" look, and I sigh.

"I have no idea, but he's been weird since I woke up."

"Hmm."

"What does that mean?"

"I'm thinking. Jesus. Chill out." Jeremy opens the door for us, and I walk through. Scanning the area, I find Paul sitting with Carpenter and Willis, smiling at something Willis is saying. What the fuck?

He turns his head, and when he sees me, the smile drops, and an emotion I can't name covers his face. Damn. What the hell did I do?

Jeremy whistles quietly, and all I can do is nod. I fucked up big.

Anxiety eats at me, making me fidgety and nervous. I grab a few things to eat and check out with my meal card. Even Preston is aware of the tension because he didn't say shit about the bacon or toast on my plate. Jeremy leads us to the table where the guys are sitting, and as we set our trays down, Carpenter looks between Paul and me, who stands.

"I was just leaving. Later." Without a backward glance, he deals with his tray and leaves the hall.

I drop heavily into my chair and look at Carp. "What the fuck happened last night?"

"You two assholes were drunk as fuck." He motions between Jeremy and me. "While he was digging a foam tit out of Albrooke's pants, you jumped on Albrooke's back and wrenched Johnson's shoulder pretty good."

Preston's head snaps toward Paul, eyes wide with possessive fury. Jeremy reaches for him under the table, but all I can do is watch the love of my life walk away from me.

Eventually, they all get annoyed by you and leave. It was only a matter of time.

Fuck. Did I seriously hurt him?

I shovel the food into my mouth, not paying any attention to the conversation around me, then stand and leave. Hustling to my dorm room, I hope he hasn't left for class already.

I burst into the room, ignoring Nikki standing outside

again, and Paul jumps at the unexpected entrance, but turns his back to me again.

"I'm sorry I hurt your shoulder." The words come out sounding almost like gibberish in my rush to get them out.

"Whatever," he huffs, grabbing his backpack and slinging it over his shoulder.

"No," I almost shout, grabbing his arm. "I don't remember most of last night, but whatever I did that made you angry, I'm sorry. I'm sure I didn't mean anything by it."

Paul clenches his jaw hard enough for the muscle in his cheek to jump, then sighs and leans into me, his forehead against my cheek. "I have to get to class."

My entire body slumps. Resigned and heartbroken. It's stupid, right? Weak? To be this hurt that someone is mad at me. Paul is my person. He has been for a long time. Even when I was sleeping with Jeremy, Paul was my comfort.

Now my skin tingles, and ice shoots through my veins as the fear of losing my best friend settles on my shoulders.

I love you, Paul. Please don't leave me.

I know I'm broken. I've expected him to get tired of me forever, but now that it's happening, I can't breathe.

With tears running down my cheeks and shaking hands, I drop my face into my palms and cry.

What did I do?

CHAPTER 28

Paul

I need to get my shit together. I'm punishing him for my own issues, and it's not fair, but I don't have the words yet to explain it. He didn't do anything wrong. It was my own imagination fucking with me. My insecurities playing with my fears.

But I'm scared.

Scared to allow myself to love him as deeply as I want to.

Scared to admit just how obsessed with him I am.

Scared I'll lose him.

And being angry is easier, so I've funneled the fear into anger. When I look pissed, people leave me alone. Someone may ask what's wrong, but I just tell them to fuck off and they do.

So, I'm fuming. I have been all goddamn day. I could barely pay attention in classes, and I'm sure practice in a few hours will be a shitshow.

Stomping my way to my room, I freeze with my hand on the doorknob when I hear noise inside. Sounds like Brendon is sick again. Fuck. He's extra clingy when he doesn't feel good, and I'm the worst fucking husband for not checking in on him. I should have. I knew he wasn't feeling well today, and I'm sure he can tell I'm in a shit mood, which will stress him out.

I hear the toilet flush and his stumbling steps back to bed. Opening the door quietly, I find him curled up in a ball on his bed with his blanket pulled over his head. He's pathetic when he's sick, like a big baby who just wants to be cared for. It's so opposite to how he normally is.

I hate when he doesn't feel good, but it's always made me happy to take care of him.

I set my bag down and stand there staring at him for a few minutes. Part of me wants to curl up behind him, pull him into my chest, and rub his stomach until he falls asleep. But I'm struggling to let go of the anger and fear.

After a few minutes of arguing with myself, I kick off my shoes since we have a few hours before practice and feel his forehead. He groans at the touch, reaching for my hand to pull me closer.

As much as I don't want to, I pull my hand back.

"Do you need anything? Water? Something to eat?" I ask.

"Just you." His voice is sad and needy. "I need you, Paul." His voice is thick with emotion.

"What did you do after you jumped on Jeremy's back, wrenching my shoulder?" I need to know. I hate that I'm questioning him, but I need the reassurance anyway.

"Why was your hand up Jeremy's pants?" he asks defensively and rolls over to look at me.

"Don't change the subject." I grip his chin in my hand, not letting him turn away from me.

"I did shots and went bobbing for dicks." Brendon's answer is not what I was expecting. "I screamed into a karaoke machine while twerking on a porch railing."

Fucking what? "I was wasted." He stands, forcing me to take a step back. "Why? What is going on with you? Did I do something I don't remember? Did I out you?"

There's a pain in his eyes that isn't normally there. One that cuts me to the core.

"I'm fully aware that I'm a shitshow, that you could do a lot fucking better than my pathetic ass, but I love you, and the last thing I want to do is hurt you." Brendon holds my gaze while his turns glassy.

I grab the back of his neck and pull his forehead to mine, close my eyes, and take a deep breath.

"I want you." I press my lips to his in a soft kiss and align our bodies. Brendon opens the blanket and wraps it around us. "But I'm fucking scared of how much I love you."

He shakes his head and shoves his face into my neck. "I want more."

My heart sings at his muffled words. "More what?"

"Of you."

I wrap my arms around him and smile. "You're mine, understand? Only mine."

Brendon nods into my neck, his unshaved cheeks scratching against my skin. "I'm yours, you're mine. I want all of you. Don't hold back."

We stand in the middle of our room for several minutes, just holding each other.

"Will you cuddle me now? I feel like shit," Brendon whines, and I chuckle.

"Yeah, come on." I step out of his hold and grab his hand, pulling him along with me to my bed. I lay down and get situated before Brendon lays on my chest and throws a leg over mine.

I run my hand through the long hair he still has on top

of his head, and he shudders. Since he doesn't feel good, I expect him to fall asleep quickly, but he doesn't.

"Something on your mind?"

He rubs his cheek against my chest a few times before he speaks. "Why did you want to know what I did last night?"

I sigh but let the words out instead of keeping them in. He deserves my honesty. If I want this to work, really fucking work for the long term, I have to talk to him even if it hurts.

"I saw someone I thought was you go into one of the frat houses and get a BJ." My face heats and tears sting the backs of my eyes. "I couldn't believe it, so I followed him in to get a better look at his face, and I still thought it was you." A tear falls, trailing down my temple into my hair. "It hurt." That pain starts in my chest again, and I rub at it. Brendon shifts to look up at me. "I tried to walk away, but I couldn't. It wasn't you."

He's quiet again, and I don't know if he's processing what I said or working himself up to tell me off.

"I'm sorry I disappeared on you and made you doubt me." He burrows into the blanket, covering most of his face. "I hope you know I would never do that to you, doesn't matter how drunk I was."

"Logically, I know that." I'm trying to keep my body relaxed, but something he said is circling my head. *I'm a shitshow. You could do a lot fucking better than my pathetic ass.*

"Has someone told you you're hard to love?" My words are quiet in the dark of our room, and Brendon tenses against me. I don't push him for an answer. His reluctance to respond is a resounding yes.

"Yeah." He takes a deep, shuddering breath.

"Hey." I reach into the blanket and lift his chin so he's looking at me. "Whatever was said to you is not true."

Tears spring to Brendon's eyes, and he chokes on a sob. I wrap my arms around him as he cries, his body shaking from the emotional release, and I run my hands up and down his back while I murmur to him.

I love this guy more than I thought was possible. He fills the holes in my heart that my parents left, completes a part of me that I didn't know was incomplete.

"I love you," I murmur into his hair, and he falls asleep wrapped around me.

CHAPTER 29
Brendon

After workout the next morning, I'm feeling better, less vomit-y, and on my way to the dining hall for breakfast with the guys before class. I'm digging in my bag, not paying attention, when I run into someone and knock them over.

I reach for her arm to keep her from falling to the ground.

"Shit, I'm sorry," I say in a rush. When she straightens up, I recognize Nikki and force myself not to groan. Jeremy pats me on the shoulder, and he walks off with Preston smirking at me. Paul looks between us, then shakes his head and follows, leaving me alone to deal with her.

"You okay?" I ask her as she straightens her backpack.

"Yup." She watches Paul for a second, then cocks her head and looks at me. "Have you ever thought about doing porn or OnlyFans? I'm betting you could make some cash, especially if you have a *partner*."

I jerk back and stare at her. "What the fuck? Who asks that?"

She shrugs like it's a very normal question. "OnlyFans is a thing these days."

I swing my bag over my shoulder and start toward the dining hall again. "Pretty sure my contract with the hockey team, and my scholarship, says no sex work."

"Hmm . . . I could read through it for you if you want."

What the actual fuck is this conversation?

"That's all right, thanks."

I open the door, and she steps through ahead of me. Of course I was hoping she would bug off, but I'm not lucky. After filling my tray, I head to the table where the guys are sitting and drop down next to Paul who's clearly annoyed with Nikki if his expression is anything to go on.

She sits next to me at the table and leans into my space, snapping a selfie with me while I'm trying to eat. It's annoying, and I'm tired of getting tagged on social media with her.

Paul grumbles something under his breath that I don't catch and stabs his eggs harder than necessary. I loop my foot around his ankle where no one is paying attention and encircle his leg with both of mine. He takes a deep breath and relaxes some, which makes me feel better.

I know having Nikki show up all the time is annoying as fuck, but I can't just tell her to fuck off.

The conversation around us comes in waves, talking about the upcoming game, spring interim, and homework. Nothing of any substance since none of the guys like Nikki much. They all call her my stalker, and yeah, she's intense, but I really think she just needs a friend.

Paul looks at the screen of his phone laying on the table and nods at me. "Gotta get to class."

Nikki's phone starts making an alarm clock sound, and we all turn to look at her.

"He's right." She shrugs and turns it off. Okay, that had stalker vibes.

Paul clenches his teeth, the muscles in his cheek jumping. He stands abruptly, grabbing my arm and pulling me up. "Come on, I'll walk with you."

I quickly pick up my breakfast stuff and follow him. Once we're outside of the dining hall, he looks behind us and lets out a breath.

"Dude, you have got to stop hanging out with her." Paul shoves me into an empty classroom. "She's not right. That girl is creepy."

I sigh and lean against the wall.

"She's harmless." I cross my arms when what I really want is to pull him against me and kiss him, get lost in him, have him hold me.

He stands there, hands on his hips, looking at me like he wants to yell, but instead he scrubs his hands over his face and growls.

"I don't want to fight with you." I lean my head back against the wall too. I'm tired. Tired of not knowing where I stand with him, tired of this argument, tired of homework, tired of hiding parts of myself from everyone but him. Hell, I'm tired of hiding parts of myself from him too. Since we got married, I feel like I'm walking on eggshells sometimes. He doesn't touch me like I expected; we haven't had sex, just a few handies and blowjobs.

"I love you," I say as he opens his mouth to respond. His shoulders slump, and he steps into my space, pressing his forehead to mine and a soft kiss to my lips.

"I love you too," he whispers, wrapping his arms around my lower back. I slide my hands up his chest and around his neck, finally able to breathe.

Closing my eyes, I let the words tumble out of my mouth that have been circling my brain for a while.

"Is there a reason you don't want to have sex with me?" Paul tenses against me and more words pour from me without clear thought. "If you aren't into it, that's fine, some people aren't into penetrative sex, there's nothing wrong with that, but is that what it is? I expected you to want to fuck after Vegas, but you don't seem to want to, so I just want to make sure I didn't do something or—"

Paul's mouth crashes into mine, effectively shutting me up, and he grinds his hips into mine. His cock thickening against me, which only turns me on. Fuck. Paul lifts a hand to my jaw and moves me the way he wants, deepening the kiss and the connection between us. I swear I could come just from this, from him controlling my mouth and rubbing against me. I love the way he commands my body.

He swallows my whimper and groans, licking the inside of my mouth and exploring all the edges. Paul nips on my lip, sucking on it while grinding hard against me. My balls are full and heavy, I'm panting, and I want to come so fucking bad.

"Please," I whisper against his lips. "I'm so close."

He smiles against me, reaching into my pants and wrapping his hand around me. My hips thrust my cock into his hand, and he chuckles. "Desperate, dirty cumslut."

The words have goose bumps prickling along my skin and stealing my breath. "Don't come, hold it."

My moan is pain-filled, and he snickers at me.

"I want to fuck you, Brendon. Fill you with so much cum I need electrolytes." He trails his nose along my neck. "Both your stomach and your ass. I want you to fuck me, till you're so close to the edge you're desperate and can't hold back. I want to use your dick to get myself off and leave you hard until I'm ready to go again."

His words and the mental image they force into my

head have me dripping. I love that I can leak precum, that I have proof of how much I want him.

"Paul." It's the only word I can force past my throat. There's nothing else, just sensation and anticipation.

"After class," he says against my skin and bites my neck over the tattoo. "Your cum is mine. Don't you dare take care of this on your own."

I whimper again, clenching my hands into fists in his shirt and wanting to sob. My entire body is trembling and tense and on edge. I can't think of anything except orgasming.

"I hate you," I moan, shoving my face into the crook of his neck and sucking on his skin just to the right of the that little hollow at the base of his throat. I suck hard, knowing it'll leave a mark and not giving a shit. If I'm going to be uncomfortable for the next few hours, so is he.

"That's right, baby, mark me," Paul growls, gripping my hair in his hand to keep my mouth on his skin. "I want everyone to know I'm yours."

Paul lets go of my dick and removes his hand from my pants, then rubs his palm against the ridge in my jeans.

"I promise I'll make sure it's worth the wait," he says, and I release his skin with a pop. I pull back enough to see the dark purple mark on his throat, and my eyes widen. Okay, that's way darker than I meant. Fuck.

"Shit, I'm sorry," I ramble as I feel the blood drain from my face. "I didn't mean for it to be that dark. The guys are definitely going to ask about it."

"Hey." Paul lifts my chin so I'm looking him in the eye. "It's okay. I've never had a hickey before."

The smile that splits my face hurts my cheeks, but I don't try to dull it. I love being his firsts. While I wasn't sleeping with *everyone* who offered, I definitely got around for a while there, but Paul's innocence reminds me of the butterflies and excitement. I like showing him new things.

"I can't wait to rim you." I smirk at him. "It's fucking amazing."

Paul smiles and nods. "Noted."

He gives me another quick kiss, and we both adjust ourselves to make the hard-ons less noticeable, then turn to the door. Nikki is standing in the window of the door, watching us. What the fuck?

My stomach drops to the floor, and I swear my blood turns to ice.

Fuck.

No one knows about Paul but Jeremy and Preston. Will she tell anyone? Ask questions?

Paul growls behind me and lets out a huff of breath. I guess he saw her too. She lifts an eyebrow, meets my eyes, then walks away.

Dread sits heavy on my shoulders, and I'm afraid to turn around. I don't know what I'm going to see on Paul's face and that scares me.

"Let's get to class," he says and puts a hand on my shoulder.

"I'm sorry," I mumble miserably.

"Nothing to be sorry about. Let's just get to class."

CHAPTER 30
Paul

N
ikki has got to go.

That chick is like an invasive pest. She shows up where you least want her, pushing her way in, and taking over. I hate her.

She makes me want to act like a caveman and tell her Brendon is mine.

All through classes, my brain is bouncing between fucking Brendon and Nikki telling people I'm gay or bi or whatever term she uses. I'm tense and frustrated and tired of myself when I get back to the dorm.

Brendon isn't back yet, so I drop my bag and lay down in the dark, just needing a damn minute to chill out, but before I know it, I'm asleep.

I wake up slowly, to something grinding against my dick. My lungs suck in a little gasp and my eyes flutter open to find Brendon between my thighs and leaning over me.

"Please fuck me," he murmurs. "I need you."

I reach for him, bringing his mouth to mine in a slow, deep, lingering kiss. I'm relaxed from sleep and just want to explore him for a while. Brendon trembles, pants, and whimpers into our kiss. He's so desperate and needy it's intoxicating. I love him like this, that I can do this to him.

"Roll over," I command, and he wastes no time switching spots with me on the bed. I get to my knees and pull his pants and underwear off, dropping them on the floor. He sits up to pull his shirt off, and I remove my clothes too, finally getting skin to skin with him. We groan in unison at the connection, at the warmth of our bodies together.

Brendon's hips cradle mine, his legs wrapped loosely around me as I lean over him to kiss him again. He can't keep still, too worked up from being edged for hours.

He's whimpering and panting, his hands demanding and trying to rush.

"Shh," I say with my lips on his chest. "I'll get you there."

"Please . . ." His voice is heavy with desperation, almost a sob in the quiet of the room. "I need you."

I bite at his flesh, worshipping his body, sucking on his nipples and as much of the surrounding flesh that I can get into my mouth. His back arches off the bed, making my dick rub against his abdomen, and I moan around his skin.

I release his nipple with a pop and wrap my hand around his cock, stroking him fast with a tight grip. Brendon whimpers long and loud, his hips rolling and arching into my touch, thrusting into my palm. His face is red and shiny with perspiration, eyes closed and eyebrows pulled together.

"Please, Paul, fuck," Brendon whines. "Coming!"

Cum splatters on his chest, drips down my hand, and pools on his stomach. He's breathing hard, like he just did an hour of drills, but his body is limp now. The tension of just a few minutes ago evaporates, and I smile at him. I love that I can do this to him.

Swiping my fingers through the cum on his chest, I slide my fingers between his cheeks while leaning on my elbow next to his head.

He mewls when I circle his hole, still breathing too fast.

"Are you going to let me in?"

I get more cum and paint his hole with it, making sure my fingers are slick with it and push against him.

"Relax for me," I say against his lips. One finger pops through the tight ring, and he moans. "Good boy."

His cheeks brighten again at my words.

"Hmm, you like being good for me, don't you, baby?" I lick along his bottom lip, and he turns into me, hiding his face in my neck while I pump my finger in and out of him. "You're taking it so well."

Gathering more cum, I slide two fingers into him, watching his body and listening for any sounds of pain. His chest is flushing red, and his hips are starting to move again, like he can't keep them still.

"You like being full, don't you?" I suck on his earlobe, and he shudders.

His cock twitches, and I smile, knowing he isn't just tolerating this.

Two fingers become three, and it takes me a while, but I find his prostate, hooking my fingers in a "come hither" motion to find that magic spot. Brendon shouts when I find it, damn near jumping off the bed.

"There it is." I chuckle.

"Fuck me, please," Brendon begs with his face still in my neck. "Hard, deep, please."

I sit up and grab the lube from the bedside table to slick my cock, then settle back against his hips. I swipe his cum across his bottom lip, line my head up with his stretched hole, and suck his lip as I push in. His salty taste bursts on my tongue as he arches into me, groaning into my mouth as he takes me deep. One steady thrust has me settled as deep as I can go.

Fuck. I drop my forehead to his and breathe through the urge to come already. He's hot and tight and wet. It's been so long since I had sex that I'm already close to the edge, but I want this to last. I need to show him that I can love his body just as much as his mind.

"Paul," Brendon whines, gripping my arms hard enough to leave bruises.

I start with slow, deep thrusts, making sure he's stretched enough. The last thing I want to do is hurt him and make this bad for him.

"Harder," he demands, but I don't do what he wants. I slow down, making him feel every inch of me. Brendon lets out a frustrated sob and grips at his hair. I take one of his hands, lacing our fingers together above his head and grip his thigh where it meets his hip in the other hand. My lips take his, and my thrusts get hard and deep, fast going in, but slow pulling out. It's enough to keep him on the edge, to keep my own orgasm at bay for a while, but still feels possessive and almost dangerous. I have control of his body, his pleasure, and I'm addicted.

"Tell me you love me," he begs, and my heart aches for him. I hate that he needs that reassurance during this. He must feel vulnerable like this.

"Look at me." I wait until his eyes open. "I love you, Brendon. You are mine, always."

A tear trails from the corner of his eye into his hair, but I don't take my gaze from his. In this moment, we are sharing the same air, finding pleasure and comfort in each other, and solidly in this second of time. Nothing matters but us, right here, right now.

My body moves on instinct, keeping us connected and chasing the high of orgasm. Brendon wraps his legs around my ass to keep me close and bites his lip as he watches me.

"Touch yourself, I want to see you come again."

He whimpers but reaches between us to jack off while I fuck him.

I've never had sex like this. Powerful. Connected. All-consuming. World-ending.

I love this boy, this man, with everything I am. It's terrifying, but I can't stop it. Putting distance between us only hurts both of us. I have to embrace it, embrace him, and hope he isn't taken from me. It would destroy me, but not having him at all would be worse.

Brendon's body tightens around me, pulsing and clenching as he empties himself again. His eyes stay locked on mine while he finds euphoria, and it pushes me over the edge. I fill him with me, shuddering and groaning against him until I'm weak and sated.

I collapse on Brendon, not giving a shit about the cum mess that we'll have to clean up.

"Okay," Brendon pants. "That was awesome, and we should do that more often."

I chuckle and turn my head to kiss his neck.

"Definitely."

"If you don't get up, you're going to be glued to me, and that's just not my kink." Brendon runs his hand through my hair and pulls on it playfully.

"Shhh, I'm sleepy."

He laughs, making me bob up and down. "You could sleep through a tornado, I swear."

"You love my dive alarm, and you know it." I nip his neck, then sit up, unsticking my chest from his.

"I'm going to throw your phone out the damn window one of these days."

I run my hand down his side and smile at him. "Come on, let's rinse off. We have to get to practice."

"Oh sure, fuck my brain into jelly, then make me go to practice. Real nice." Brendon rolls his eyes but sits up. His gloriously naked body is so distracting, even in my post-nut haze.

He's not super cut, there's some padding on his muscles, and I love it. He clearly works out but loves food too. I love his body.

I climb off the bed and grab his hand to make sure he follows me into the bathroom. The shower isn't huge, so we bump into each other as we try to clean up, but I don't mind. I like the contact.

"Does this mean I can touch you whenever I want?" I ask as he rinses the soap off his stomach.

"Was that ever not allowed?" He turns to look at me like I've lost my mind. "I always want you to touch me. If I could ride on your back like a backpack all day, I would."

I chuckle and lean in to kiss him quickly.

"I've loved you for a long time," I tell him quietly, looking at my feet. In the steamy shower, it feels safer to tell him this. "I was afraid you would see it and stop coming to me when you needed to cuddle or whatever."

Brendon cups my cheeks and lifts my face to his.

"How long?"

I sigh and close my eyes.

He's your husband, you can be vulnerable with him.

"Basically, since you joined the Lumberjacks." I hold my breath and wait for his reaction. Wait for him to be angry or disgusted or something. It's stupid and logically I know that, but it doesn't stop the fear.

"Paul." My name is sad on his lips. "Why didn't you ever say anything? I thought you were straight up until a few months ago."

I chuckle and look at him.

"Definitely not straight." I wrap my arms around his lower back, comforting myself with him. "I was scared you didn't see me the same way, that you would stop talking to me." I shrug and lay my head on his shoulder. Normally this position is reversed and he's leaning on me, but I like that I can rely on him to be strong for me sometimes. That's what relationships are all about, right? Switching who is strong.

"I keep waiting for you to get tired of me and leave."

I lift my head and take in the truth of those words on his face.

"What? Why?"

He shrugs and rotates his wrists in that nervous way he does sometimes.

"Because of the bullying?" I can't imagine talking about it is fun, but I feel like this is something I should know.

"Partially, but I've been told my entire life to lower my voice, sit still, stop making noise. I don't have friends from childhood. I had to make new ones every year, only to join a hockey team where they hated me. Fucking Chad Fenwick had it out for me bad. He was a dick, and his dad was the coach, so he got away with everything."

I pull Brendon into a tight hug and just hold him. I can't imagine what he's lived through, and I'm so glad Jeremy and I found him.

"Your quirks don't bother me. I like that you're you. You make me smile; it's impossible not to have fun with you around, and some of my favorite memories involve you."

Brendon lets out a quiet sob and grips me hard, digging his fingers into my back as he fights with the demons in his head.

"And if I ever hear anyone say anything like that to you, I'll knock them out. You hear me?" I say into his ear. He nods and relaxes some, letting go of the ghosts that haunt him from his childhood. "I love you the way you are."

Brendon presses his lips to mine. It's salty with tears but healing.

"I can't imagine my life without you," he says, his voice rough. "You're it for me."

CHAPTER 31
Paul

W e get to the locker room with barely enough time to get our gear on and most of the team already filing out onto the ice. Brendon and I race to get out on the ice before Coach rips us a new asshole and just barely make it.

"Oiler, Johnson, nice of you to join us," he barks across the ice, and I just nod. I know better than to fuck with Coach.

I can see Brendon open his mouth from the corner of my eye, and I quickly say, "Don't do it," under my breath. He snaps his mouth closed and lifts his stick in acknowledgement.

We start with warmup skates, going around and around the rink until we're breathing hard and starting to sweat. Coach yells out drills, and we get into position for them. It's standard practice, and since Carmichael is back on the ice, his voice is a lot closer when he yells insults at us. I really thought getting laid regularly would make him nicer, but I was wrong.

"Johnson!" I grind my teeth together at Carmichael's

voice. "Albrooke's baby niece has better puck control than you!"

I flip him off and keep going while Oiler chuckles.

"For once, it's not me," Oiler yells with his arms in the air.

"Riggs! Have you ever been on a pair of skates before?" Carmichael yells, and our baby player fumes but doesn't say anything. Smart kid.

We run some passing drills with insults as a soundtrack, though most of us just ignore him these days.

"Oiler!"

"Fuck." Brendon groans. "I know! Slower than your one-legged, dead grandma running through peanut butter in the snow. Got it."

Everyone laughs, and Coach calls the end of practice. We grab water bottles and trudge back to the locker room. I'm going to get changed, then head back to the dorm to crash. I should eat, but I just don't care. Maybe I'll order pizza or something.

I pull my practice jersey off and hang my pads in my cubby to dry out. As I'm pulling my base layer over my head, someone grabs my arm while my head is covered in the fabric and turns me.

"Johnson!" Willis yells, and I fight to get the damn shirt off. "You find yourself a hoover?"

I get the shirt off and lift an eyebrow at him. Jeremy snorts behind me, and Brendon comes up next to me, dropping an arm over my shoulders. This is either going to be hilarious or awful.

"You jealous? I can give you a matching one if you want." Brendon shrugs. "You guys can be twins like me and Jeremy."

I sigh and shake my head while Willis looks between us, clearly trying to decide if Brendon is full of shit or not.

It's on the tip of my tongue to tell Brendon not to touch him, but my gut tightens, and I hold it back. Logically, I don't think anyone on the team will care if they find out Brendon and I are together, but the only people that I've come out to are Brendon and Jeremy. It's terrifying to put myself out there like that. Will I be judged? Will people start making fucked-up comments about me or what I like? Will the team think less of me?

"Knock it off," I tell Brendon and smack his bare stomach with the back of my hand before heading to the showers. Brendon is not far behind me and smacks my ass on his way past me. "They're going to start thinking you're serious, you know."

Brendon turns to the room and cups his hands around his mouth and fear courses through me. What the fuck is he going to say?

"Hey!" he yells. "I'm bi or whatever. I like holes *and* poles. Anyone got a problem with that?"

I turn and watch everyone react to his words. Everyone looks around confused for a few minutes before Riggs calls from the back, "Are we supposed to be surprised?"

Everyone starts laughing, and I can't help but join in too. I love that Brendon doesn't hide who he is, isn't afraid to show affection to other guys, isn't intimidated by toxic masculinity mentality. Being around him has helped me accept myself too.

Once we're dressed, we head out of the arena, and I run smack-dab into the back of Brendon who has stopped dead in his tracks.

"What the fuck?" I look over his shoulder and grit my teeth when I see Nikki standing there with a grocery bag.

"Hey." Brendon sighs. "I brought you a snack, figured you would be hungry after practice. And a Gatorade so you can hydrate."

I manage not to make any noise, but I roll my eyes behind him where she can't see me. I'm so tired of this girl.

"Uh, thanks." Brendon takes the bag awkwardly.

"Dude, get outta the way! I'm starving!" Riggs yells from the back of the line. Brendon flushes but moves to the side, his neck and ears turning pink. It's clear he doesn't know how to get out of the situation, so I clench my teeth and handle it for him.

"Come on, we gotta get going." I reach for his hand and pull him along behind me, not giving him time to respond to her.

"Uh, sorry!" he calls but hustles along with me. "Thanks. I never know what to say to her."

His hand is so warm in mine, so right, that I don't want to let it go. I should, but I'm so fucking tired of hiding.

"What's in there?" I nod to the bag as we walk toward the dining hall, most of the team behind us. "Anything good?"

Brendon takes his hand back to open the bag and starts naming things off. "Zero sugar beef jerky, peanut butter protein bar, low sugar cherry Gatorade, and cheddar Sun Chips."

"She's really concerned about your sugar intake, huh?" I open the door for him, and he walks through, but I don't hold it for Jeremy, so it smacks him in the shoulder, and I laugh when he glares at me.

"Dick," he mutters as he gets in line behind me.

Brendon starts eating the snacks while loading his tray with dinner. Preston lifts an eyebrow at him but doesn't comment. I'm glad we could finally break him of that particularly annoying habit.

We find a table and sit with Carp, Willis, and Nick. Nick is Carp's friend that's on the football team, and Brendon likes him because he showed us where to go get good cinnamon rolls. Brendon is very food motivated. Like a puppy.

"You guys going to be ready for finals?" Carp asks, and everyone groans.

"Shhh, we don't use those types of words." Brendon throws a cherry tomato at him.

"What words?" Nick smirks.

"Finals, tests, midterms, lima beans, burpees, Brussels sprouts, surprise anal." Brendon ticks them off on his fingers.

Caught off guard by his last one, I inhale my water instead of swallowing it and have a rough coughing fit. Fuck. My throat is sore by the time I'm done, and Brendon has gone back to his food while everyone at the table either laughs or is staring at him.

"The fuck, dude? What kind of list is that?" I wheeze.

"It's the naughty word list," he says like it's obvious.

"I swear, your brain is a weird place sometimes." I shake my head and take another drink of water.

I can't help but watch Carp and Nick. There's something going on with them. They keep looking at each other and smiling, like they're having a telekinetic conversation. It's giving me a couple vibe.

"Surprise anal is never a good time," Nick agrees, shoving a fry in his mouth. "But I like Brussels sprouts and burpees.

"Excuse me?" Brendon sputters. "You can't sit with us if you like burpees. I can almost excuse the Brussels sprouts, but not burpees. Get out." He points away from the table, and Nick laughs but stands up.

"That's fine, I was done anyway. Gotta go *study*." Nick leans over Carp, hand on his throat, and kisses him. Everyone at the table freezes before Willis shouts, "I fucking knew it!"

Carp flushes bright red, all the way down his neck and into his shirt, and ducks his head. Nick grins like the cat that caught the canary and kisses Carp's head before winking at us and walking away to dump his tray.

"Dude, this team has more than its fair share of queers." Brendon shoves another bite into his mouth. "We should start a queer league in the off season."

"Do you have to be queer to join, or can we just be supportive?" Willis asks.

"I guess that would depend on how many people sign up." Brendon shrugs.

"If you need players, I'm in," Jeremy adds. "And Preston will play too."

Preston sighs. "Good, you'll keep in shape during off season."

I roll my eyes. Of course that's his thought.

"Paul, make notes. You're going to have to organize this." Carp points at me.

That pisses me off. Brendon is fully capable of handling his own shit. He's not stupid.

"I will help if he asks for it, but he can do it himself if he wants to."

Brendon smiles shyly, hiding his face from the table, and hooking his foot around my ankle.

It drives me nuts when people think he can't handle things or take anything seriously. Is he a goofball? Yes. But that doesn't mean he can't focus when he needs to. I love how his brain works. He's quick-witted and makes me laugh, thinks outside the box, and finds solutions to problems other people can't figure out.

Carp raises his hands, palms up, and dips his head. "I'm sorry, you're right."

The conversation flows again as we finish eating, then clean up.

Brendon and I are the last to leave and walk slower than the group, just enjoying the cold night. I miss the clear nights full of stars from back home. I need to go back and visit my grandparents before summer camp starts.

When we make it back to the room, Brendon strips down to just his underwear, which has dancing cheeseburgers on them, and climbs onto my bed before I do. He lies on his back, one arm behind his head, making his torso stretch in a long, lean line.

I kick off my jeans and strip my T-shirt off before crawling on the bed to collapse on his chest. He chuckles and wraps his free arm around my shoulders while I lay my cheek over his heart. I slide one knee between his and pull him closer with my arm around his waist. Brendon tosses my crocheted blanket across us, and I breathe a sigh of relief and contentment.

"I love you," I mumble into his chest.

"I love you too."

"This is really comfy. Now I see why you like sleeping like this." I turn my face enough to nip at his skin, and he hisses.

"Right?" Brendon agrees and settles more into the pillows. "It quiets my brain."

I close my eyes, breathing in the smoky pine scent of his deodorant, and absorb the comfort he freely offers.

"I'm afraid of what will happen to me if I lose you." The words are quiet in the dark of our room, a place where secrets can be told. "When my mom died, my dad lost it. He mentally checked out. Couldn't handle life without her."

Brendon's arm tightens around me, but the dam has burst, and I can't keep the words in anymore.

"He came to the hospital, found out she was dead, and left me there. I was fourteen. I needed my dad. I needed him to tell me he didn't blame me, that we were going to be okay, but he just . . . left." Tears fall from my eyes onto Brendon's chest, but I don't try to wipe them away. "My grandparents basically raised me after that. Dad couldn't be bothered to care where I was or what I was doing. When I was at home, I had to fend for myself. He spent more time out on the lake than with me, so I moved in with my grandparents. It was obvious they were trying to make up for him not caring, but it hurt so fucking bad."

A sob escapes, and my grip on Brendon tightens as I let the pain from the last few years out.

"Why wasn't I enough?"

Brendon wraps his body around me, arms and legs, to hold me as tight as he can.

"You are enough," he says into my hair. My chest heaves with the emotions that I've kept locked up in a cardboard box in my heart. But it's been ripped open, and no amount of tape will put it back together. For the first time since my dad left me in the ER on my fourteenth birthday, I mourn the loss of my father. I let myself purge the fear of being in love, the fear of turning into my dad, the fear of never being enough.

"Don't leave me, okay?" I lift my face into the crook of Brendon's neck while my chest heaves and my skin feels too tight. "I don't know if you want to do the kid thing or have twelve dogs, but if you die, I promise I won't abandon them. You have to promise too."

"I promise not to abandon our hypothetical children if you die before me."

I know it's stupid, but his words make me feel better. They ease the pressure cinching around my ribs so I can suck in a full breath.

Easing back from his neck, I look up at him with tears drying on my skin. He doesn't hesitate, just drops his mouth to mine in a deep but soft and slow kiss. It's not meant to get the blood stirring, only to bring comfort. And it does.

Brendon may have been the one to need touch first, but he's made me crave his nearness. Nothing calms me like he does, like his skin against mine, his heart beating with mine. The raging, turbulent emotions ease into a calm, flat sea.

"Get some sleep, love," he says against my lips, and I smile, lying down on his chest once again. I know it will take time to process the scars left on my heart that day, but I'm on my way.

CHAPTER 32

Brendon

I'm awoken a few hours later by a weird noise.

Is that groaning?

Is there a werewolf transforming in here?

What time is it?

I force my eyes open, and once my eyes adjust to the dark, I find Paul on his side, curled up into a ball, kind of rocking back and forth, and groaning. Not the sexy kind of sound either. Sitting up, I rub my eyes and reach for Paul.

"Hey, what's going on?"

"It hurts," he moans. "I think I'm gonna be sick."

He jerks upright and hustles toward the bathroom, moaning in pain the entire way. I get up and follow behind him, getting a washcloth wet and a cup of water while he throws up, and it sounds like he's choking back tears.

"I think you should go to the hospital," I say as I hand him the cup to wash his mouth out and wipe the back of his neck with the cloth.

"We have a game tomorrow," he argues and tries to stand up but cries out and drops back down to the floor.

"And you think you're going to play like this?" I cross my arms and lean against the sink. "You can't even stand."

Paul leans his head against his arms on the toilet. "It hurts so fucking bad."

"What hurts? Like, your stomach or the muscles?" I've never seen him like this, and honestly, it's scary. I don't know how to help him, but he's obviously in pain.

"I don't know." He breathes for a second. Panting, almost whimpering in pain. "It's, like, inside."

"Did you eat something weird?"

Paul tries to stand again, and this time I pull his arm around my shoulders to help him shuffle back to the bed. This isn't normal. I've seen him get the flu, food poisoning, all kinds of shit, but this is so much worse.

"Maybe you should go to the ER?" I ask as he curls into a ball on the bed. Grabbing my phone, I google "stomach pain." Sitting on the bed next to him, I scroll through the results and narrow my search down to "how to tell when stomach pain is serious."

"How long has this been going on?" I ask him as I read. This is bad. He needs to go to the hospital, and he's not going to like it.

"I don't know," he whines.

"You need to go in, dude." My heart rate skyrockets as "emergency surgery" and "sepsis" hit my brain. I stand up and grab him some pajama pants and a zip-up hoodie. "Come on."

"I don't want to go to the hospital. I'm just going to sit in the waiting room for three hours and be told to take pain reliever." He turns his face into his pillow and yells a pain-filled sound that solidifies my determination.

Without waiting for his agreement, I slide his feet into the pants and work the fabric up his legs as far as I can while he's lying down.

"Come on, lean on me. We're going."

Paul doesn't argue, but it takes him a bit to get up enough for me to finish getting him dressed. He's gritting his teeth and breathing too hard; pain is etched into every line of his face.

The walk to the elevator takes so much longer than it usually does, inching our way with him leaning on me and the wall.

Worry eats at me the entire time. What's wrong with him? Will he have to have surgery? Will he be able to play hockey? If he has surgery, how long will he be in the hospital? How long until he can play again?

He's sweating, and a tear falls down his face by the time we get into the elevator. I brush the tear away and kiss his hair.

The ride is quick since it's the middle of the night and no one else is awake at this hour. It's cold outside, but he won't be able to make it all the way to his car in the parking lot.

"Sit here," I tell him and help him sit on the curb. "I'll get the car and be right back."

He doesn't argue, just curls into himself and breathes.

I run to his car and get it unlocked. It's been a while since it's been driven, so I have to try twice before it starts, then hustle my way to him. It's in park and I'm around the front of the car before Paul even looks up. I help him into the car, buckle his seat belt, then pull up the directions to the closest hospital on my phone.

Luckily, it's not too far and there's no traffic, but every bump in the road and turn has Paul groaning. I hate how helpless I feel right now. I'm not a doctor, I don't know what's wrong with him, but it's bad. There's a deep pang in my bones, vibrating through me with every beat of my heart. Paul takes care of me, not the other way around. I'm a fucking mess.

At the ER entrance, I stop and run inside for a wheelchair so he doesn't have to walk, then help him from the car. Once he's inside talking to the nurse, I hurry out to park. Of course, it's a weird parking garage, and I end up going in the out driveway because it's dark and I'm not paying attention.

I have to back out and hope not to hit anything, which I barely manage. Once I'm inside and find a parking spot, I run down the ramp toward the ER, but Paul isn't in the waiting room anymore. There isn't anyone in the waiting room, actually. That seems weird for a city like Denver, but I'm not going to look a gift horse in the mouth.

"Excuse me, did Paul Johnson get taken back? I just brought him in," I ask the lady at the desk.

She flicks her gaze at me, then back at the computer screen. "Yes."

I wait for her to continue, but she doesn't say anything else.

"Can I go back there with him?" I ask, pointing to the door.

She sighs heavily but hits a button, and the door buzzes. I hustle to the door and push it open. I have no idea where I'm going, but I'll figure it out.

A tall woman in blue scrubs and black cat-eye-shaped glasses stops me with a raised eyebrow.

"Can I help you?" Her no-nonsense tone has me swallowing my own damn tongue.

"Um. Uh." I swallow and try again. "I'm looking for my friend who was just brought back here, Paul Johnson."

"Brendon." Paul's voice comes from behind a curtain to my left, and the woman nods, letting me pass.

Paul is propped up in a hospital bed looking miserable.

I grab the plastic chair and pull it up next to his bed and hold his hand.

"Hey, what are they saying?" I'm eager for information, to know he's going to be okay.

"Nothing yet. Gotta talk to the doctor." Paul turns on his side facing me and leans his forehead against the edge of the mattress. I lean in, my arm around his head, and press my lips to his forehead.

I fucking hate this. He's clearly in pain, and there's not a goddamn thing I can do about it. It's just a bunch of hurry up and wait.

His skin is sticky with sweat, probably from being in pain, and he's tapping his foot. It's making me antsy. I want to fix it.

A woman with dark hair pulled back in a ponytail, blue scrubs, and a white lab coat over the top comes in.

"Hi, my name is Dr. Nora Prow," she says as she pulls up Paul's chart.

He tells her about the pain and vomiting, how he woke up with it, all while not moving from the crook of my arm. She asks him some questions, then asks him to roll onto his back. He groans but does it, throwing his arm over his eyes and not letting go of my hand.

The doctor lifts his shirt and pushes on his stomach. His hand tightens around mine to a painful grip, and he yells. His legs try to come up like he's going to curl into a ball, but he's able to force them back down.

"Okay, let's get some labs drawn and some pain meds on board." She makes a note in the chart. "How would you rate your pain on a level from one to ten, with ten being the worst pain you could ever imagine?"

Paul thinks about it for a second, then says, "I don't know, like five or six?"

He's panting again and turns back toward me, this time

pulling my hand wrapped around his into his chest to hold against him.

She asks some more questions about allergies, surgeries, diagnoses.

"Okay, I have a feeling we're dealing with appendicitis. I'm also going to get some imaging done to see if we can see anything, okay?" Dr. Prow says. "Do you have any questions for me?"

Paul shakes his head, and the doctor pats Paul's foot, says "Hang in there," and leaves again.

I lean my forehead against his and watch his face as he deals with the pain.

"Is there anything I can do?" I whisper.

"Just don't leave me," he whispers back. I wish I could crawl onto the bed with him, but I don't want to jostle him since moving seems to be making it worse. So I just hold him the best I can, kissing his forehead and running my fingers through his hair.

I don't know how long it takes for a man in green scrubs to come in and talk to Paul about surgery and fill out paperwork, but it feels like hours yet only a few minutes. The surgeon and the anesthesiologist both have crap for him to sign and questions for him. Apparently, they are pretty sure he has appendicitis and will need surgery. Once the papers are signed, one of the ER nurses takes blood for labs and gives him morphine for pain before taking him to get imaging done.

He's high as fuck, which is amusing. I'm so relieved he's feeling better, but this waiting shit sucks. I want definite answers. I want to know he's going to be okay.

"Are there clouds in here?" Paul asks, staring intently at the ceiling. "Are we outside?"

I snort and shake my head. "No, that's the morphine."

"Morphine . . . what does it make you morph into?" He turns his head to stare at me.

"You're adorable." I lean my elbows on the mattress and smile at him. He's so relaxed. For once there isn't anything going on in his brain. His eyes are glassy, but his smile is easy. It's sexy, that quick upturn of his lips. I want to kiss him.

"Why are you so fucking beautiful?" Paul blurts out much louder than necessary since my face is two feet from his.

"You're high."

"Does that change your bone structure?" Now he looks confused, which makes me laugh at him.

"Only you would be high as fuck and talking about bone structure." I shake my head, but he reaches for my chin and pulls me into a kiss. I expect it to be a quick press of lips or sloppy from the drugs, but it's neither. Paul makes love to my mouth, sucks on my tongue, and explores every corner of me.

Would he still be demanding and bossy, or would he want me to take the lead? The kiss is deep but slow. There's no rush, no fire lit in my blood demanding I fuck until I can't stand. It's love and comfort and a slow burn kind of heat. The kind of languid kiss you can get lost in and forget about time.

The screech of the curtain sectioning off the bed sounds, and I jump back from Paul, my face immediately flushing hot. I hate that I have to hide him. It was his decision to keep us quiet, but it still sucks. I want to show everyone how proud I am that he's mine.

"Okay, Mr. Johnson, it looks like your appendix is very infected and swollen. We're going to give you some antibiotics through your IV, then get you moved to the OR for surgery. With as enlarged as it is, it needs to be removed." Dr. Prow stands with her hands in her pockets as she delivers the news.

Anxiety has my knee bouncing, and there's a boulder in my stomach. Fuck. My head buzzes with what ifs and what happens next. Even though he filled out the paperwork, I was hoping he wouldn't have to have the surgery, that some antibiotics and pain meds would be enough. Surgery is scary as fuck.

"How long is that going to take? When will he be discharged?" I ask the doctor.

"We'll give the antibiotics a bit to get into his system, then the surgery should be quick, as long as there aren't any complications. The surgeon will have more information on discharge."

A nurse comes in, tells us she's putting broad spectrum antibiotics in Paul's IV, uses a syringe to add it to the line, then leaves again.

"Any other questions for me?" Dr. Prow looks between us expectantly.

"Can I play hockey tomorrow?" Paul asks.

She laughs and shakes her head. "Uh, no. You won't be playing hockey for a few weeks."

"Ah man. That sucks." Paul groans and lifts his hands, only to drop them back to the bed.

Right. Hockey. I have to call Coach.

"Thank you." I nod to her, and she leaves the room. "I'm going to call Coach. It's time for gym anyway." Somehow, we've been here for three hours already.

Digging my phone from my pocket, I find our head coach's number, suck in a deep breath, then hit call.

My knee is still bouncing, and I lean my forehead

against the mattress while I wait for the grumpy man to answer.

"Oiler, where the hell are you and Johnson?" he barks.

"The ER, sir. Johnson has appendicitis." Paul's fingers run through my hair and to my neck, making me shudder.

"How long have you been there? Is he okay? Is he having surgery?" The tone change is immediate, and he's in problem-solving mode.

"A few hours, I think we got here about three a.m.?" I glance up at my husband and find him dosing off. "He's high on pain meds, but he's okay. They're going to take him back for surgery in a little while. They just gave him antibiotics."

"Are you going to be able to play tonight?" he asks, and I can hear the scratch of a pen on paper as he probably takes notes.

"Yeah, I'm fine to play." I'm always fine. Even when I'm not.

"Are you still at the hospital?"

"Yes, sir."

He sighs, and I swear I can see him pinching the bridge of his nose.

"Listen, son, I know you guys are close. I'm not going to tell you to leave him there alone, but if you're playing tonight, you gotta have your head in the game. You hear me?"

I take a deep breath and sit back in my chair, staring at the man that has taken my heart and run away with it. He's my life, my air, the reason my heart beats.

"Once I know he's okay, I'll be good, Coach. I promise."

"Good. Get some rest and eat." He ends the call, and I'm left mentally drained while anxious at the same time. I want to pace, demand an update that doesn't exist, yell, and crawl into bed with the man who anchors me. I don't know how to do this. How to be an adult. Paul is the adult, the comfort, the level-headed one. I'm a fuckup. A clown. No one takes me seriously.

Needing to move, I stand and pace next to his bed. It's only a few feet, but it's better than nothing. It gets my body moving, gives the nervous energy an outlet, and makes me feel like I'm doing something.

I don't know how long I do it, lost in my head, and the worry. Is he going to be okay? Will there be complications? How long will he be in the hospital? Will I be able to sleep without him in our room? How long will he be down? Will he be able to play hockey next season?

A different nurse comes in with some kind of fabric hat on and looks at me. "Hi, I'm Allison." She smiles at me. "I'm here to take Mr. Johnson upstairs. You are welcome to follow us up. I'll point out where the waiting room is."

My stomach clenches, but I nod.

Paul has already changed into a gown, so I grab his bag of stuff and follow along behind the wheelchair they transfer him into.

"Do you do this surgery a lot?" I find myself needing reassurance as we move through this.

"Yeah, it's pretty straightforward. With the laparoscope, it only takes fifteen to twenty minutes once he's out. Healing is much faster too." She smiles at me, and I breathe a little sigh of relief.

"Thank you," I mumble to her, trying to keep my emotions in check. I don't know how to do this. How to handle this. I should call his grandma.

Allison points out the waiting room for me to sit in and lets me kiss Paul's head before pushing him down the hallway and through the doors that say No Entrance.

With a knot in my throat, I type in Paul's password and call his grandma.

"Good morning, Pauly." Her warm voice fills my ear, and I break into tears. "Pauly? Paul, what's wrong?"

All the fear and stress that's been forced into the back of my mind for hours escapes my grasp and floods my brain. Suddenly I have no control over myself or my emotions. I'm sitting in this fucking waiting room, sobbing, rocking back and forth while folded in half.

I can't lose him. I just can't. I need him so badly it hurts.

"Brendon," I barely manage to get out.

"Brendon? Where's Paul? What's going on?" She's so worried, and I know I'm not helping, but I can't get a hold of myself. I'm so fucking worried about him. I'm so far outside of my element. At twenty-one years old. I'm still a fucking child. I can't take care of myself, much less anyone else. What the fuck does he even see in me?

"Brendon, breathe." Her command cuts through the fear and gives me something to focus on. What I wouldn't give to have her here with me, to hug me and tell me what I'm supposed to do. I don't want this fucking responsibility anymore. It's too much. This is all too much.

It takes me a minute, but I manage to pull it back enough to get the words out.

Through my sniffling and tears, I tell her he's in surgery for appendicitis.

"Oh, thank Christ." She breathes a sigh of relief. "He's going to be okay." It's a statement not a question. What does she know that I don't? How is she so confident?

Tears are still trickling down my face and dripping onto the floor as I lean on my knees.

"Brendon, take a deep breath. Why are you so panicked? Baby, why are you so upset?" Her voice is soft like she already knows the answer or at least expects it, but I'm an idiot for calling her. I doubt Paul has told her that we're even dating, much less that we're married. Hell, I don't even know if she knows he's into guys. Fuck. I'm fucking up everything by not thinking things through, again.

"Sorry, I'm just tired, I guess. I'm sorry to bother you. He's gonna be fine. I'll make sure he calls you when he's awake. Bye." I hang up quickly before any more words can fall from my lips and fuck up Paul's life. I don't know if his grandparents are homophobic, but I really hope they aren't. After being all but abandoned by his dad, he needs his grandparents.

The surgeon comes in not long after the disastrous phone call, and I hop up out of my chair so fast I get light-headed.

"Are you Paul's family?"

"Yeah," I say it quickly, but my face heats, and I hope against hope he doesn't think I'm lying and refuses to tell me anything.

"He's out of surgery; it went as expected. He's in recovery and will be until he's awake, warm, and the pain is managed. It could be half an hour, could be multiple hours." The doctor shrugs. "It all depends on how his body responds. Once he's out of recovery, he can have a visitor or two, but he'll likely be very tired still. We'll keep him for twenty-four hours or so, make sure he's on the mend, then discharge him."

I'm nodding along but none of the words are really sinking in. My brain is noisy, but there's no distinct thoughts, just enough background noise to stop me from being able to process what he's saying.

"So just wait here or . . ." I trail off, not really sure what other options there are.

"You can wait here or go home and wait for him to call you from his room. Get something to eat, take a nap, something like that. You've been here a while." The doctor puts his hand on my shoulder in a comforting gesture, and it's all I can do not to break down again.

"But he's going to be okay?" My voice is tiny, like the fucking child I am.

He smiles warmly at me before nodding. "Yes, he's going to be just fine."

The tension and fear that's been keeping me going breaks just long enough for a sob to escape my mouth. I slap a hand over my mouth like I can keep it in or take it back. The doctor squeezes my shoulder and pats my back.

"He's all right. Take a deep breath."

I force myself to close my eyes and focus on breathing. Long, slow inhales that fill my chest and belly, then slow exhales. I don't know how long we stand there, but he doesn't leave my side, for which I'm appreciative.

Once my heart rate slows and I feel like I can handle life for a second, I open my eyes and look at the man in front of me. He's not much older than me, maybe ten years with clear gray eyes, and a *PAW Patrol* fabric head covering.

"Thank you," I manage to choke out. He pats my shoulder and heads back to save more lives.

CHAPTER 33

Brendon

L ooking at the time on my phone, I cuss under my breath, scrub a hand down my face, and head to the parking lot. It's later than I thought, and I need to sleep for a few hours, or I'll be useless tonight. I already missed morning skate, so I hustle down to Paul's car and get back to campus as quickly as I can without getting a ticket.

As I get off the elevator on the third floor, Preston and Jeremy are standing at my dorm, knocking on the door.

"Hey," I call to them, and they both turn to look at me at the same time with the same confused expression. It's kinda scary, actually.

"Where they hell have you been? You missed morning skate. Where's Paul?"

I unlock the door and push it open, only to come to a stop when I see someone sleeping on my bed. What the actual fuck?

Jeremy runs into the back of me, and Preston grunts.

"Is there someone in your bed?" Jeremy asks, his head peeking out around me.

"Excuse me?" Preston growls. "I don't give a shit what you guys get up to in here, but we are not joining in on your orgies."

Jeremy starts laughing, and I turn around to face Preston with a serious set to my face. The urge to fuck with him is just too strong. After the morning I've had, I need this moment of normalcy.

"What makes you think Jeremy hasn't joined in?"

Jeremy stops laughing abruptly, gaping at me. "Dude. Why would you do that to me?"

Preston stares daggers into the back of Jeremy's head, and I smile.

"Excuse you?" Preston wraps his arm around Jeremy's chest and yanks him back against his own chest, speaking quietly into Jeremy's ear. A split second of fear flashes on Jeremy's face before it melts into lust, and I shudder. Nope. I can't watch Jeremy get his rocks off by Preston.

Rustling sounds behind me, so I turn my focus back to the trespasser.

Nikki sits up and stretches, the blanket falling to pool at her waist. Thank fuck she at least has a shirt on. I am so past giving a shit, though, and probably would have made her leave naked if that's how I found her. I'm done.

"Get the fuck out of my room!" I demand, squaring my shoulders. "How did you even get in here?"

She looks surprised, like the idea of finding her in my damn bed wouldn't at the very least annoy me.

"The door was unlocked."

"And you took it upon yourself to come on in and sleep in someone's bed?" Preston asks. "You don't know what he does in there. Or when he washed his sheets last."

"Hey!" I yell at Preston. "Rude."

"I thought you left it open for me," she says, scooting to the edge of the bed and sliding her feet to the floor.

"What the hell made you think that?"

"Why else would you leave the door open? You know I was going to be here before first skate!" she throws back, standing and putting her hand on her hip.

"I don't know what you thought this was, but I'm not interested." There. I finally said it. "You need to leave me alone."

She walks straight at me, rears back, and slaps my cheek.

"What the fuck!?" I cup my hand over the abused skin that burns way more than it has a right to.

"How dare you lead me on only to embarrass me in front of your friends!" she screams before storming out the door.

"So where were you this morning, and where is Paul?" Preston asks as he shuts the door.

"The hospital." I sigh and drop down onto Paul's bed and pull his crocheted blanket around me. Preston and Jeremy are instantly serious and waiting for details.

"He has appendicitis and had to have surgery this morning."

"Did you tell Coach?" Preston asks.

"Is he okay?" Jeremy smacks Preston's arm and gives him a look that clearly says "wrong question, dumbass."

"Yes to both." I rub my face and lean my elbows on my knees. "It's been a long night, but he's okay. Surgery went fine. He's in recovery and should be moved to his own room anytime now. The surgeon said Paul can call me once he's settled."

"Does he know your phone number?" Jeremy asks.

Fuck. I didn't think of that. I have his damn cell phone.

"Goddamn it."

"What hospital?" Preston has his phone out and is typing something.

I give him the details he asks for, and he leaves with his phone to his ear.

When I look at Jeremy confused, he smiles at me. "Preston's dad was a surgeon, remember? He knows how to get information through."

Oh, that's right. Dude was fucking nuts, and I'm glad he's dead.

"Are you playing tonight?" Jeremy sits next to me and wraps his arm around my shoulders. I lay my head on his and close my eyes, leaning into the comfort I need so fucking badly right now.

"Yeah, Coach said I could, but I don't know who he'll replace Paul with on our line."

Jeremy rubs my arm as Preston comes back in. I can feel the tension radiating from him for the mere fact that I'm touching Jeremy, but right now, he can fuck off. Jeremy was one of my best friends before he came into our lives.

"Do you need anything?" Jeremy asks.

"I need to sleep," I mumble. "But I don't want to be alone."

Tears clog my throat at the weakness. I'm supposed to be a grown man, but I still can't handle anything on my own. I need reassurance that my friends don't hate me, that my husband still loves me, that I'm not too much.

"Lay down. We'll stay." Jeremy kisses my hair, and I hear Preston come closer. I open my eyes and watch as he struggles with himself. His hand flexes, lifts a few inches, then drops back to his side a few times before he finally reaches out and lays a hand on my shoulder. The touch has tears flooding my eyes and falling down my cheeks, but this time, there's no body-racking sobs. I know he's weird about being touched. Jeremy is the only one that can get away with it, and Preston doesn't touch anyone unless causing harm, so this simple, comforting gesture is everything.

"Thank you." My voice is thick with exhaustion and overwhelming emotions. Jeremy squeezes me, then stands so I can lie down. I kick my shoes off, then crawl across the bed to lay my head on Paul's pillow, wrapping my arms around myself so I don't feel so alone. I breathe in a deep lungful of his scent and close my eyes, wrapped in his blanket.

"My sheets are clean, asshole," I mumble, and I barely hear Jeremy snicker before I fall deep into the blackness of sleep.

When I wake a few hours later, there's a white takeout container sitting on the bedside table with a note that says, "Eat this, dumbass," in Preston's sharp handwriting. My stomach grumbles as I sit up and reach for it. A chicken sandwich with lettuce, tomato, and red onion on wholegrain bread, packets of mustard and mayo, a bag of baked chips, an apple, and fresh veggies.

I inhale the food without any thought. I didn't eat breakfast, and it's about lunchtime, so I'm starving. There's nothing left but the apple core and packaging when I'm done. I find a water bottle and chug that too, then search for my phone. When it's not in the normal places I leave it, like the bedside table, desk, or bathroom sink, I check my pockets and find it.

There's a missed call from a local Denver number and a voicemail.

"Hey, Little Menace, I'm okay. Super tired but in a room now. Kick ass at the game tonight. I want to hear all about it. Don't let that shit stain from Minnesota get in your head. I love you."

A watery smile turns up my lips, and I listen to it again.

271

He sounds exhausted and a little scratchy, like his throat is dry, but in good spirits. He's okay. The weight of what could have been lifts, and my shoulders finally drop, and I can suck in a deep breath.

There's a knock on the door as it opens, and I look to find Jeremy and Preston coming in already dressed in suits.

"Did you eat?" is Preston's first question, which makes me chuckle.

"Yes, Daddy, I ate."

Preston shudders, and Jeremy laughs while I lift the food container to show him I did in fact finish my food.

"Smartass."

"Your life would be boring without me." I smile at the big grump and stand to stretch.

"Did you hear from Paul?" Jeremy asks, handing me the suit from my closet.

"Yeah, he's in a room now."

"Good."

I strip out of my clothes without thinking twice about it, and Preston grabs Jeremy, turning both of them around.

"Both of you have seen my naked ass," I say as I pull on the slacks.

"And I wish I hadn't," Preston deadpans.

"That's disrespectful. I work hard for this ass." I throw my balled-up T-shirt at him, hitting him in the back of the head.

"What makes you think I want to smell like you?" He glances at me with disgust and brushes the shirt away.

I grab my shirt and button it up while Jeremy leans into Preston. Honestly, I'm glad they found each other. Jeremy deserves to be loved completely, and while I don't know all the details, I know Preston needed to be shown how to love. There was no one else that could have gotten through to him like Jeremy did.

It took a second, but Preston and I have managed to understand each other. I know he doesn't like to be touched, probably because of his trauma if the news reports are at all correct, but I tease him about it while knowing he will not allow it. I would never actually do it, and he knows that too. I'm pretty sure threatening to murder me is his love language.

I tuck my shirt in, adjust my clothes, and tie my tie. Preston huffs and steps in front of me, grabbing the silk and adjusting it while I grin up at him.

"Ohh, who knew getting pulled around by the tie was so hot?" I wag my eyebrows at him, and Jeremy snorts.

Preston freezes and looks like he's about two seconds from punching me in the face.

"Are you trying to get your nose broken?" Jeremy shakes his head and opens the door for us to leave.

Preston finishes adjusting the tie, and I wink at him as he walks away. Jeremy and I follow him down the hallway where we meet up with some of the other players as we make our way down to the rink.

Everyone asks where Paul and I were this morning and where he is now. I tell the story for what feels like a hundred times by the time we're changed into warmup clothes.

Through warmups, I'm able to get lost in the familiarity of each movement. My muscles remember how to do it, though I still have to think about what's next and how many sets I've done. It keeps my mind busy, which I need right now.

My head is such a messy place that it's not until we're on the ice for the team skate that I realize what Paul said in his voicemail. We play Minnesota tonight. I'm going to have to face Chad. I'm afraid of falling apart again, spiraling and not having Paul to pull me back from the edge.

The weight of the last twenty-four hours pulls on me once again. I don't want to do this. I don't want to go back to my dorm alone. Sleep alone. Then get up and do all this all over again tomorrow.

Coach put Riggs on our line for the game, so he'll get some good ice time today, but I'm not sure how well the game will go since we haven't practiced much with just the three of us. Riggs is eighteen, and while he has the potential, he's still green. Jeremy, Paul, and I played together for years on the same line before Paul came out here for a year. We know each other inside and out.

Jeremy and I slap sticks and head out onto the ice, but it doesn't feel right. Paul not being here, not even in the stands, puts me off my game. Is he watching on TV in the hospital?

Our first line gets set up for the puck drop and the game starts. I love how fast the game moves; there's no time for anything except watching the puck. Guys are constantly in motion, the puck flying back and forth, the lines changing. It's exhilarating.

Coach switches out the lines a few times, and we're sent out. Albrooke and Riggs follow me out, racing for the puck before they can get it in the net. Jeremy intercepts a pass and flings the puck to Riggs who somehow loses it between his own legs and kicks it to me. I manage to get a breakaway, rear back, and slap the puck toward the goal. The goalie tries to stop it but barely misses it. The lamp lights up, and we are on the board!

We're smiling when our asses hit the bench and the next line goes out. We get drinks of water or Gatorade and watch the game, knocking gloves with our teammates in celebration.

The game moves on, we get another two in the net before they score, but I can't help but watch Chad and his stepdad. The way they talk in the box, motioning over here and looking at me. It makes my skin crawl, and I have to force my head not to go back into that locker room.

In the second period, Chad is on the ice at the same time as I am, and he's on me like a virus. I can't shake him. Every chance he gets he's slamming me into the boards, waits until the ref turns his back and trips me, hits my back with this stick. It's infuriating.

"Come on, birdy, you gonna chirp for us?" he calls loud enough for some of the guys around us to hear him. He makes a squawk sound, and a few of the other guys on his line do the same. Embarrassment heats my cheeks, and I want to hit him so fucking bad.

"You really need some new material," Jeremy tosses back after hearing the same line a few times. This period of the game, Coach Williams has decided to throw Chad and his line out every time my skates hit the ice, so I can't get away from them.

"I packed a bar of Irish Spring just for you." Chad smirks as he shoves past me, and I swear I can almost taste it.

Even Preston is getting fed up with the bullshit and has started targeting the asshole when given the chance.

If I just look at the puck, that fucker is on my ass.

Chad shoves me into the boards, his stick against my throat and his face in mine.

"Come on, birdy, cry for me. It gets me hard when you act like a bitch."

"Why don't you grow the fuck up, huh?" I shove him off me.

"Because getting under your skin is a favorite pastime."

He smirks and turns his back to me. "The memory of you choking on my dick is a particular favorite of mine."

God, I fucking hate him. My body trembles with rage and humiliation, but I refuse to let him see that it's getting to me. I am not a victim, not anymore.

I get back in the game, racing after the puck and blocking a pass. I turn to hustle back up the ice, making it about halfway before I slam into a hard body. A shoulder gets me in the middle of the chest, and my face hits his helmet. White hot pain explodes across my face as my ass hits the ice, blood gushes from my nose and tears fill my eyes.

"Fuck!" I cup my face and lay on the ice for a second. There are whistles blown and people yelling, but I can't see shit. I can barely fucking breathe! I think he broke my fucking nose!

From the sounds of the yelling and grunts, a fight has broken out, and I'm pissed I can't get my own shot in at Chad's fucking face. EMTs come out on the ice and pull my hands off my face. One of them shoves some gauze against my nose, and I yell as the pain intensifies.

"That fucking hurts!"

"How's your neck?" a male voice asks, pushing on my neck.

"I'm fine," I growl as I push his hands off and sit up. The crowd cheers, and I pull my gloves off so I can wipe my eyes enough to be able to see. Four of our guys and five of the other team are in the penalty box, and I can't help but smile despite the blood dripping down my chin. Preston, Jeremy, Willis, and Carpenter are looking unamused behind the glass but, fuck, I love those guys.

I'm helped up, still holding the gauze to my face, and I leave the ice for the back where I can be looked at closer. On my way off the ice, I see Coach Williams screaming at a ref and Chad with a towel pressed to his forehead in the penalty box.

Scott, one of the assistant coaches, pulls my skates off, and I sit on the gurney for the EMTs.

A man with black hair pulled back in a man bun takes the gauze and looks at my nose.

"Yeah, that's broken," he tells his partner. To me he says, "Lay back, you're going in."

I drop my head forward to hang from my shoulders. "Come on, man. Just numb it up and reset it."

"Absolutely not." He shakes his head, and I huff. Fuck's sake. "Can I get a change of clothes?" I holler at Scott who gives me a thumbs-up and heads back into the locker room. I'm sure he'll meet me at the hospital. I don't know how he got tasked with medical duty, but he's always the one who goes when someone gets hurt.

In the ambulance, I take my jersey off one arm so they can get my blood pressure, I'm asked a hundred questions, and they call it in to the ER. Maybe once they release me, I can sneak upstairs to see Paul since I won't be back in time to play the rest of the game anyway.

The ER is busy since it's a Friday night, and I'm already frustrated. The blood on my shirt gets some looks, and it's starting to itch as it dries on my skin.

I get moved to a bed, and the EMTs leave to go back to the game. A nurse comes in with a folded sheet and gown.

"Can you get changed yourself, or do you need assistance?" She looks a little frazzled, so I don't try playing with her.

"I can do it."

She puts them on the foot of the bed, and I start stripping out of my gear. Now that the adrenaline is fading, my face hurts like a bitch. It's still bleeding pretty good too, so I get blood on fucking everything before sitting back down.

I push the call button on the bed when blood starts running down my arm.

The nurse opens the curtain, takes a look at me, and without a question grabs more gauze. She tosses it on the bed, then puts gloves on and takes the dripping pads from me and disposes of them in the biohazard container.

She asks me another twenty questions, then tells me the doctor will be in to see me in a minute.

Dr. Nora Prow comes in and cocks her head at me. "Hello again."

I nod at her as she puts on gloves, asks me the same questions I've already answered twice, then takes the gauze from me.

"Okay, we're going to get the ENT doctor in here to take a look at you." She puts the gauze back, takes her gloves off, and leaves my bed.

It's hopping in here, but luckily, they don't make me wait long. Another doctor with a mop of curly dark hair comes into the room putting on gloves.

"Hello, I'm Dr. Gray. I'm the ear, nose, and throat doctor. Can you tell me what happened?"

I groan but tell the story again while he takes a look at my nose and feels around, then presses on my forehead, cheeks, and eyes.

"Okay, let's get a CT scan," he says to the nurse I didn't notice come in. "If that comes back clear, we'll set this and use a Rhino Rocket to stop the bleeding."

She asks something I don't understand, and he agrees.

Scott comes in with my suit and asks for a bag for my gear since I didn't get around to it.

The nurse hands him one, and he packs up my bloody shit.

"That's going to smell amazing by morning." He laughs.

"Yeah, hopefully I remember to take it back to the locker room when I'm done."

I'm pinching the bridge of my nose, trying to get the damn bleeding to stop, but nothing seems to be helping.

"What's the word?" he asks, leaning against my bed.

"Probably a broken nose."

He nods with a sigh. "Right."

"Hey, can you check in on Paul?" I give him the floor and room number. I don't know if visiting hours are over or not, but I hate that I haven't talked to him in hours. If he was watching the game, he'll know I was hurt and probably worried too.

"I'm not supposed to leave you, but I'll see if I can get up there really quick." He puts my suit on the back of the chair and heads out.

I get wheeled to the CT room by a nurse named Jessica, asked if I have any metal in my body or on my body, then am laid on a bed. Blood drips down my throat, and I have to force myself to hold still instead of gag on the taste of copper from lying flat.

It only takes a few minutes for the scan, but it's a weird whooshing sound that's louder than I expected as it zooms around me.

The table is removed from the big circle, and I'm able to sit up, but it turns my stomach, and saliva fills my mouth.

"Puke," I manage to get out, and the nurse with me hands me a trash can for me to vomit into. Dark red puke is very disturbing and hurts a broken nose like a motherfucker.

She takes the bag from the can and leaves the room for a few minutes while I sit on the plastic bed thing. I would kill for some water right now. Jessica comes back with the wheelchair and pushes me back to the bed. I feel like I've been here forever yet only a few minutes. It's weird.

I wish I had my phone so I could find out the score of the game and call Paul. I hate that he's not with me. Being on my own sucks.

CHAPTER 34

Brendon

By the time I'm released, I've been poked, prodded, had a balloon shoved up my nose, and got no Paul update because they wouldn't let Scott in. I'm finally able to put clothes on and leave the ER with tape on my face, but I'm free. In the waiting room, Jeremy rushes toward me when he sees me while Preston ambles.

"You okay?" Jeremy grabs me to look at my nose. "That looks awful."

"Thanks, you look great too, asshole." I'm hungry, irritated, and just want to be fucking cuddled.

"Do you have a ride back to campus?" Scott asks, and Preston tells him yes. I hand Scott my discharge papers for Coach, and he leaves us.

"I want to see Paul," I tell them and head toward the elevator.

"It's late, man, I don't think they're going to let you in," Jeremy says as he trails after me.

"I dare them to stop me." After the shitshow that has been the last twenty-four hours, I need to see him.

It doesn't take me long to find the post-op ward, but the lady at the desk is not amused to see me.

"Visiting hours are over," she says in a firm voice.

"I just spent hours downstairs in the ER. I haven't gotten to see him since he was taken back for surgery. I just want to see him for like five minutes!" I'm so far past done it's ridiculous. I'm tired, hungry, frustrated, and in pain—both physically and mentally.

"Only family members are allowed back after visiting hours."

"He's my husband!" I shout at her. My entire body is tight with tension, and I'm ready to snap. Christ's sake, I just want to see him. Why is this so fucking hard?

She looks at me for a second while my chest heaves and my jaw aches. I'm sure I look like a fucking wreck, and I hope it's pitiful enough to get what I want.

"I won't stay long. I just want to see him for a few minutes," I reiterate.

"Fine, five minutes," she snaps. "Room five forty-six."

"Thank you," I tell her and hustle down the hallway before she changes her mind. I follow the numbers on the doors until I find the right one and stop just outside of it. Nerves flutter in my stomach. *What if he doesn't want to see me?*

I roll my wrists and crack my fingers while I stare at his door, working up the nerve to open it. I hate that I question everything. He fucking married me, but I still don't know if he wants to see me.

Just do it. Go in. Maybe he's asleep anyway.

Reaching for the handle, I let out a slow breath and push it open. The low hum of a TV is on when I enter, but I can't tell what it is yet.

I peer around the corner to see two beds, one empty and one with Paul sitting up, looking at me. A big smile spreads over his face, and I race toward him, not able to hold back anymore. He opens his arms, and I collapse next to his bed on my knees, wrapping one arm around his back, one across his lap, and laying my cheek on his chest.

He holds me as tightly as he can, kissing my hair and rubbing my arm.

"Hey, it's okay," he murmurs. "That was a nasty hit you took. Did you break it?" Paul lifts my face with his fingers under my chin, but I can't speak, only nod as tears fill my eyes and fall down my cheeks. I'm so fucking weak.

Paul brushes the tears away with his thumbs and places a gentle kiss on my lips. "You're okay. I'm okay. We're *okay.*"

"I love you."

He smiles at me again and kisses my forehead. "I love you too. I'll be back tomorrow, okay?"

I lay my cheek against his chest again and inhale his scent. It's not right since he's wearing a hospital gown, but it's better than nothing.

"I was so scared," I whisper, and he cups my head. "I called your grandma but probably made her panic, so you might want to call her to tell her you aren't dead."

He chuckles, and the sound makes my heart a little lighter.

"Hey," he says as he lifts my face to his again. "Thank you for taking care of me."

I pull my eyebrows together and look at him as sternly as I can. "Don't ever make me be the adult again. That shit sucks."

He laughs and kisses me again. "I'll do my best."

Reaching for the back of his neck, I kiss him a few more times. Quick presses of our lips, not nearly enough, but better than nothing, then sigh and rest my forehead against his.

"I have to go. The nurse gave me five minutes."

Paul runs his hands through my hair again and kisses my head.

"Thank you for coming up here to badger the nursing staff," he says with amusement. When I look up at him, he's got a half smile on his lips. I sigh and stand, cupping his face and kissing him carefully so I don't hit my swollen, bruised nose.

"I love you," I breathe against his lips.

Paul nips my bottom lip and says it back to me.

"I'll see you tomorrow?" he asks. "Or are you on concussion protocol?"

"No concussion. I'll come get you if you're released early enough."

He holds my hand as I walk away and doesn't let go until we are physically too far apart to touch anymore.

On my way past the nurses' station, the woman lifts a strict eyebrow at me as I walk down the hallway.

"Thank you."

"Mmhmm."

Jeremy and Preston are waiting for me with arms crossed, both wearing stern expressions. It's kind of scary how much Jeremy is starting to look like Preston.

"What?" I hit the button for the elevator, but neither of them says anything until we're out of the hospital and I've been locked in a car with them.

"You're fucking married?!" Jeremy finally snaps and yells, making the Uber driver jump and swerve a little. "Sorry."

Oh.

Shit.

"Uh. Yeah." I shrug like it's not a big deal, but I know Jeremy is not going to let this go easily. I'm not embarrassed about being married to Paul, but I don't know how he'll react to Jeremy and Preston knowing. We agreed to keep it quiet until he was ready.

Now I have a healthy dose of guilt heaped on top of everything else.

I lean my head back on the headrest and sigh. I'm so fucking tired. Today has sucked, and all I want is to be wrapped around Paul in bed, watching TV until I pass out, but I can't. I have to just fucking manage.

We stop at the pharmacy on the way back to campus to pick up the pain meds the doctor prescribed, then finally go back to the dorms. I'm running on empty by the time my feet hit the hallway of the third floor, and I have to force myself to keep moving. Jeremy puts a hand on my back, and for once, Preston doesn't growl. They make sure I get inside and help me get my suit hung up, apparently Preston has a *thing* about suits, then I'm allowed to go to bed. I take a pill and lie down on Paul's pillow, needing any part of him I can get, but I don't sleep. Not until the pain pill kicks in and forces my eyes closed.

CHAPTER 35

Paul

Get. Me. The. Fuck. Out. Of. Here.

While I've been allowed to get up and move around and take a piss on my own, I'm going stir-crazy. I've been on the go for years. Between school and hockey, I'm only still if I'm injured or sick. Hospital beds suck ass, the food is bland, and it doesn't have Brendon.

Watching my team play on the TV sucks too. I want to at least sit in the stands and cheer for my team. I want to be there in the locker room after the game to celebrate the win or console them after a loss. No athlete was made to sit in a hospital bed while their team plays.

My abdomen is sore, the three little puncture wounds from the surgery are glued shut and bruised, but I feel a lot better than I did before the surgery. I have to be careful moving around for a while, I get that, but I want out of here.

The doctor comes in finally, looks at the surgery site, and tells me I can go home.

Picking up the phone, I dial the only other number I have memorized besides my grandparents'—Brendon.

"Oiler's Pizzeria and Crematorium, our ovens are always on." There's noise in the background that sounds like he may be at breakfast.

I chuckle and have to put a hand on my stomach when the muscles pull.

"You're an idiot."

"P Dawg!" His shout is so loud I have to pull the receiver away from my ear. "It liiiiiiiives! Bwahahaha!"

In the background is a chorus of "Paul" and "Johnson," and it makes me smile.

"Your evil laugh needs some work, my guy."

Brendon must turn the phone away from his mouth or covers the speaker because I can't hear what he says, but when he comes back, it's quieter.

"Hey, husband." His voice is softer this time. It's intimate and quiet. The tone warms my heart. Seeing him last night was exactly what I needed, and he obviously needed it too since he was a mess. That's it. I can't hide him anymore. From the moment I opened my eyes after surgery, I've only wanted him with me. It's killing me not to be with him. I'm done hiding.

"Hello, husband." I close my eyes and picture him in my mind. "Come get me?"

"Seriously?! They're letting you out?" I can feel his excitement through the phone. It's so pure, almost childlike, and it's infectious. I love that he still gets excited over things, doesn't try to be cool or fit in. He wasn't meant to fit in.

"Yeah, come get me, baby."

He moans, and I wish I could see his face. "I love when you call me that."

I will definitely remember that . . .

"I need clothes. Will you bring me something? And my phone."

The chuckle that leaves him is devious.

"Brendon, normal clothes from my dresser."

"Aww, you're no fun," he huffs.

"Yo!" someone yells in the background. "That Johnson?"

"Yeah, I'm gonna go grab him some clothes and go get him."

"Cool, man," whoever it is says, then yells at the phone. "Hope you feel better, man!"

"Everyone says hi and shit," Brendon tells me. "I'll be there in a bit."

"Thanks."

Brendon arrives wearing my hat and a dopey grin on his face, carrying a bag.

"Your clothes, sire." He bows and lifts the bag to me.

I grab the bag and his hand, pulling him toward me, and lift my mouth to his. He kisses me with a smile on his face. His nose is swollen and bruised with white tape across it. He also looks like he's got black eyes, probably from the pooling of the blood in his face.

"How's your honker?" I press my lips against his again, in a soft, easy pressure that I feel low in my pelvis.

"What's wrong with it? I got a booger or something?" Brendon taps at his upper lip carefully. I shake my head and toss the blankets back so I can move to the edge of the mattress and put my feet on the floor. I have to move slowly, but I manage.

Brendon moves back to give me room, but I reach for his purple Darby U hoodie and pull him between my thighs. Wrapping my arms around him, I lean my cheek against his chest and sigh. I needed this. Brendon wraps his arms around my shoulders and holds me while I snake my hands under his shirt to find his skin.

"Do we have time for mostly naked cuddles when we get back?" I ask with my eyes closed, breathing him in.

"Maybe for a few minutes." Brendon runs his hand through my hair and down my back.

"Okay, untie me."

He pulls the strings on the back of the gown and pushes it down my shoulders.

"Is it weird that this is turning me on?" Brendon asks, and I smirk as I look up at him.

"Which part? Me being injured or undressing me?"

"The undressing of a hospital gown so . . . both?" He thinks about it as he hands me a shirt. "I guess I have a doctor-patient fantasy?"

"Okay, but that does sound hot. Do you want to be the doctor or the patient?" I pull on underwear, grateful he didn't bring one of his weird pairs or something. When I stand to pull the underwear and sweats up, Brendon reaches for the waistband and does it himself while keeping our eyes locked together.

"I don't like having to be the adult here, but right now I'm desperate to touch you." His words are quiet, like he's afraid of being overheard, but so full of need it hurts. "Please don't make me adult anymore."

"I'll do my best." I kiss him again, just a quick brush of lips while my dick thickens.

"How long until you can fuck again?"

"Doctor said about two weeks."

Brendon groans and drops his forehead to my shoulder.

"You'll be okay, cumslut. I'll still be able to get you off."

He shivers, a breath catching in his throat, and thrusts his hips against my leg.

I kiss his hair, and he backs up, pulling socks and shoes from the bag.

"Sit," he instructs, and since I don't really want to bend that far, I do what I was told.

He finishes getting me dressed, helps me into a matching hoodie, and I steal my hat back.

A nurse comes in with my discharge instructions and a brown bag with the pain meds I'm being sent home with. I'm told what to look for in case of problems, and that if I don't rest, I'll fuck myself up.

Brendon grabs my hand and leads us back to my car. I don't pull my hand away even though a nagging voice in the back of my head says I should. Someone could see us, and the news could spread through the team in a heartbeat, but I just don't care right now. I need the comfort of his touch more than I need the secret.

We get in the car and get out of the parking garage with my hand on Brendon's thigh.

"So . . ." He trails off, and I wait for him to figure out what he's going to say. He cracks his knuckles and rotates his wrists before sucking in a deep breath. "Preston and Jeremy know we're married."

I don't know what I was expecting him to say, but that wasn't it. I sit back in the seat and think about it for a minute.

Did I want to be there when they found out? Yes.

Am I upset they know? No.

"What did they say?"

"Well, Jeremy is not amused that we kept it from him, but he doesn't care otherwise. And who the hell knows what Preston thinks?"

I chuckle because that's fair. Dude isn't a big talker.

"Are you mad?" Brendon sounds so small, so fearful, it

breaks my heart. Even if I was mad, his fear would take the wind out of my sails.

"No, I'm not mad. Tell me what happened."

He visibly relaxes, his shoulders dropping, and one hand starts moving as he talks.

"After I was released from the ER last night, I wanted to see you. They had come after the game and waited for me, so when I came up here, they followed. The nurse was not very nice and said only family could go back after visiting hours." He takes a deep breath and clicks his tongue. "I *may* have yelled at her that you're my husband, so she gave me five minutes."

This story is so Brendon that I can't help but laugh. It hurts to laugh, but Jesus, that's funny.

"I love you," I say between chuckling and holding my stomach.

"I love you too, obviously."

Brendon lifts my hand from his lap and kisses my palm, then bites the fleshy part between my index finger and thumb.

"Hey, we don't bite!"

He lets go but has a devious smile on his face. "You do too bite. I have it tattooed on my neck."

Out of nowhere, Brendon stops the car in the middle of the road and climbs out. I don't even have time to ask why. The cold air blasts me from the open door, and I watch as he rushes into the street and picks something up, then runs back.

Is that a dog?

Brendon gets back in the car and slams the door closed holding a shaking white puppy.

"What the hell are you going to do with that?" I ask him and take it as he hands it over. The poor thing is shivering and wet. I look in the back and find a T-shirt to wrap around it and hold it against my chest so it's not pushing against the surgery site.

The puppy has a light brown patch around the left eye and right ear. It's adorable, and I love dogs, but we live in the dorms which have a strict no pets policy. Plus we have nothing for it, and we have classes and hockey.

"I couldn't just leave it in the middle of the road where it would get hit by a car!" Brendon blasts the heater, and I point one vent toward the dog to help dry it. "Do you know how to tell the sex of it?"

I roll my eyes and lift the puppy up to look. "Boy."

"My little buddy." Brendon scratches the puppy's chin.

"You can't keep him. You know that, right?"

The puppy puts his head on my shoulder and settles against me. Damn it. That's cute as fuck.

"You don't have dog food or toys or bowls or a leash or—"

"But I can get it." He shrugs. "He's a baby. I'll figure it out."

I cuddle the puppy for the last few minutes of our drive, then wrap him up better for Brendon to carry inside. He basically looks like a lump of laundry, which is fine.

It's lunchtime, so the hallway is pretty empty, thankfully.

We get inside, and Brendon sets the puppy on his bed, scrubbing his fur carefully to help dry him, then finds a ratty towel to wrap him up in.

I sit on the bed and yawn. I'm exhausted.

"Why don't you rest for a while? I'll get lunch and bring you back something, then we can get dressed for the game."

I check the time, and we have a few hours before we have to be there, so I kick off my shoes and settle back on the bed.

"Bring me the puppy." I sigh and turn on my side. Brendon's smile is triumphant as he hands me the wrapped-up dog.

I get him situated against my chest, and he gives my chin a little lick before sighing and laying his head on my arm. It's adorable, I can't deny that. He's cute as fuck, and if we didn't live in the damn dorms, I would absolutely be down to keep him, but we can lose our housing if they catch him in here.

Brendon leaves, and before the door is closed, I'm out.

CHAPTER 36
Paul

B rendon lets me sleep for two glorious hours. Once I'm showered and dressed, he's in his suit looking sexy as fuck, even swollen and bruised. He pulls out a blue collar with a green-and-blue plaid bow tie on it and a matching leash.

"When did you get that?" I ask.

He kneels to put it on the pupper and squishes his little face.

"When you were sleeping. I got him some puppy chow too."

I'm impressed he didn't get distracted and end up spending all his money on dog toys.

We head down to the rink, and Brendon encourages him to run around to get some energy out. There's a ball shoved in his pocket so we can play with him during intermission and before the game. Hopefully, he'll chill during the game.

The locker room is loud as usual as the guys get changed and ready.

The puppy lets out a sharp bark, and it's instantly

quiet. My eyes widen as everyone looks around for the source of the sound.

Brendon has a shit-eating grin on his face as he poses with the dog at his feet.

Everyone comes over, wanting to pet the dog and ask questions. I shake my head and head over to sit on the bench at my cubby. Preston lifts an eyebrow at me and nods toward Brendon.

"We found him in the middle of the road." I shrug.

"Of course you did." Preston sighs and grabs his workout gear to go change in a bathroom stall.

Jeremy appears behind Preston with a stern grimace and his arms crossed.

"I know, you're pissed. We can talk about it later." I nod at him with my hands up.

"You feeling okay?" he asks, pulling on his gym shoes.

"I'm tired and sore but okay."

Jeremy pats me on the shoulder. "Good."

The guys get ready for the game, stretching and warming up on the ice while Brendon and I head to the stands with the puppy. Someone found him a blanket so he can lay on the floor or be wrapped up in Brendon's lap without getting fur all over his clothes.

Brendon takes the pup outside to run around and get some energy out while I find our seats. It's weird to sit here and watch my team on the ice. I've of course been to hockey games before, gone to friends' games so I knew players on the ice, but this is *my* team, and I'm not out there with them.

There are some die-hard fans that say hi to me as I pass, ask me questions about the game and the other team or why I'm not playing. I drop down into the seat and look around, the frigid air of the rink, the excitement of the crowd, and try to find it in myself. But I'm struggling.

Not only do I hate not being on the ice with the boys, I'm tired of not being myself outside of my dorm room. I'm tired of hiding. Brendon deserves to be shown every day that I love him proudly. In public. Out loud.

My knee bounces as I watch. The announcers introduce the players as a smiling Brendon sits down next to me with the puppy under his arm.

"I had to tell security he was the team pet." He chuckles and spreads the blanket out next to our feet. He sets the puppy down and wraps a corner over him. It doesn't last long. About half a second later, he's up and begging to be picked up, which Brendon does.

I lay the blanket on Brendon's lap so he can put the puppy down. It's only a few minutes because he calms and lays down. Just in time for us to get the biscuit in the basket and the crowd goes wild. The poor dog jumps and lets out a scared bark as people cheer and whoop and clap.

I chuckle and pet his head.

"It's okay, little buddy."

"How come you never talk to *my* little buddy like that?" Brendon smirks at me, and I lift an eyebrow as I lean in close so no one overhears me.

"Your *little buddy* doesn't like to be talked to nicely." I drag my lower lip between my teeth and watch his mouth. "Your *fuck stick* likes it when I'm a little rough on him."

Brendon's cheeks pinken at my words, and I sit back in my seat to watch the game.

The next time we light up the lamp light, I jump out of my seat and immediately regret the abrupt movement. My surgery site screaming at me to calm the fuck down, so I do.

"You okay? Did you rip your glue or whatever? Do you need a doctor?" Brendon's panicked tone cuts through the pain a bit, and I'm able to focus.

"No, I just moved too fast. I'm okay." I reach for his hand and thread our fingers together, holding his hand against my thigh while I turn back to the game. It takes me a few minutes to realize he's quiet. Too. Damn. Quiet.

When I look at him, he's smiling at me, but I have no idea why.

"What?"

"You're holding my hand."

I look down at our hands and smile at it. It was so natural that I didn't pause to think about it. He's it for me, and I'm done keeping him a secret.

With our eyes locked together, I speak my truth.

"I love you, Brendon, and I'm done hiding it." I don't know how, but his smile gets bigger, brighter. "You're my husband, and I don't care who knows it."

Even with a swollen nose and the bruising under his eyes, he's still beautiful. Brendon's eyes turn glassy with happy tears, and he ducks his head, shaking it and wiping at his eyes.

"I don't deserve you," he says with a gravelly voice. "But I'm selfish enough to not let you get away either."

It's a stab in the heart to hear him think he's unworthy, but I'll spend the rest of my life proving him wrong. He is the *most* worthy.

"Look at me." I wait until his eyes meet mine again. "Your past doesn't determine your worth. No one is a better fit for me than you, and I will spend the rest of my life proving that to you."

A tear escapes his eye, and he swipes it away, leaning in for a kiss that I don't deny him. It's a quick kiss, a brush of lips, but it's comfort. It's home. Brendon is my home. And as much as that scares me, I won't let it stop me from loving him out loud.

He rests his forehead on mine with his eyes closed.

"Thank you," he whispers.

The puppy chooses that minute to pop up and lick Brendon right across the lips. He jerks back, and I laugh at the look of surprise on his face.

"Someone's jealous, huh? You need love too?" He cuddles the dog to his chest and scratches his ear while the pup licks furiously.

"What are you going to name him?" I scratch under the puppy's chin.

"Me? Don't you mean *we*? He's *our* dog. Or do you expect me to name all the children too?" The hoity tone is so amusing. I love that he assumes we'll have kids because, why wouldn't we?

"Letting you name the children by yourself is slightly terrifying. They would end up with initials that spell something weird."

Brendon throws his head back and laughs hard.

"You're not wrong."

I look at the pup, at the square shape of his muzzle and his soft floppy ears.

"How about something like—"

"Lizard Brain. I was thinking the same," Brendon interrupts.

"Lizard Brain?"

"Butt Breath?" he tosses out.

"What the hell is wrong with you? Have you never named an animal before?"

He scoffs and rolls his eyes. "Let me guess, you want to name him something boring like Bob. Carl. Spot."

"He's distinguished. Look at him." I point at him. "He has a bow tie and will probably be pictured with the team a lot. He can't have a weird-ass name."

"If you suggest we name him Darby, I'm leaving you."

It's my turn to laugh, but fuck, it hurts.

"No, we aren't naming him Darby."

"Oh good, I didn't want to leave you."

Reaching for his chin, I pull his mouth to mine and take his mouth in a quick but dirty kiss. It sizzles my blood and has lust licking my skin.

"You aren't going anywhere."

Brendon blinks a few times while his neck turns pink.

"How about something like Seymour?" I offer. "He looks like a Seymour to me."

"Butts!" Brendon shouts. "Yes, he can be Seymour Butts."

"I'm going to start calling you Bart."

He cackles and squishes the dog's face in his hands. "Hello, Mr. Butts."

The dog's tail wags, and he licks Brendon's face again.

"See, he likes it. Don't be a party pooper, P Dawg."

Intermission is about to start, so Brendon takes the puppy out again to run around.

"Grab me a Dr Pepper on your way back in." I smack his butt as he leaves with the dog.

I watch the last few minutes, then flip through my phone while I wait. When I open Instagram, I have a hundred new tags that weren't there before the game started. *What the fuck?*

All the blood drains from my face at the pictures of Brendon and me kissing being shared on social media. Who the hell takes pictures of random people in the stands and posts them? Goddamn it.

My heart starts pounding, and my body has so much anxious energy I want to get up and pace. Instead, my knee starts bouncing, and I scroll through the pictures. One looks like someone zoomed in from somewhere behind us. One is cropped from the selfie of the couple directly in front of us. I stare at the back of her head for a second. Seriously? Who does this?

The last one is from a strangle angle, which means the person who took it was looking directly for us, probably watching us, and when I flip through the pictures posted with it, I have no doubt it was Nikki. Us kissing in the hallway the day she saw us and images of the way we look at each other. It's so clear we're together. Fuck her.

Well, the cat's out of the bag now. Part of me is grateful it's out and I can just deal with it and be done with it, but I'm also mad that the opportunity was taken from me. Coming out is a big deal, and I wanted to do it my own fucking way. Now I'm going to be bombarded with questions, and people will want me to put a label on myself. I've seen how Jeremy and Preston get asked when they go to press conferences. Preston refuses to answer, just staring at the reporter until it's awkward, but Jeremy gets flustered.

Shoving my phone back in my pocket, I stew in my irritation while I wait for Brendon to get back. Is he already being bombarded with questions? Does he already know about the pictures?

A few minutes later, Brendon and Seymour are back, both looking like they had a good run. Brendon drops into the seat and grabs the blanket before picking up the pup. Seymour sits on Brendon's lap with his tongue hanging out, panting and gazing up at the man who saved him.

"The internet knows about us."

That was not how I expected to tell him. Jesus.

"Huh?" Brendon looks at me with confusion creasing his face.

"A few people got pictures of us kissing and tagged us on social media. They've already got a few thousand views, and it's been like half an hour."

Brendon goes very still like he doesn't know how to react.

"Are you okay?"

I sigh and scrub a hand over my face. "I think so. Irritated that people shared a picture they didn't have a right to. Frustrated that we're going to have to deal with the questions."

Brendon reaches for my hand and gives it a squeeze.

"You're not alone. I won't let you face it alone. Okay?"

I nod and chew on my lip. "What if we make our own post?"

For a split second, Brendon is excited, but he shuts it down so fast I can almost convince myself it wasn't there.

"Do you want to?"

I shrug. "Yeah, pull the Band-Aid off and get it over with. If you're okay with it."

A huge grin splits Brendon's face, and I find myself smiling back.

"I'm done hiding us."

We both pull our phones out to look for a picture to post. We decide to do our own and as much as I'm nervous for whatever Brendon's is going to say, I'm excited too. I'll probably laugh.

I find one that I look a while back of him asleep on my shoulder lying on my bed with his face in my neck. It's perfect.

I load it up onto Instagram and think about what to say.

I don't think people should have to "come out" but just be accepted for who they are. You love who you love, gender shouldn't matter. So this isn't me coming out, it's me saying I married my best friend a few weeks ago, and I'm tired of feeling like I have to hide that fact. He's an amazing man, and I am honored to call him mine.

I tag him and post it to my socials. It's empowering and scary, but I'm glad it's done.

Only a minute later, I get a tag from Brendon and I'm smiling before it even loads.

The picture is of us standing next to each other at the costume party, his arm around my shoulders, and I'm looking at him with love in my eyes.

Somehow, I managed to trick this guy into putting up with my shit for the rest of my life. Or his. He's told me I can't name the kids by myself, which is probably best for everyone. He keeps me grounded but lets me fly. He's the Batman to my Robin. The peanut butter to my jelly.

"You're a dork and I love you."

CHAPTER 37

Brendon

T he game is over, we won, and I'm on cloud nine. I've got Señor Butts on his leash looking dapper as fuck as we walk into the locker room after the game. The boys are excited and rowdy, as they should be. It was a hard-won game, and they did great.

"Hold the fuck up!" Louis, Carpenter's roommate, yells. "Are you two fucking married?" He points between Paul and me.

"I didn't think that sentence was going to end that way." Paul laughs. "Yeah, we got married in Vegas."

The locker room goes silent, and everyone turns to look at us. I can see Paul tensing up, waiting for a bad reaction, so I do what I do best, distract.

"Honestly, did you really think anyone else was going to put up with my shit? Good thing I've got a nice ass, huh?"

"New rule!" Carp yells. "No one talks about their sex lives. No details."

The entire room says "Agreed" in unison, and I laugh.

"Oh, come on, you sure you don't want to hear about

when Paul jack—" Paul puts his hand over my mouth, and I laugh.

"That's enough of that." He gives me *the look*, and I shiver. I wish he could fuck already, but he can't. Stupid surgery.

I bite his palm, and he pulls his hand away while I smile.

"Also," I say as I pick up the dog. "This is Señor Butts."

"Seymour!" Paul shouts.

"That's what I said." I shrug.

Everyone laughs, and they go back to celebrating.

"See, that wasn't so bad." I nudge my husband and put my arm around his shoulders.

"You're lucky you're cute," he grumbles.

We hang out while everyone is getting changed. Since it's the last game of the season for us, I'm glad it ended with a win. Maybe next year we'll make it to the Frozen Four.

"Brendon, we have to figure out what we're going to do with the puppy. We can't keep him in the dorms." Paul is the killer of dreams.

"I know, but I don't want to let him go. Look at his sweet face." I hold the dog up at face level.

"If we had our own place, this wouldn't be a question, but we can't get kicked out of the dorms."

I huff, and my heart hurts at the idea of giving him up.

"Maybe one of the coaches can take him so you can still see him all the time."

Someone clears their throat behind me, and I turn to find Assistant Coach Scott.

"What if he slept at my house?" The words coming out of his mouth sound like English, but it takes my brain a second to understand them. "I'll bring him with me in the morning, you can have him all day, he'll hang out at the bench during practice, then come home with me at night."

Hope bursts in my heart.

"Really? You would be willing to do that?"

He looks at the pup and nods. "I'm gonna let him sleep on the bed, though."

"That's perfect! He's definitely a bed dog."

Paul sighs and mutters, "We're going to need a huge bed."

"And when we graduate and leave the dorms, we can have him?" I need the clarification because I'm not giving him up.

"Of course. You'll need to chip in for dog food and that kind of stuff, vet bills. He's your dog, just sleeping at my house." Scott reaches out to pet the puppy, and Seymour licks his hand.

"He's obviously a good judge of character," I say begrudgingly. "Okay, we can try it."

Paul puts a hand on my lower back and leans into me a little. "It's a good option."

"Doesn't mean I have to like it," I grumble.

"Thank you, Scott," Paul says. "We really appreciate it."

"Of course. I've been thinking about getting a dog but didn't want it stuck at home all day by itself, so this is a good alternative." He pets the dog again, and Butts lays his head on my shoulder.

"Okay, let's get some dinner, celebrate the win with the boys, then get to bed." Paul leads me out of the locker room and down the hallway.

Something about this moment reminds me of the years I spent jumping at shadows. I almost gave up hockey just to get away from Chad, but if I had, I wouldn't have Paul. I no longer jump at loud noises or flinch when someone touches me. I'm able to smile and sleep and be me. I'm sure I'll still have setbacks, things that trigger a memory that I wasn't expecting and send me spiraling, but I know that Paul will love me through those times. He'll hold me while I break down and not judge me for it, close the cabinet doors that I leave open, and only grumble a little when he finds the milk warm on the counter.

We get to Rocky's, and the fans have already gotten the party started. It's loud and crowded, which is the best way to celebrate. Paul and I aren't drinking tonight, but we sit around and enjoy the conversation of our teammates and their significant others.

Football Guy sits next to Carp, and if I'm not mistaken, reaches over to put his hand on the captain's thigh. Carppy's face turns hungry as he looks at the other man, and I swear I get singed from it.

"Carp and Nick are going to fuck so hard later," I whisper into Paul's ear. He turns his head and watches the exchange that's all eye contact.

"Oh shit, yeah they are," he chuckles. "I can't wait to be able to fuck again."

I take a second to look at Paul, really look at him. He's sagging in his chair, eyes heavy. He needs to go to bed.

"All right, time for bed. Come on, sleepy pants." I push back from the table and pick up my pupper.

"What? We just got here. You didn't even order yet." Paul turns in his seat to argue.

"You are about to fall asleep. You just had surgery and need to rest." I kiss his forehead, and there's a bunch of "Awww" around the room. I flip everyone off and head to Scott. It hurts my heart to give up the pup, but I know I have to. It's just a few hours before I'll see him again.

I lean my head down to kiss him, and he jerks back,

smacking my nose. My eyes water and white-hot pain shoots through my face.

"Fuck," I yell and cup my nose. Scott reaches for the dog and takes him from me while I breathe through it. Goddamn, that's brutal.

Paul stands next to me, rubbing my back. "Do you want ice?"

"Maybe."

"On it," Jeremy says.

I check my upper lip, and I'm not bleeding again, thank God, but I sit down since my eyes won't stop watering. Jeremy appears with a bag of ice and some napkins to wrap around it. I lean my head back and groan when the ice is placed on my nose. It feels so good.

Paul runs his fingers through the long hair on top of my head, then pets the short hairs on the sides.

"Are you bleeding?"

"No, I'm okay." I sit up and take the ice off my face. Seymour is sitting on the floor next to Scott, just watching everything going on. He's a good pup.

"Okay, we're going to go back to the dorms," Paul tells everyone. "We've had about enough excitement as we can handle for one day."

The guys chuckle, and I say good night, then reach for Paul's hand and let him lead me from the restaurant.

"That could have gone worse," I say.

"What are you talking about?"

"Telling everyone we're married." I shrug. "It could have gone worse."

"I'm going to tell myself not to read the comments on our posts. I'm sure there's some dickheads on there."

"Fuck them." I pull Paul closer and wrap my arm around his lower back. "They don't matter. The only opinions that count are yours and mine."

"And Seymour Butts."

I laugh so hard I have to brace myself on my knees. I did not expect that answer or for Paul to say Butts. Best name choice ever.

I'm still chuckling when we get to the elevator and into our room.

"I don't know what you were worried about. My name picking ability is on point. His name is perfection." I pull off my jacket and start unbuttoning my shirt when Paul stops me.

"I've always wanted to do this," he says quietly as he undresses me. My nose is still throbbing a little, and I know we can't have sex yet, but him touching me, looking at me like this, is making it hard to remember that. His fingers dance over my skin, teasing me with the touch he knows I crave.

"I don't have the energy for much, but I just want to touch you tonight." Paul's eyes drag over my body like a physical caress.

"But I get to come, right?" My dick is already hard and wanting attention.

He chuckles and leans forward to place open-mouth kisses on my chest.

"Please," I whimper.

"Shhh," he says against my skin.

Paul gets me undressed, kissing and nipping at the exposed skin until I'm naked while he's still dressed. He pulls me against him, the fabric of his suit rubbing my skin is strange, but I like it.

"Are you going to get naked too?" I run the back of my pointer finger down the buttons of his shirt.

"You do it." His gaze locks on mine, and I quickly open his shirt without looking away. I slide the shirt and jacket off his shoulders and hang them up before opening his pants. He toes off his shoes so I can get the rest of his clothes off.

I take in his body, the long, muscle-packed thighs, the tight, trim abdomen, wiry arms, and defined pecs. His body screams speed and agility. One of the puncture marks from his surgery is bruised, but the other two are just a little red. So far it looks like they're healing up well.

Paul takes my hand and pulls me to the bed. Normally, he lies down first so I can lie on him, but I don't want to put my weight on his injury, so I climb on first.

"Roll over," he tells me, and I flip to my stomach. I don't know what he's going to do, but it doesn't matter. I trust him.

Paul straddles my thighs, resting his cock on my crack, and leans forward to pepper my shoulders with kisses. Sometimes he bites, sometimes he sucks, but most of it is light kisses.

"I love your shoulders," he whispers against my skin. "You're so strong, powerful."

I smile into the pillow and wait to see what he does next. Paul licks down my spine and digs his fingers into the muscles of my ass. It feels amazing to have those muscles massaged, even if it doesn't last very long.

"This," he cups my ass and jiggles it, "is a work of art."

I snort as he bites me, not hard, just barely pressing his teeth into my flesh.

This is so much more than sex—it's savoring, loving, sweet. I haven't had a lot of sweet interactions with sexual partners, but this is like coming home. My insecurities try to tell me that I'm not worthy of his attention, of his care, of his love, but the way he loves me proves to me that Paul thinks I am. That's what matters.

Paul doesn't leave even a centimeter of my skin untouched. My body is worshipped, slowly, purposefully, while he whispers words against my flesh. I'm not hard or buzzing with lust; I'm relaxed and sated. Would I like an orgasm? Of course, but that's not what this is about. This is about comfort, both his and mine after the shitshow that was the last few days.

Paul makes his way back up my body, kissing and nipping until he's at my neck.

"You know, I wasn't so sure about this tattoo," he says as he traces it with his tongue, "but it does something to that Neanderthal part of my brain that wants to claim you."

I smile against my arms. "I am yours. Even before this started, I was yours. I just didn't know it yet."

"Mmmm," he growls with my skin in his teeth, sending a shiver through me. "You were mine then, but I didn't feel like I could touch you. Not like I wanted to. You weren't exclusively mine. Now, if someone tries to make me share or tries to take you, I'll hurt them."

My heart flutters at his words, at the seriousness of them. I think I love that possessiveness. And I may just have to rile him up on purpose sometimes, just so he'll fuck me extra hard. My dick twitches at the thought.

"I love you, Brendon, until my heart stops beating."

"Then I'll make sure it never does."

CHAPTER 38

Paul

Winter finals are over, and hockey is over for us, so Brendon and I pack some shit into my car, grab Seymour, and head for Michigan. I don't know if my grandparents have seen the social media posts or news articles talking about our marriage, but Grandma hasn't said anything about it. A part of me was hoping Dad would call. Even if it was just to tell me that I'm an idiot, something is better than nothing, right? It shows that he pays attention, that he cares. I'm trying not to dwell on it, but it stings.

I'm healed up, and Brendon's nose is on the mend. We're both back to working out, though we have to go slower to make sure we don't push too far and set ourselves back. Once the doctor gave the go-ahead, Brendon and I have been fucking like bunnies. We don't go more than twelve hours without an orgasm . . . or two. My recoup period is like five minutes. We take advantage.

The drive is long, seventeen or eighteen hours depending on traffic, construction, and weather. It's a long fucking day of sitting in the car, but with Brendon's nonstop brain, it's entertaining most of the time. He sings lyrics, acts out scenes from movies or TV shows, tells stories with ten tangent stories. I love listening to the way his brain works.

By the time we pull into my grandparents' driveway, my ass is numb, my back hurts, and I'm pretty sure I'm going to need someone to lift me out of this car because all my joints have solidified.

"Baby." I run a hand down Brendon's arm to wake him. He fell asleep about two hours ago, which means he probably won't sleep tonight unless I wear him out. "We're here."

I shake his leg, and he mumbles something I don't catch, so I run my hand up the inside of his thigh, under his basketball shorts, and tease the crease of his groin. He groans this time, shifting his hips.

"Pauly," he moans, shifting so he's leaning against me. "Don't tease me."

I kiss his cheek and smirk at him. "But teasing you is *so* fun for me."

When I start to pull my hand out, he grabs my wrist through the fabric and stares at me with heat in his eyes.

"Please."

"In my grandparents' driveway?" I scratch at the tender flesh, and he hisses, but it's not from pain.

"I can't get out of the car like this!"

He lets go of my hand, and I sit back in my seat and take in the red cheeks and messy hair.

"I'll make it up to you later, I promise."

He groans again, pushing his palm against the ridge in his shorts.

I can't help but chuckle as I get out and groan myself, but this one isn't from lust; it's from the ache in every muscle in my body finally moving. Grandma comes out the door with a smile on her face, making a beeline for me while Brendon gets the leash on our beast.

It's cold as fuck when I get out of the car but it's March so that's not surprising.

"There's my boy!" She wraps her arms around me, and I have to bend over to meet her height, but I hug her back just as tightly. She will always be home. Even before my mother died, she was my safe place. Mom was amazing and I miss her all the time, but there's nothing like a grandma's love.

"Hey, Grandma." I breathe in the perfume she's worn my entire life, some kind of soft floral with rose mixed with Downy fabric softener. Age has made her softer, which makes me a little sad. I know some day I'll have to say goodbye to her, and that day will crush me, but I know I will survive with Brendon by my side.

"How was the drive? Are you hungry? Grab your bags and let me at my other favorite boy." She pats my back and kisses my cheek before releasing me.

"We will definitely eat."

I open the trunk of my car and grab our bags while Brendon picks up Grandma and swings her around carefully while she laughs. Seymour jumps around and barks happily. The scene makes my heart happy. These little moments will be permanently branded into my heart. He puts his arm around her shoulders and walks her back to the house with the puppy, letting me carry his shit.

It's so damn cute that I don't argue or give him shit.

When I get inside, Mr. Butts is in Grandpa's lap, licking his face while he laughs.

"I don't know what you're cooking, but it smells amazing," Brendon says as he rubs his stomach.

"Venison stew," she says and heads to the kitchen. "Bedrooms are made up upstairs." She points, and I stop with both bags. Brendon looks at me, asking me what I'm going to do without words.

"Uh, we only need one." My voice shakes, and I brace for their reaction.

Grandpa looks between the two of us and shrugs like *duh*, and Grandma says, "That's fine, pick a room then."

Well, that was anticlimactic.

I'm not sure how to feel about that. Relieved, sure, but seriously? That's it?

Brendon laughs at whatever expression is on my face, and I huff at him.

"I'm giving you the itchy blanket," I tell him and head upstairs to my old room. It's weird to stay in the guest room when I lived in this one for years.

It's been changed a little. My posters of hockey players were taken down, but my trophies are still on the shelf Grandpa put up, and my team pictures are still framed on the wall. I'm lost in the memories I have in this room, the wins and the losses, the smiles and the tears. This room makes me proud. I've come so far, overcome so much, and I'm still standing.

Warmth at my back and hands on my hips have me smiling and leaning back into my husband. The love of my life.

"I love how they kept this room yours," he says as he lays his chin on my shoulder.

I drop the bags on the floor and reach for his hands to wrap his arms around my waist. Even though we spend so much time together, I don't get tired of him. He's my air.

"I'm glad we're here." Brendon closes the little distance between us and squeezes me while I hold on to his arms.

"Me too."

"We're fucking after they go to bed."

I chuckle and turn my head to look at him while I grind my ass against his dick.

"I'm sure we can work something out."

His touch turns from comfort to arousal. In the blink of an eye he's damn near desperate for me. It's a high I never expected to experience. It's romance movie shit, but it's my life, and I love to tease him, work him up, and leave him hanging.

"I hate you," he groans as he thrusts against me.

"You love me and my ass."

He's starting to pant, his cock once again hard because of me, and he digs his fingers into my skin.

"Please," he whimpers and licks his lips. "It'll be so quick."

"You can wait. It'll be worth it, I promise." I turn in his hold, one hand sliding into his hair to pull his head back while the other slips into his underwear to cup his balls. I slam my mouth over his, swallowing his moan. His hands grip my T-shirt in tight fists on either side of my hips, but he lets me play with him. He always does.

"Such a good little slut, aren't you? So needy but so eager to please." I lick his upper lip and bite his lower lip. Brendon's body is tense and so ready to come. This power he lets me have over him is intoxicating.

"Boys! Wash up for dinner!" Grandpa yells up the stairs, and Brendon almost sobs.

"You have ten seconds, give it to me." I drop to my knees, pull his dick out, and suck on his head while jerking him fast in my hand.

His body bows, and he shoves his hand in his mouth to keep the sound in. He grips my hair and fucks into my hand. I hold up my free hand, counting down the seconds. I'm breathing hard now too, lust licking my veins at the control I hold in my literal hands. The challenge I threw was bullshit, and I knew it. I knew he wasn't going to be able to finish that fast, but he's trying so fucking hard. There's a small part of me that feels bad. It's really fucking small, though. Like miniscule.

Precum hits on my tongue at nine and at ten, I pull off him, leaving him hard and throbbing.

"Noooo! Fuck!" he yells against his hand while he trembles. He squeezes his eyes closed and covers his face with his hands. The red blush of arousal has climbed up his neck to his face, and I know it's spread over his chest as well.

It takes a minute, but he grips his hair in his hands and pulls hard. The bite of pain giving him something else to focus on, I'm sure. I wait it out, knowing my grandparents are downstairs waiting for us but not willing to leave him alone like this. His dick is still hard when I stand up and tuck him away.

"This time I mean it; I hate you." He opens his eyes and glares at me. I smile at him and lean my forehead against his.

"But think about how good it will feel later when you finally get to fill me with cum." I chuckle when he shivers on a gasp.

"Boys!" Grandma yells this time, and I kiss Brendon quickly, then step away from him, moving to the door to go wash my hands. It's probably a good idea since I just had my hand on his balls, plus it'll give both of us a few minutes to cool down. I'm hard and aching for touch, but I know waiting will make it so much better. When did I become such a masochist to myself?

My flushed face catches me by surprise in the mirror when I step in front of the sink. I've never seen myself heated from lust, only post-orgasmic, I guess. Interesting. I splash some cold water on my face and am washing my hands when Brendon comes in glaring at me.

I smile at him in the mirror, giving him a wink for good measure, and he breaks into a disgruntled smile. He's trying so hard not to, but he can't hide it from me. It's fucking adorable.

"They go to sleep early; we have all night." I wink again, and he grumbles something, slapping my ass as I walk past him.

At the table, Grandma and Grandpa are at each end, leaving Brendon and me on either side. The stew pot is in the middle of the table with mashed potatoes and yeast rolls with butter. It smells so good. Venison stew is one of my favorites. It's hearty, full of protein, veggies Grandpa grew in the garden, and delicious carbs. I serve myself a bowl, layering the mashed potatoes then stew on top as Brendon comes bounding down the stairs making a "meep meep" sound.

Seymour sees him and yips, jumping off the couch to chase him into the dining room.

"Hey, monster," he says in a baby voice and scratches the dog.

Grandma sighs and shakes her head but doesn't say anything. I know she thinks he just washed his hands and is now touching the dog, but she lets it go. He's an adult.

Brendon falls into his seat and pulls one foot up because he can't sit normally for long if he's not touching me.

He serves himself, and we all start eating.

"How was the drive then?" Grandpa asks.

"It was fine, I guess. You know, for being locked in a car for a bazillion hours with random cell service and the piss break warden." Brendon points his spoon at me and rolls his eyes.

"Excuse me? You wanted to stop for snacks every fifteen minutes, not piss."

Grandma chuckles, a smile lighting her face and enhancing her smile lines. She hasn't had an easy life, and burying her only child had to have been crushing, but the lines of her face tell her story. While there were hard times and sorrow, there was also lots of love and laughter.

"I was hungry!" Brendon says around a mouthful of food.

"If I stopped every time you said you needed more snacks, we would still be in Nebraska." I shake my head and shove more food in my mouth. "How's Drumstick? Is she still broody, or did you feed her to the bears?"

"We got a rooster from Carol Lewandowski down the street. You remember her? Her boys went to high school with you, Jake and Timmy?" Grandma asks, and I nod.

"Shit For Brains is the dumbest damn rooster I ever seen," Grandpa grumbles. "He gets up in them trees when we open the coop and can't get down half the damn time. Sometimes I just leave his ass up there and hope a bear will come get him, or a racoon."

I snort and choke on my food while Grandma sighs, and Brendon just nods along like this is completely normal. I guess it is for kids like us, growing up in the small towns around the big cities. We're technically an hour from Muskegon in Bitely, Michigan, but it's easier to tell people I'm from the city. I grew up going to games and practices in Muskegon anyway. Grandma worked there too.

Brendon and Jeremy were from Muskegon, though, so I spent a lot of time crashing with them, especially if the weather was bad and Grandma didn't want to drive home in the dark during a whiteout.

"Do you eat roosters?" Brendon asks.

"You can if you butcher them at the right time,"

Grandpa tells him. "Most of our chickens are laying hens, but some of them damn birds get pissy about us taking the eggs, so we have to get a rooster for a while or give her rubber eggs to lay on."

Brendon gets into an intense conversation about chickens and rubber eggs with Grandpa, and Grandma nudges my hand.

"One bedroom, huh?"

I smile, dipping my head toward my bowl. "Yeah, one bedroom."

"When did that start?" She reaches for my hand and holds it. "You've had feelings for him for a while, haven't you?"

I lift my gaze to hers, finding acceptance and sympathy.

"How did you know that?"

She cocks her head. "Sweetheart, you think I can't tell when my boy has feelings for someone? He was all you talked about for a long time."

A knot clogs my throat, and I lift my water to my lips to force it down.

"Are you disappointed?" I can't meet her eyes as I wait for her answer. It might crush me.

"That you found a partner who loves you? That you're happy?" She shakes my hand and waits for me to look up at her. "No, Pauly, I'm not disappointed."

Tears well in my eyes, and I cover them with my hand, dropping my head again. She gets up and wraps her arms around me, pulling my head against her chest.

"Any good parent figure just wants their kids to be happy. Who you are happy with shouldn't matter."

Seymour lifts his front paws onto the seat of my chair and nuzzles my leg while wagging his tail. I pet his head and scoot back enough to pick him up.

"I'm not making this a habit, little dude," I tell him. "Dogs don't belong at the table."

Brendon scoffs. "He's gonna have a seat at the table."

"Absolutely not! You are not feeding the dog at the table."

Brendon drops his head back on his shoulders and groans like a petulant teenager. Grandma snickers and whispers in my ear, "It's like looking at Grandpa at the same age."

That is a mental picture I did not need since I know what we were just doing in the bedroom upstairs.

I snuggle our pup for a minute, then put him down and stand to hug my grandma. I'm so glad I have her and Grandpa. I don't know what would have happened to me or where I would be if they hadn't stepped up. I barely know my dad's parents, so after Mom died, I was left alone until these two figured out what was happening and took me in. I don't think Dad ever noticed I was gone too.

"So," I take a deep breath before I continue. "We actually got married when we were in Vegas for a game."

Grandma pauses for a second, then looks at Brendon who looks like a deer caught in the headlights. Grandpa starts laughing, and Grandma smacks me upside the back of my head.

"Hey!"

"I know! I had to read about it in a news article like everybody else!"

I rub at the spot on my head.

"I was waiting to see how long it would take you to fess up to it." She puts her hands on her hips and stares at me. "Congratulations, but why didn't you tell us? We would have flown out."

"It was spur of the moment." Brendon comes around

the table, pulls my chair back, and sits on my lap. "We didn't plan it."

I wrap my arms around his waist and lean my face against his strong back, breathing in the scent that's just him.

"Pain in my ass," she mumbles and starts to clear the table. Brendon pops up and grabs dishes too. I take the food in and set it on the counter, then help get it put away. Brendon takes the dishes from her and loads the dishwasher, shooing her from the kitchen.

We work together to get it cleaned up, and I remind him to close cabinet doors. He babbles, sings random song lyrics, and flicks water at me. Even this mundane task isn't boring with him around.

We're laughing and fucking around when Grandma comes in with a smile lighting up her face.

"You two are having way too much fun in here." She looks between us and the wet spots on our shirts. "Make sure you get the water cleaned up so no one falls."

"Yes, ma'am." Brendon salutes her. She chuckles and kisses both of our cheeks. "We're headed to bed. Good night."

We both say good night at the same time, and my grandparents head upstairs, Grandpa waving at us as he passes us.

The second we hear their door close, Brendon spins around and pins my hips to the counter I'm wiping down.

"You owe me an orgasm." His tone is rough and guttural.

"You gotta wait for them to fall asleep first, damn." I push back into him and grind my ass against his dick. "Are you up for a flip fuck?"

Brendon sucks in a shuttering breath through his teeth and bites my shoulder through my T-shirt.

"I'll take that as a yes." I reach behind him, pulling him closer, and roll my hips. "Be a good boy and help me finish this up, then we can get to the good shit."

He groans into my skin, digging his fingers into my hips for just a second before he steps back and gets his work done. It only takes us a few minutes before he's done and takes the puppy out to pee.

When I get to the bedroom ahead of Brendon, I see someone put a dog crate with a bed and blanket in it for Seymore. Thank fuck. I did not want to try to have sex while the dog wanted attention.

"Señor Butts is such a good pup," Brendon says, carrying the dog.

"In the kennel. He can come out once we're done."

Brendon looks scandalized, holding the dog to his chest like he can't believe the words that just came out of my mouth.

"Excuse you. First you take him away from the table, and now this?"

"You want to try to fuck while he's climbing on us and trying to lick your face?" I cross my arms and wait for that mental picture to hit him.

"Yeah okay, you have a point." He puts the pup in the kennel and puts a blanket over it. "No child needs to see his dads fucking."

Brendon flicks the light off, leaving only the light from the moon peeking in through the curtains, but it's enough.

"Strip," I demand, and Brendon doesn't hesitate. His Darby U T-shirt hits the floor only a few seconds before his shorts and hockey puck underwear. He's gloriously naked, that beautiful blush already spreading across his chest and up his neck, and his cock is jutting out from his body. Even in the dim lighting I can see him so fucking clearly. "Your fuck stick looks like it wants some attention."

Brendon's breathing increases until he's damn near panting, and I haven't even touched him yet. He opens and closes his fists, watching me like he expects me to pounce.

I strip my shirt off and let Brendon rake his gaze over my body before dropping my pants. He whimpers when I wrap my hand around my cock and stroke. I'm hard as fuck and want to come too since I've been edging myself along with him.

"Sit." I nod to the bed, and he sits on the edge, eyes never leaving mine. I get him adjusted the way I want, so he's farther back, leaning on his hands, and I can ride him.

I grab the lube and one of the butt plugs I brought from our collection.

"Lay back. I want you stretched around this plug while you fuck me."

"Fuuuck," he moans and lays back on the bed. I lift one of his legs and open him wide to get better access to his hole. This plug has a long taper so I can prep him with it without needing fingers first, and once I'm ready, I can remove it and fuck him without more prepping. It'll burn a little, but he can take it.

In and out, I work the plug into him until it's fully seated, and he can't keep his hips still. His hands are in his hair, pulling at the long strands, and his back is arching off the bed.

I lick a line up his neglected cock, and he gasps. He throbs like he's going to come, but I grip his base hard to keep him from losing it.

"I hate you," he groans, and I dribble lube over him and spread some on my hole as well. Sometimes I like going right for it and not prepping. That stretch, that burn, makes me weak.

I straddle his lap, the soft hair on his legs tickling my ass until I lift up and position him at my hole. Brendon's eyes pop open and watch me as I tease myself with him. He's so fucking close to the edge I should be able to get a second one out of him.

Once his head is inside me, I sink down on him, grab the back of his neck, and pull him back up to sitting.

He's a whimpering mess, leaning back on his hands so he can't touch me but wants so desperately to. I tangle my hand in the back of his hair and pull his head back, then fuck myself on him. Rolling my hips first, circling them, then rocking before lifting up and slamming back down on him.

He moans, and it's music to my ears.

"Such a good toy," I croon as I take him as deep as I can.

"Please," he whines as his body tenses and trembles. "Pleaaase. I need to come."

Putting my free hand on his knee for better leverage, I pick up my pace and make him wait for my answer.

"Paul . . . please!" He's desperate and almost there, almost to the point of no return, and he's afraid I'm going to make him stop. I love this part. "Paul!"

"Give it to me. Fill me with your cum." My words are a harsh demand as I ride him hard. "I want your cum dripping from me while I fuck you." The pace I set is fast, and I'm already sweating. Red splotches explode across Brendon's skin as he shudders and comes inside me. The warmth and throb of him inside me pushes me closer to the edge too, but I'm not there yet. Brendon relaxes, weak and sated. Sitting up, I wrap my arms around his shoulders and kiss him. He tosses his arms around my waist but doesn't have the energy to put any pressure into the hold.

The post-orgasm weakness, when his head is quiet and his body is relaxed, is such a turn-on. I love that I can do this to him. That I can work him up, push him to his breaking point, then watch him fall is a high no drug will ever touch.

Once his breathing slows, I lift off him, and he falls back on the bed.

"Come here." I pull on his thighs to bring his ass back to the edge of the bed and lift one so I can get to his hole. The plug slips out easily with only a little moan from Brendon.

I slick myself up and push against him. He tenses up just a little, but the slide inside is easy thanks to the stretch of the toy. I push his knee to the bed and use his other thigh as leverage to snap my hips against his ass. He's tight and hot around me. So fucking perfect.

Watching this strong man give in to the pleasure I force on him gives me an appreciation for strength that I didn't have before. It takes so much power to submit.

He takes me so beautifully, letting me use him in any way I want with no hesitation.

Brendon moans as I use his body, his spent dick twitching against his stomach.

I'm not going to give him enough time to recover and come again. I want my own too badly. I need to mark him, fill him, use him.

"You take it so well," I groan, and he tightens around me.

"I want it," Brendon begs. "Please."

Electricity shoots through me, tingling concentrates in my balls, and I shudder as I empty myself into him. Brendon hooks his leg around me to keep me close as my knees threaten to give out. I lean on his chest to stay upright and breathe through my orgasm.

"Fuck, I love you," I mutter with my eyes closed, sucking in as much air as I can.

"I love you too, Pauly boy."

I smile and open my eyes, seeing the love I've always been so afraid of shining back at me. I kiss his chest and step back so he can get up.

With cum dripping from both of us, we stand in an embrace and just hold each other. Surrounded by love and support and comfort, I know I've found my one and only.

CHAPTER 39

Paul

W e've been in Michigan for a few days, just hanging out with my grandparents. Brendon is learning all about keeping chickens and goes out to collect eggs every morning with Seymour. Pretty sure he's now planning to raise chickens once we leave college. My little weirdo.

I'm sitting on the couch, the pup curled up in my lap when the front door opens and my dad walks in. He freezes with his hand on the knob when he sees me, half in the doorway as we stare at each other. We look so much alike it's startling. Like looking into my future. His hair is longer and turning gray, his beard is going gray too, but his eyes are empty. There's no light in him, not like when I was a kid.

Seymour barks, and I drop my gaze and set the dog aside to stand.

I clear my throat and straighten my T-shirt just to give my hands something to do.

"Hey, Dad." I look up, standing tall while I try to sort through my feelings. "I didn't expect to see you."

"Shouldn't you be at school?" He closes the door. "I was going to tell Richard that I grabbed the poles I left in the garage."

He starts past me to go look for my grandpa, and I can't help the punched-in-the-gut feeling.

"That's it?" I demand, clenching my jaw. "I haven't seen you in years and all you want to know is why I'm not at school? You didn't even wait for an answer."

He stops but doesn't turn to look at me, and I swear I'm fourteen again, just wanting my father to tell me that he loves me, that it's not my fault my mother is dead, that I'm enough. I never got those words, and I hate myself for still wanting them over seven years later.

"I'm on break, by the way." I move to stand in front of him so he can't hide from me anymore. "I had my appendix taken out a while back. Did you know that? I got married too. How about that?"

He won't look at me. He's staring at his shoes.

"I hate you for abandoning me." My words are quiet, but he flinches like I struck him. "I needed you, and you left me at the hospital. I deserved a lot better from you."

My lip trembles, and my chest is tight as I stare at the man who was beaten down by life and he let it win. He wasn't strong enough to fight to live.

"But I have to thank you." My voice breaks. "I learned I will never give up. I'm a fighter, and no matter what life takes from me, I will keep going. Should I ever be blessed to have a child, I will spend every day of my life making sure they know I love them more than life itself. I will no longer be afraid of love because, what has that gotten you?"

The sliding glass door opens behind me, and I hear Brendon's laugh cut off.

"Ryan, I didn't expect you this weekend," Grandpa

says, and Brendon comes to stand behind me, his heat radiating against my back.

Dad looks between Brendon and me and nods. A tear rolls down his cheek, and it breaks my heart.

"I'm glad you're a better man than I am." His tone is rough, like he's been smoking two packs a day for twenty years. Hell, it could be the truth, for all I know. "I'm sorry I wasn't stronger, but every day I'm glad you had your grandparents."

My throat burns with the warring emotions threatening to drown me.

"I'm proud of you. I hope you can believe that." He turns to leave but pauses in the doorway. "I love you, son. You were always enough. It was me who wasn't." Then he's gone, and I crumple to the floor.

A sob rips from my throat, and I mourn the loss of the parent that still breathes. I never let myself grieve him. Instead I wrapped my anger around me and used my fear of being him to keep people at arm's length. Until a smart-mouthed redhead came into my life and made me fall in love with him.

Brendon pulls me against him and holds me tight as I finally let the pain out. It's been years since I saw my dad, and I've never been bold enough to call him out on his shit. I was scared it would push him further away, make me harder for him to accept. But thanks to Brendon, to his unending love, I don't need him like I used to.

"I love you," Brendon says against my temple. "You are more than enough."

I wrap my arms around him and let the rapid waves of sobs ease into a stream. Seymour's cold nose touches my underarm, and I open up enough for him to burrow in between us.

"We're a fam-damn-ily," Brendon says, petting the pup. "No getting away from us now."

I lift my face to his and kiss him softly. "We can't keep chickens in our dorm room."

"You are the sucker of fun!" he groans.

Grandma sniffles and comes over, chuckling at us.

"You were never the problem, baby." She cups my face and kisses my forehead. "And your momma would beat that man for leaving you, but his shortcomings are not your fault. They never were."

"Thanks for taking me in." Another tear streaks down my cheek, and she brushes it away.

"It wasn't ever a question, and we loved having you around."

"Except your damn hockey gear smelled like shit," Grandpa says, taking the basket of eggs and moving into the kitchen.

We all laugh because he's not wrong, and it has not changed.

This right here is what family is about, and I'm so fucking lucky to have it.

Grandpa starts cooking eggs, and Grandma leaves Brendon and me to our moment.

I sit up so I can see Brendon's face but don't move out of his arms. "I want to get rings. I don't care if they're just those silicone ones for now until we can afford good ones."

"Those come in crazy colors and shit, right? Can they do patterns? Can you have them, like, engraved or stamped or whatever?" His mind is spinning with possibilities, and I love that about him.

"I think you can get custom ones." I shrug. "Why? What do you want on yours?"

"What *don't* I want on it? Hockey sticks, obviously. A

puppy face. Pizza. Michigan. The date we got married, 'cause I already forgot it."

I start laughing and can't stop until my stomach hurts and there are tears in my eyes. God, I love this man and the way his ridiculous mind works.

"Okay, the date is a good idea," I concede.

"Come eat," Grandpa calls, setting plates on the table. Brendon gets off the floor and offers me a hand up. Without a word, Brendon moves the chairs so we're sitting next to each other and he can hook his leg over mine.

Brendon starts telling me about the eggs we're eating—he collected them and is very proud—how the color of the yoke is an indication of what the birds are eating, and the taste can change depending on their diet. All of a sudden, he's a chicken guru, and it makes me smile. I grew up with chickens; I'm well aware of what he's telling me, but I won't stop him from sharing what he's learned. He's excited about it, and I want to share in that with him.

Once everyone is done eating, I start clearing the table since it was usually my job growing up anyway.

"Since I was out with Gramps this morning doing men's work, you can clean up," Brendon says with the fakest straight face I've ever seen.

"Men's work?" I scoff, picking up his plate. "You mean checking for eggs?"

"Mmhmm."

"You realize that is typically a child's job, right?" I laugh at his scandalized expression.

Grandma and I get the dishes done and the kitchen cleaned up pretty quickly while Brendon falls asleep on the couch. We should be doing some kind of workout stuff while in the off season, but we're tired. I'll get him back in the gym when we get back to Denver.

The mailman pulls up to the box at the end of the

driveway and stops. He opens his door and steps out, coming toward the house.

"Grandma, Mr. Phillips is coming to the door." She's had the same mailman for twenty years.

I open the door, and he smiles at me.

"Hey there, Pauly. I found this in the mailbox and didn't want it to get lost." He hands me what looks like a metal wedding ring with a piece of receipt tape with words scribbled on it in pen.

"Oh, thanks." I take them from him, confused when I see my dad's handwriting.

> *Paul-*
> *I've followed your hockey career for years. I loved your mother more than I loved my own life. I hope you can forgive me.*
> *Dad*

I stare at the ring in my hand that I never saw my dad take off. The silver band doesn't look like much, but it has a story to tell. The story of a man who lost himself in grief.

I don't know what this means, if it's his way of extending an olive branch or his way of saying goodbye, and that hurts. As hurt as I am by his actions, I hope we can repair some of the damage and maybe start over.

Grandma rubs my back, reading the note in my hand, and she closes my fingers around the ring.

"I think your mom would love to have you wear that. It was a symbol of a promise he never broke."

I give her a hug, the metal warming in my palm.

"I'll think about it."

She pats my back, and I sit on the couch next to my husband and puppy. Brendon stirs and shifts, leaning against me, and falls back asleep. Seymour grumbles and lays his head on my leg.

I don't know how I expected my life to go or where I would end up. I definitely didn't expect to be married to Brendon, but nothing and no one is more perfect than this moment.

CHAPTER 40

june

Brendon

Summer training has started, and we're already bitching about being up so early every day, but it's the weekend, and we get to sleep in.

It's also Paul's birthday.

Thanks to Preston not being a total douche and liking Paul, he had cinnamon rolls delivered fresh and warm this morning.

There's a knock on our door, and I get up out of bed in my chicken boxer briefs to answer it.

"Good morning, dear." The warm smile of the bakery owner, Debbi, greets me. She's a middle-aged woman with blonde hair that's starting to go gray and lines on her face that prove she's laughed a lot.

"Good morning, Pastry Fairy!" I give her a quick hug, which surprises her, and take the warm goods. "Thank you!"

She pats my arm, and I duck back inside the room. Thank fuck Paul sleeps like the dead and is still softly snoring.

I open the containers and set them on the bedside

table, then swipe my finger through the frosting and paint his lips with it. It takes a minute because he moves and starts to wake up, but I manage.

Lying back down in bed, I slide my hand into his underwear and grip his morning wood, stroking him in loose strokes, and kiss him. He wakes with a groan, tasting like sugar and cinnamon. Paul thrusts into my hand, and I smile into the kiss when he reaches for me.

"Why do you taste like frosting?" He moans, leaning his forehead against mine as I squeeze his cock in a rhythm I know will get him to the edge quickly.

"That's for me to know and you to find out." I kiss his lips again quickly, then slide down his body and under the blankets to wrap my mouth around his dick.

His back arches when I suck on his head, my hand still working him over.

"Fuck, baby," he moans, reaching to tangle his fingers in my hair. He uses the grip to fuck into my mouth. "Are you ready for breakfast?"

His words are a growl a split second before his salty cum hits my tongue and I'm swallowing around him. Paul moans, his legs tightening around me and his hips arching and thrusting into my mouth until he's spent and weak. The tight grip on my hair loosens, and he cups my cheek.

I lick him clean, the frosting and cinnamon from my finger leaving just a hint of sweetness on his skin that I lap up.

Paul hisses when I suck on his tip to get the last few drops of him, and I climb up his body.

"Mmm, sweet." I run my finger over my lower lip and suck on it to make sure I didn't waste any. "Breakfast of champions."

Paul's red, relaxed face smiles at me, and he pulls me in for a kiss. He drapes his legs over mine, trapping my hips against his as he explores my mouth, tasting himself on my tongue.

"Happy birthday, lover," I whisper against his lips. "Get dressed for a day on the lake. We gotta go." I wag my eyebrows at him, and a smile covers my face. I'm so fucking excited to spend a day on the water with my husband, best friends, and pup.

There's a knock on the door, and I get up to answer it again. Scott is standing in the hallway with a wiggly, white puppy with adorable brown patches.

"Butts!" I reach for my excited boy, and he licks my face while slapping me with his whip-like tail. "Go say good morning to Daddy," I tell him and set him on the floor.

Paul chuckles and reaches down to pick up the puppy who instantly attacks his face with kisses. Paul yells and wrestles with the puppy, laughing and twisting Butts in the blanket.

"Thanks for bringing him over today, I appreciate it."

"No problem. Enjoy the weekend, and happy birthday, Paul." Scott holds his hand up in a wave, and Paul shouts "Thank you" while hiding his face from the dog.

I start to close the door, but something stops it. Turning to look, Preston has his foot in the doorway and is looking unamused in swim trunks and a rash guard shirt.

"You aren't even dressed yet. Let's go. If we're late, there won't be any parking."

Jeremy steps up behind Preston and slides his hand under Preston's shirt. Preston grits his teeth but allows the touch. I think this is the first time I've seen them touch besides a hand on a thigh—okay, besides the time I walked in on them—and it's fascinating.

Jeremy whispers something I don't catch, and Preston's

head snaps to the side, looking over his shoulder at his fiancé.

Seymour jumps from the bed and charges for Preston and Jeremy, going between their legs and wrapping around their ankles, tangling his leash around them.

I laugh and step back to get some swim trunks. I have zero shame, so I change right there in the room, not giving a shit if they all look at my ass. It's a nice ass.

My trunks are board shorts with dancing tacos on them. They're awesome.

Paul sighs and does the same, changing in the middle of the room while Jeremy untangles them from the leash.

We grab supplies for the day, including the cinnamon rolls that have sadly cooled, and head out to Paul's car. He gets in the driver's seat, and I take the front passenger's seat, making Preston fold his huge ass into the back with Jeremy and Mr. Butts. It's better for everyone this way.

As Paul drives, I rip parts off the pastry and feed it to him. He nips at my fingertips and licks the frosting off every once in a while. Jeremy pretends to gag in the back seat, but it just makes me want to do it more.

Pulling a piece of the treat off, I turn and reach back to offer it to Preston, but he glares at me. When the bread brushes his lip, he slaps my hand, and I laugh. I offer it to Jeremy, but Preston takes it from me and feeds it to Jeremy himself.

Shaking my head, I sit back in my seat and bop my head and dance to the music. Sometimes I sing too, using my fist as a microphone.

Jeremy and Paul join in with the singing, and we roll the windows down. Mine and Jeremy's longer hair flies everywhere, but we don't care. This takes us back to the Lumberjacks, to a time when things were simpler. For the few years we were together there, we would do short road trips every chance we could, driving a few hours to go to a lake we hadn't been to before, to see a game, or go skiing. Any excuse we could find to just drive. There's something freeing about being on the freeway on your way to an adventure with your best friends, with the windows down and music blasting. Just a couple of dumb-ass kids eating junk food and seeing where the road takes them.

I'm singing "What's My Age Again?" by Blink-182, serenading Preston just to get a rise out of him. Jeremy grabs my fist, singing into it with me, and Preston growls, which makes me burst into a fit of giggles. Paul reaches for my leg and rests his hand on my thigh as he drives, singing along and smiling.

Seeing him enjoying himself makes my heart burst with happiness. He's usually pretty shut down and grumpy on his birthday. I always make sure we go out and do something, try to get his mind off his mom's death, but it's not very successful. Nothing will make me stop trying, though.

We've done movie marathons in the theater, mini golfing, rock wall climbing, and volunteered to help a kids' hockey league. I have a feeling I was going about this the wrong way, though. Instead of distracting him from his pain, I have to celebrate his mom's life and make today special. I plan to do both.

We get to Horseshoe Reservoir about eight thirty, which gives us plenty of time and decent parking. Jeremy goes inside to get the pontoon boat keys that we reserved for the day while the rest of us unpack the car. The ice chest is heavy with drinks, ice, and food. Not to mention all the food we packed in a big box so we shouldn't have to come back in.

"Shirts off, time for sunblock," Preston orders, holding up a spray can.

"If you wanted to see us half naked, all you had to do was ask, big man." I wink at him and pull my shirt off. Paul smacks me upside the back of my head, and I laugh. Preston sprays us down with the sunblock, and I double-check that my backpack is with our stuff since it has most of my surprises. One is food, so it's hidden in an ice chest that we bummed off Scott the other day.

Jeremy comes out of the office with paperwork and keys, sliding his sunglasses on.

We all grab our ball caps and sunglasses and lift shit to carry, following along behind Jeremy to our boat, with Seymour's leash around my wrist.

In slip 16 is the twenty-foot pontoon boat we rented with bench seats and a cover over half the boat so we can get out of the sun if we need. We load all our shit up, only having to make two trips each, and we're off. Jeremy is driving while Preston hovers behind him. He doesn't give up that precious control often, but he's never driven a boat while the rest of us grew up doing it during the summer. Paul stretches out on a bench and pops the top off a Dr Pepper. I stand at the front of the boat and take a picture of the guys, then grab some blue Takis from the snack box and park my ass on the other bench with Señor Butts to keep the weight even as we head out to a quieter spot on the water. He lifts his little feet onto the edge to look out over the water and lifts his snout to sniff the air.

This place is beautiful, all blue water and deep green pine trees on the hills. The reservoir is long, so if you look in the right direction it seems like the water goes on forever. The water is calm except for boat wakes, and the wind on my face puts a smile on my lips.

Music starts playing from behind me, and I turn to see Preston messing with his phone and holding a Bluetooth speaker.

He swipes through his phone and changes the playlist to some kind of summer hits.

"Uptown Funk" starts, and I get up, raising my hands in the air and start singing with Jeremy singing backup. Paul gets up and dances with me, wrapping a hand around my hip, while Seymour jumps around our feet.

I spin around and lean over to brace my hands on my knees, doing the worst twerk in history against my husband's crotch, and try not to get my face licked by the puppy. He laughs and grabs a handful of my hair, pulling my back to his chest.

"How many of your holes am I going to fill today?" His sultry tone sends goose bumps over my skin and hardens my nipples.

"All of them." I grind against him. "Hopefully more than once."

He hums and bites the tattoo on my neck.

"Hey, hey!" Preston yells. "This is not a porno. Knock it off!"

The song changes to "Shape of You" by Ed Sheeran, and I roll my body, dragging my hand down my throat and chest to my hip while making awkward eye contact with Preston.

"Maybe I planned a gang bang for Pauly boy's birthday," I yell, and Preston clenches his jaw.

"He is not touching me." Paul pulls me closer to him, swaying his hips in a sensual movement, leading my movements, and getting my attention back on him.

He sings in my ear as Jeremy finds us a little cove that doesn't currently have anyone else in it. I'm sure that won't be the case all day, but we'll enjoy the solitude while we have it.

Jeremy drops the anchor as close to shore as he's

comfortable getting, and he drags Preston to the open space where Paul and I are.

"I'm not dancing."

Jeremy is not deterred and steps in front of him, holding his hips and moving against him. The big man just watches him with a stern expression and his arms crossed. I'm not sure why, but I find it hilarious and start laughing.

"You're going to marry him, and you won't dance with him?" Paul asks.

Preston lifts an eyebrow at Paul. "That's correct."

"But why? It's only us out here." I shrug, spreading my arms. "Even if you dance like a dumbass, it's only us."

"Not happening."

I sigh and turn to face Paul, putting my forearm on his shoulder and interlacing our legs. His hand on my hip moves to my lower back, using it to lead.

The music changes, and my stomach growls. Paul chuckles, kisses me quickly, and steps back. I skip to the ice bin and pull out a premade peanut butter and honey sandwich, devouring it in about three bites, and chugging a water.

Jeremy opens the gate at the end of the boat so we can jump off and steps back under the shade for Preston to spray him down with sunblock.

I toss my hat and sunglasses onto a chair and get into a running stance.

"Everyone in the water!" I yell and run across the deck and into the water. It's cold on my sun-heated skin but feels amazing, even for nine a.m. I hear Paul shout, "Yee haw," and I swim out of the way so he doesn't land on me. I turn just in time to see him cannonball into the water.

Mr. Butts stands at the open gate and barks at us, wagging his tail and whining. We call him and encourage him to jump, but he won't do it, so I swim over and grab him. He swims around, then clings to me.

By some miracle, Jeremy convinces Preston to get into the water.

Okay, maybe it's because I told him he wouldn't be able to stop me from touching Jeremy's butt if he didn't.

We spend some time splashing around, wrestling, laughing, and swimming. It's amazing how freeing it is out here. Nothing exists except the water, my people, and my puppy.

Preston starts talking hockey and how the new guys look. Since a few guys graduated, we have to break in new players and rearrange the lines. We talk about the good and bad points of each of the guys we've seen while we float in the water.

"I'm hungry. Feed me," I complain. My arms and legs are wrapped around my husband.

"Come on then." He pats my legs, and I release him. We all make our way back to the boat and grab food.

Preston grabs a turkey sandwich and takes a bite.

"You know you would play better if you didn't eat that bread," I tell him as I add potato chips to my sandwich.

He sighs heavily as I take a big crunchy bite and smile at him.

"Why do I put up with you again?"

"Because your scratching post likes me." I ball up my trash and throw it at him. Jeremy snorts, and Paul sighs. I love fucking with Preston. He's just so easy to rile up.

"Angh!"

Everyone turns to look at Paul when he makes a weird sound and is spitting his bite out into his hand. Seymour is there to try to help him out with that food, and Paul has to push him back with his foot.

His confusion as he looks at the mess in his hand and

sees the black silicone band in his food has me holding my breath. We both want rings, but he's been going back and forth about what he wants to do. These are cheap and can be replaced when he comes to a decision. I don't care what the rings are made of as long as we have them.

He pulls the band out and cleans it off with a napkin.

"February twenty-fourth?" he asks, looking at me.

"It's our anniversary date. I looked it up." I'm proud as fuck of myself for that. I had to check the schedule to see which days we played Vegas, but I did it.

"You got married before or after the game?" Preston asks. Of course his weird ass would remember the exact dates of games we've played.

"It was the day before the game," Paul says.

"Then your date is wrong."

Oops.

"I looked it up!" I grab my phone and flip back to February to check the dates and, fuck, Preston is right. I huff and cross my arms. "Whatever, it was the thought that counts."

I reach into my backpack and pull out the ring I had made for myself. It's white, black, gold, and red. The Lumberjacks team colors. It's where I met Paul and Jeremy. It's where my life turned around. It's where I was finally safe again.

Paul smiles when he sees it and takes it from me. He kneels on the deck at my feet, and I see Jeremy dig for his phone and I assume start recording. Preston grabs the puppy that's trying to lick Paul's face and settles back on the bench with Jeremy.

"Since I didn't get to do this the night we got married, can I do the honors now?" Paul holds my left hand and the ring. He's looking at me with so much love in his gaze it's hard to keep eye contact. I know he loves me, but sometimes, it's still hard to remember that I deserve that unconditional love.

"Do it, hubs." My voice cracks, and he smiles at me while he slides the colored band onto my finger, then leans over and kisses it.

I slide off the bench to sit on my shins and reach for his left hand. Paul gives me the band he almost ate—okay, it probably wasn't my best idea to put it in a sandwich—and I hold his gaze while I slide it on his finger.

Paul pulls my lips to his with a hand on the back of my neck. His mouth is warm against mine, full of happiness and acceptance that I never expected to find. He's my everything.

CHAPTER 41

Paul

All day, I've caught myself staring at my wedding ring. The black band is simple, but it represents everything I grew up wanting and ended up terrified of. I'm still a little scared, but I can't let that fear control me. Loving Brendon is worth the risk.

After a long day at the lake, we're all exhausted but content. Jeremy, Brendon, and Seymour passed out in the car on the way back to school. Preston is a lot more relaxed when Brendon is asleep, I've discovered. We dropped off the puppy, and Brendon didn't even stir.

Now we're back at the dorms, slightly sunburnt, exhausted, and I'm waiting for Brendon to come cuddle me so we can go to sleep. The lights are off but the curtains are open, allowing the moon to light his way, and I'm already down to my underwear, lying in bed.

"Come on! I'm tired!" I call to my husband who is taking his sweet-ass time.

The bathroom door opens, and the light from two lit candles casts his face in shadows in the dark room. He's holding two cupcakes, each with a single candle.

I sit up, confused, and wait for him to come to me, a little nervous that he's going to drop one and catch something on fire.

"Two?" I ask when he stops in front of me.

He lifts one with a blue candle. "This one is for your birthday. Make a wish."

I wish to love you for the rest of my life.

I blow out the candle and look up at him, waiting for whatever he has to say next.

"This one," he holds up the cupcake with a pink candle, "is for your mom."

That sentence is a punch in the gut. I don't know what I expected him to say, but that was definitely not on my radar. A knot forms in my throat as I stare at the flame.

I miss you, Mom.

I blow out the candle but can't take my eyes off the wick. It's been eight years since Mom passed—since my life was flipped upside down—and not once has anyone thought to include her in my birthday. Every year, my grandparents and friends would try to distract me, not that I blame them, but no one tried to include her.

Every year, the closer it gets to my birthday, the more I worry about forgetting her. I can see her smiling in my mind, but her face isn't as clear anymore. The edges of my memories are blurring, the sound of her laugh is just out of reach.

I didn't know I needed someone to remember her on my birthday until this moment.

Closing my eyes, I lean my forehead against Brendon's stomach and let the tears gather and fall. Not shuddering sobs, just the release of being reminded that she existed.

"She loved you," Brendon says, putting the cupcakes on the bedside table and running his hands through my hair. "The way you love shows me that."

I smile and press a salty kiss against his skin before looking up at him. I can't really see him, but I know every centimeter of his flesh so I can picture it in my mind.

"Thank you for celebrating her today too." My words are rough around the knot in my throat, but I don't care. I'm not embarrassed to show this emotion to him.

Brendon cups my face and slides onto my lap, straddling my thighs and deepening the kiss a little. Our chests are flush, arms holding each other close, and fingers spread to cover as much as we can.

Our kiss is slow but deep, powerful, and meaningful. It's comfort, a promise, and understanding all wrapped up in a hug.

"I love you so much," Brendon says against my skin and wraps his arms around my shoulders to pull me close. I kiss his neck and inhale his scent. Sunblock, sweat, and deodorant, but under it is Brendon. My husband. My best friend. My person.

"I love you too, baby, so much more than I thought was possible."

We sit there for a while, just existing. Breathing together and feeling our heartbeats until he starts to squirm.

With a smile, I lean back on my palms and wait. He's itching for those cupcakes, I know it. I can picture his face if I told him I wanted to eat both, and it makes me chuckle. He would let me, but he would not be happy about it.

"Can I eat this frosting off you?" Brendon picks one up, pulls the candle out to lick clean, then tosses it over his shoulder.

Called it.

"We should just eat them. You can have one," I tell

351

him, reaching for one of the cupcakes. "What flavor did you get?"

"I got red velvet for your mom 'cause Grandma said it was her favorite." He points to the one I'm holding. "And something with Oreo cookies in it 'cause it looked amazing."

I didn't think I could love this man any more than I already did, but here he is, making me fall harder. It warms my heart to know he cares. That he went out of his way to make this special means the world. He cares so much, but people don't see that. It's their loss.

"You can have the Oreo one," I say, pulling the wrapper down and taking a bite of the red velvet cake.

Brendon is almost vibrating with his excitement over this treat. I don't know where he gets the energy from to be that excited after the long day we had, but here he is, damn near dancing in my lap over a cupcake.

He takes a bite and moans, dropping his head back on his shoulders.

"Damn, I thought I was the only one who got you to moan like that." I smirk at him.

Brendon circles his hips over mine, grinding his ass over my dick.

"Oh my God, sex while eating this would be a hard one to beat."

I finish my own cupcake and toss the wrapper in the trash.

"I'm way too tired for that. Come cuddle me so I can sleep." I sit up and taste his lips. The cookie-cake mixture mixing with my own is delicious.

Brendon starts to pant, rolling his hips in a sensual glide.

"Even if I do all the work?" He pants against my mouth, a shiver making him tremble.

My cock is definitely taking notice, thickening under him, and my skin is starting to heat.

"You want to fuck me, baby?" I bite his lip and pull on it until he whines. "Fill me with your cum while you lick mine off my skin?"

The pitiful whimper he lets out is the only convincing I need.

"Get the lube."

Brendon shoves the rest of the treat into his mouth and scrambles off my lap to find the lube and take his balloon underwear off.

I take mine off too and stroke myself lazily with one arm behind my head. He finds the bottle he never puts away and holds it up victoriously before climbing between my legs. He nuzzles my trimmed pubic hair and licks my balls. I hold his head still with a hand in his hair and continue to stroke myself.

The cap on the lube clicks open, and I spread my thighs to give him better access. His slick fingers slide down my crack and swirl around my hole. I groan when he pushes against it and sucks my ball into his mouth.

"Fuuuck, I love the way your mouth feels."

Tingles of electricity dance along my skin as I start to pant. It feels so good to have all his attention directed at my pleasure.

One finger quickly becomes two as he stretches me and worships my body. He sucks on my tip, drags his tongue along my balls, and rolls them around his mouth all while fingering my ass. It feels so fucking good. I could come just from this, but I want more from him.

"Fuck me, dirty boy. Make me come." I release my dick and pull on his hair to drag his mouth to mine. I own his mouth, fucking into it and taking control with my free hand gripping his jaw. He moans into the kiss, panting and hungry for more.

"Please," he begs, and I let him move just enough to slick up his cock and press his head against my hole. He looks up at me, waiting for me to give permission with every muscle in his body strung tight. "Do it."

He pushes forward, the thick head of his cock stretching me in the best fucking way. It's a continuous thrust until he's bottomed out, his hips flush against my ass.

"Hard, Brendon." I bite out his name, demanding him to obey. He doesn't hesitate, just does what he's told. The thrusts are deep and hard, exactly the way I like them. Precum dribbles down my cock, and I wipe it off with my finger to shove it into his mouth. He sucks my fingers deep, hammering into me.

Gripping my dick, I stroke myself and watch Brendon try to hold on.

"Fuck," he whimpers. "Please." He's trembling, losing the smooth thrusts from a few seconds ago as he walks that fine line between needing to come and too far past it.

"No, hold it," I demand. I love watching that panicked determination cross his face. He wants to do what I told him, but he doesn't think he can. He's desperate to come but desperate to please.

Brendon grips my hips and leans over me, sucking on my nipple, then biting it.

Pleasure shoots to my balls, and I arch against him.

"Oh fuck," I groan, cum shooting onto my belly and taking me by surprise. My body shakes as the chemicals overload my brain and makes me shudder.

"Please!" Brendon almost shouts. The veins in his arms are standing out at the strain of holding himself back, and it's fucking delicious.

I scoop up some of my cum and shove two fingers into his mouth for him to suck clean.

"Come for me, fill me up, give it to me."

He shudders and twitches inside of me, only a few more thrusts before he stills and drops down onto me while breathing hard.

"Edging is the fucking worst, but fuck, that payoff is always good," he complains into my shoulder.

We lay in a sticky, sweaty heap for a few minutes before he bounds off to the bathroom for a wet cloth to clean us up.

I scoot over, and he climbs into the bed once we're clean enough, and I lay on his chest with his arms around me.

"Thank you for a perfect birthday," I say as I nuzzle into his neck.

"It was okay?" he asks as anxiety tenses his body. "I wasn't sure if bringing your mom into it would be a good idea or if it would just make you sad."

"It was perfect. Thank you for including her."

Brendon kisses my forehead, and we fall asleep wrapped up in each other. It doesn't matter what the future holds because we will weather it together. There is nothing I can't do without him.

Dear Reader

I know there was no satisfying ending to Chad Fenwick and Coach Williams. Much like in real life, we don't always get the justice we deserve. For now, this is where that part of Brendon's story ends. He is moving on and healing with the love of Paul, Paul's grandparents, Jeremy, and Preston. Perhaps in a future book, we will learn that some justice was served to these two horrible people, but we won't know until we get there.

Also By Andi

Other MM Stories

Darby U Boys

Hidden Scars

Blurred Lines

Broken

Rescue Me

Standalones

Curves Ahead

ACKNOWLEDGEMENTS

I don't know where to start with this book. It was a struggle from the very beginning.

Kayla went through and made notes about the timeline from Hidden Scars so I didn't mess that up and have characters in two different places at once then kept scrupulous notes on the timeline in this one. There's a spreadsheet of characters, positions they play, and any information previously mentioned. She put in the damn work for this book.

JR held my hand while I learned a new plotting method and sat on numerous video calls with me while I stared at the wall (where I have my plotting sticky notes) and wrote down nothing. He bounced ideas around with me, helped me fill plot holes, and put up with my whiny baby bullshit.

Melissa was a wealth of knowledge about Hidden Scars and kept me on track with little details that I had forgotten. She spent hours on the phone with me helping me scrape together a plot only for me to scrap it and start over a few days later.

Melissa, Kari, and Bethany were my cheerleaders. Checking in on me, telling me I wasn't a garbage writer (if you know, you know), and offered support where ever necessary.

Hubs put up with my crazy work hours, the tears of frustration when it wasn't working, offered to help plot and problem solve, and took on the full responsibility of our kids while I holed up in my writing closest. I even worked while on vacation and a trip to the midwest to visit family.

By some miracle, I was able to get this baby done.

Thank you readers for wanting this story. For telling me in your tags on social media and reviews that you wanted their story. Thank you for helping me spread the word of the book and recommending it to your friends. I don't know what I did to deserve it, but I am humbled every time.

-Andi

TRIGGER WARNING

- Car accident
- death of a parent
- abandonment of a parent
- bullying
- assault
- anxiety/depression/ADHD

About the Author

Sarcastic and snarky, I love to laugh and read dark fucked up shit. I write about tortured pasts and hot sex, a happily ever after that has to be worked for. My stories tend to be a little dark but with some comic relief, typically in the form of sarcasm and usually include two men falling in love though I sometimes dabble in other LGBTQIA stories.

Made in United States
Orlando, FL
04 July 2025

62638939R00207